THE
EXILE
AND THE
MAPMAKER

EMMA MUSTY

Legend Press Ltd, 51 Gower Street, London, WC1E 6HJ
info@legendpress.co.uk | www.legendpress.co.uk

Contents © Emma Musty 2021
The right of the above author to be identified as the author of this work has
been asserted in accordance with the Copyright, Designs and Patents Act
1988. British Library Cataloguing in Publication Data available.

Print ISBN 978-1-80031-9-431
Ebook ISBN 978-1-80031-9-448
Set in Times. Printing managed by Jellyfish Solutions Ltd
Cover design by Kari Brownlie | www.karibrownlie.co.uk

Emma Musty was born in England and grew up in Scotland. She spent her childhood crossing the border between two countries and two cultures.

In 2009, she went to Calais for the first time and met some of the many people living in 'the jungle' as they struggled to reach the UK. As a result she began to write about borders and migration, starting work on what eventually became *The Exile and the Mapmaker*.

She is an editor and writer with the *Are You Syrious? Daily Digest*, which chronicles news from the ground regarding the refugee situation in Europe, and a long term member of Khora Community Centre which works with marginalised groups in Athens. She is also a freelance consultant for Refugee Rights Europe. Emma's second novel will be published by Legend Press in 2022.

Follow Emma on Twitter
@EmmaMusty

and on Instagram
@emmamusty_author

For Anthony Musty, you are missed

And to the strength and courage of those who seek safety over the border for themselves and for the ones they love

'We are about to walk off the map...'

(George Mallory in a letter to his wife during the
failed ascent of Everest in 1921)

I shall betray tomorrow, not today.
Today, pull out my fingernails,
I shall not betray.
You do not know the limits of my courage,
I, I do...

(M. Cohn, French Resistant, written shortly before her death in
prison, 1943/44)

* * *

What is civic responsibility if, in certain conditions,
it becomes shameful submission?

(Manifesto of the 121, Paris 1960)

* * *

Let's say that all French people – or the majority of
them – were used to thinking of the Nazis torturing
people, but that the French should go and do the
same thing to others seemed incredible to us...

(Denise Barrat, French Anti-colonial Resistant who worked with
the Algerian National Liberation Front in Paris 1950s/60s,
interviewed by M. Evans, 1989)

* * *

But in time, oppression is invariably met with resistance. The impoverished and the workers rise against the rich, as do the slaves against the masters. The village militates against the chief, the weak unite against the powerful and the new erupts over the old. This is a historical truth.

(Our Struggle and Our Goals, Eritrean People's Liberation Forces, 1971)

* * *

We are not animals who live in the forest, we need a home.

(Banner displayed in Calais 'Jungle', 2015)

GLOSSARY OF TERMS

Exodus – Mass movement of Parisians, who left the city when it fell to the Germans in June 1940, during the Second World War.

FLN – National Liberation Front of Algeria.

Pied-noirs – Algerians of European Descent.

OAS – Organisation Armée Secrète, an underground organisation formed mainly from French military personnel who supported French Algeria.

CHAPTER 1

Such short shelves. Stubby. The books running along in little lines, cut off, contained in these inadequate boxes. It had never made sense. The ceilings were so tall, the room so big, where were all the other books? There could be so many more.

Theo turned back to the computer. The Google search screen blurred and refocused. He moved his face closer then further away. Where were his glasses? His hands hovered over the keyboard, they were still large for his height, but now ink-stained like old parchment, weather-beaten as an eighteenth-century sea chart. Would he find her? It seemed impossible. Yet just the other day an ex-colleague had told him about a cousin whom he had not seen in nearly sixty years. An old man, who had emigrated to Canada as a young one, running away from the war he had been forced to serve in, trying to reclaim his youth. His cousin had got in touch with him after 'googling' his name. 'Googling'. It was not even a real word, yet it connected a cabin on the edge of a frozen lake in the Rocky Mountains to an apartment on Lafayette Street in seconds, straighter than the crow flies. A voice came over the Sorbonne library loudspeaker to inform him that they would be closing in fifteen minutes. He was running out of time.

Marianne Anouar. He typed it, spelling in approximation.

He closed his eyes and saw a hand groping in a locked box, scratching away, searching for knowledge. The face was covered, the eyes blind. The map only extended as far as the hand could feel.

She could be dead. This heap of wire and plastic could tell him that she was dead. He tried to recall her date of birth, but it escaped him. She was younger than him by a year or two or three, he knew that, or thought he did, but that was all. She had a beautiful smile.

How long had it been since he had seen her? When had Algeria gained independence? When had all those bodies slipped below the dark waters of the Seine? Forty, fifty years ago, more? Such big numbers. So much had happened; life had marched forward, filling all the moments between then and now, a marriage, a birth, more funerals than he wished to count. Had she married? Had a family? Been happy?

Been happier than him?

He had messed up a lot of things with these big clumsy hands, hands that now shook at the memory of it all, like frightened children. He had made bad choices. Acted in ways he was ashamed to recall. He tried to forget. Forgetting was easy for him now, he should be pleased. Yet, while yesterday was a mystery to him, he could clearly recall the look on his mother's face the day that de Gaulle walked into Paris, the heat of the Algiers sun, the backstreets of Cairo. And Marianne, small and angry and perfect, a jagged rock in the river of his life, became sharper every day. Was it too late to apologise, decades too late? Now that all of the heat had gone out of all of the moments that had led up to here, to this particular moment, their actions seemed preposterous, as the passion of youth does when seen through an old man's eyes.

He had been looking for something else, a tie he was sure he had bought, when he had found the letters, yellow and dry as dust. It was a long time since he had seen her handwriting, but to see it now brought tears to his eyes. He had forgotten, almost, how much he had missed her. He had become used to this hole inside himself.

I cannot be both — French and Algerian — You and Me — I can only be one thing now, a force of resistance. It is time for me to give my whole self and I am ready to do so. I will return for you. With love, M, 19th November 1961.

The note had contained her new address. This was the night she had left him. He had refolded the letter carefully, had been tempted to tuck it away, hide it again, as if this act could change history, but instead he had gone back to the beginning, two years earlier, and read all her letters and notes in one sitting. It was their story, or at least a part of it. He had been capable of so much emotion, so much love. Where had it all gone? In one of the letters there was a photo of her. She stared right out of it, challenging him all over again. There was nobody else in the world that looked at him that way. It brought him right back to the day he had first seen her. The dress that moved around her, full of flowers as if she were a sapling and the dress was made of honeysuckle. He could see her cool stare, the way she leant forward, brushing her hair behind her ear when she had something of importance to say, the feel of her breath on his cheek.

The library loudspeaker came to life once more. There were only five minutes left. He would have to open his eyes. He thought of his late wife; her perfect face and distant eyes, and his daughter, her expression containing a life's worth of unspoken accusations. There were so many things he needed to explain, but they hardly ever saw each other, and how were you supposed to begin anyway? How were you supposed to find the words that made a life make sense, even to yourself, let alone to your child?

The seconds were passing into minutes. He had his hands over his eyes. He felt foolish. He was seventy-nine years old. He had been to war and survived. And yet, he was terrified.

Even if he found her she may not want to see him, or worse, may not remember him. A blank where a man used to be. But he had to try. The empty rooms of his apartment had become unbearable to him. The silence.

And if he did by some miracle find her, how would he approach her? Email? It seemed so crass. A letter? He had once written her so many, but he would need her postal address, something which, in the modern age, had become a strange intimacy. The world had changed so much yet he had stopped, stuck in some past time, in some place that no longer existed. She would help him make sense of it all. She had always been ahead of him, always running further and at a faster pace.

He peered through a crack in his fingers at the clock on the wall, careful to avoid the computer screen. One minute to six. He had to do it. The receptionist was staring at him oddly. He had to do it now.

He opened his eyes slowly and a few more seconds passed as they focused, rheumily, on the screen.

A list of incomprehensible others, strangers, but nothing with her name.

A shiver passed through his body at the hopelessness of it all and in the undertow of history he fell into unconsciousness.

CHAPTER 2

The metro map confronted Elise. Its ugliness pleased her. It suited her mood. She hunched her body into a corner on the too-bright, white-tiled Odéon platform. The map looked like the bars of a complicated cage, something designed to trick you, and as she stood to take her place in the crush of Parisian commuters, she decided that this was correct. She was trapped.

When they reached Duroc she changed onto Line 13. Finding a seat, she leant back, her head resting on the glass, and listened to the roar of the rails. She closed her eyes and concentrated on not thinking. At Gabriel Péri, chased out by the ghost of this murdered Second World War communist, she disembarked. Paris was always haunting you; everything was heavy with too much history. You could not escape it, even if you tried. As she reached the stairway she felt the vacuum of the green-and-white metro leaving the station and, for a moment, wished she could give up and be sucked back down into the darkness along with it.

Forcing herself up the steps she saw an advertisement for a Frida Kahlo exhibition. It was a large self-portrait, the one with the single monkey wrapping her in a protective embrace. Her serious eyes took Elise in. She wanted to reach out and touch the arch of Frida's eyebrows, trace their magnificence with her fingers. Once, as children, she and Celeste had drawn thick black lines above their eyes using Elise's mother's kohl, wrapped themselves in bright printed scarfs, and balanced stuffed animals on their shoulders. She almost smiled at the memory, the uncomplicated joy of childhood.

That morning she had awoken already exhausted, her dreams lingering, her body reaching for Mathieu yet finding, as always, his absence. She concentrated on getting to the top of the steps. As she reached the street she pulled her black woollen coat closer around her. There was a chill in the October air, and she wished she had remembered to bring her gloves. She was approaching the edge of the metro map. It barely even felt like Paris; the buildings had lost their height and age. The streets were almost deserted. She crossed the main arterial road that led back into the city centre and made her way down the narrower streets to her office. Outside a café with a faded sign, a group of men sat in the dust to smoke: Iraqi, Kurdish, Eritrean, Sudanese. They eyed her suspiciously as she passed, the border between them clear. Elise sighed and pulled her coat even tighter around her thin frame. Her morning mantra, 'Fuck, fuck, fuck,' running through her head.

When she reached the UK Border Agency Application Centre she was greeted by her own reflection. The front of the building was covered in blackened windows. Her thirty-two-year-old face looked pale and her reddish hair only served to highlight the circles under her eyes. She readied herself and entered through the door with the 'staff only' sign on it. The building was sectioned into two main areas: the first one for the public, a waiting area with chairs. A line of counters, which cut through the middle like a barricade, demarked the staff office space. On both sides the carpets were scuffed with use. There were also two small rooms for private interviews regarding emergency visa applications and other anomalies. These were the only places in the building designed to hold both staff and visa applicants at the same time.

As she was about to log into her computer, Simon, her manager, called her over.

'You've got an interview in room two, love,' he said in his harsh London accent.

She winced slightly at the use of the word 'love' but decided to ignore it. She nodded in response and wondered who would be facing her on the other side of the Formica table today.

Cantara Bourguiba was Algerian and spoke rapid, fluent French. Elise liked the sound of the words, the way she layered her parents' language with that of her children as if her body itself were the site of a fundamental transition. Her English nephew was ill. He had been in a car crash. Cantara paused in her tale, possibly concerned by Elise's silence, and looked her directly in the eye.

'What chance do I have?'

Elise already knew that this would not be considered a close enough family member for an emergency visa. Mrs Bourguiba was still waiting for her French citizenship, suspended between two nationalities, and the British authorities did not seem to want to let in anyone these days. People were categorised by potential problems: job thieves, benefit scroungers, disease carriers, rapists, murderers, terrorists. They were even trying to deport their own citizens.

'I'm very sorry, but there isn't much chance. We can do the form, but like I said, I wouldn't hold out much hope.'

'He is my sister's son and he may die. That is not enough?'

'If he was your son…'

'If he was my son? You are telling me I am not in enough pain already? You are telling me I do not care about my sister? What are you telling me?'

'I am telling you that under current regulations…'

'Under current regulations I am not allowed to care for my family. That is what you are telling me. I don't know what a girl like you is doing in a place like this. You must have made your mother sad.'

'My mother is…'

'Your mother is what? In the UK? Good, at least you can go and visit her.'

'I am very sorry,' Elise repeated and stood to signal that the interview was over.

On the metro home, Elise could still see the woman's face. That night she was sure she would dream of her, her worry lines and anger. She was reminded of her grandmother and the way her hands shook whenever she told the story of her own mother, a Jewish woman turned away from British shores when she sought sanctuary there.

It was only as she climbed back out into the open air that the missed calls began to register on her phone. As she was checking the numbers, it rang again.

'Elise Demarais?'

'Yes?'

'Your father is in hospital. He is currently unconscious, and his condition is serious. We would advise that you get here as quickly as possible.'

As she headed back down into the metro she tried to remember the last time she had seen him, the last conversation they had had, but she could not.

Alone in the hospital corridor, Elise bit at a ragged piece of fingernail. She had seen the doctors. Her father had stabilised, but his brain scan showed up as a rainbow, areas absorbing blue and yellow and presenting as red, areas absorbing red and yellow and presenting as green. The electromagnetic waves that were constantly vibrating to create these images, to create even the physical presence of her father, were shifting. Every scan showed Theo's synapses oscillating into non-existence, slowly shutting him down. His past and his future would disappear. He would become trapped in the eternal present.

She paused at the door to his room. When was the right time to give up on anger?

'Are you okay, Ms Demarais?' one of her father's doctors asked in passing.

'Fine, thank you. Is there anything he needs? Anything I can bring him?'

'A clean set of clothes, some pyjamas, toothbrush… it's always nicer to have your own things around you.'

'Okay.'

'And when he gets home he's going to require a lot more support. I don't know if you've considered…'

'Yes, of course. We'll be fine,' she said, but it was only as she spoke the words that she realised she would have to look after him, that there was nobody else to do it.

She hovered for a few more moments at the threshold before finally entering. Theo's body looked small in the expanse of white. She was shocked by how old he suddenly appeared. He opened his eyes when she took his hand, worked his mouth like a fish gasping for air on the beach, but no sound came out. A tear rolled down through the hills and valleys of his cheek. She wiped it tentatively with her sleeve as if he were a child and they were at the beginning of everything and not the end. She stayed there in silence until a nurse told her it was time to leave, and for the first time in many years, she did not want to.

'I have to go. I will be back tomorrow,' she whispered, and left the room without turning back.

It had been a long time since she had been to her father's apartment, the place where she had grown up, the place in which her mother had died. As she entered the building the familiar damp smell of the entrance hall greeted her. She made her way across the ancient tiles to the staircase. As a child she had thought that there was nothing more beautiful in all of Paris than this grand, curving sweep of steps with the Art Deco banister made of stylised flowers as if it were a freeze frame of a meadow. With her hand upon the wooden rail she walked slowly up the steps to the third floor.

The place was a mess. In the hall, dust covered the photograph of her grandparents; their faces peered through it, proud in front of their pile of rubble, '1944' scrawled in the corner. A discoloured snapshot of her and Mathieu dressed up for a party was jammed into the frame of the mirror. The photo curled in on itself, partly hiding Mathieu's face. Her mother's umbrella stood discarded in the stand, abandoned for twenty years, never thrown away yet never used. The apartment was always cluttered, the possessions of three generations of one family stacked upon each other, but now it carried the feel of decay. In the disarray she saw his loneliness and realised how closely it mirrored her own.

In his room the bed was unmade. A stack of old letters were balanced precariously on the night stand. She looked at the one on top, sent from an Algiers address, and moved to pick it up, but as she did so the rest cascaded to the floor. Under them was a black-and-white photograph of her father in uniform. She had always assumed that Theo had not completed National Service. He had never mentioned it. She picked up the letters and heaped them all unceremoniously on the bed. In the wardrobe she looked for clean clothes but found only a couple of old suits he had worn for work. She would have to buy him something new.

She went back to her own apartment via the shops, having picked out a pair of blue pyjamas and a shirt and trousers for when he left. At the last moment she had thought of underwear and bought a pack of three. At home she took the garments out of their bags and inspected them. She smelled the new shop smell on them and ran her hand over the shirt fabric. They were concrete symbols that her life had suddenly, irrevocably, changed.

Finally kicking off her heeled shoes, she sat on the sofa and put her feet up on the table while she called Celeste and Laila to ask them to come over. Only Celeste could make it. There was still time to wash and change. Elise tore her work clothes from her body and got into the shower. As if the day had physically stained her, she scrubbed herself to remove the stale air of the office, the antiseptic from the hospital, the dust from her father's apartment and her own fear at what was to come for both of them. She dressed in jogging bottoms and one of Mathieu's old T-shirts.

When Celeste arrived, Elise was cooking pasta in the corner kitchen, which was in the living room, which was also the bedroom. She gave Elise a long hug and uncorked a bottle of wine. Elise served the food and they both sat at the tiny kitchen table which folded down from the wall.

'Are you going to be okay?' asked Celeste, when Elise had explained the situation.

'You mean, will I survive?'

Celeste laughed, 'I suppose.'

'Of course, but am I happy about it? That's another question.'

'Well, of course you're not happy, he's sick.'

'That's not what I mean, and you know it.'

'Look, Elise, it's true that just because your dad is sick it doesn't mean you have to like him, but I'm not sure you've ever hated him as much as you say you do. He's just a man, isn't he? Just an old man who's led a complicated life.'

'If his life was complicated, it was his choice to make it that way.'

'You still blame him for what Monique did.'

'Is it crazy?'

'No, but it doesn't mean it's right. She was her own woman, Elise, someone who made her own choices. Remember how she used to act on those weekends we spent in the country? Like she owned the fucking universe. I'm not saying she wasn't depressed, and I'm not saying she wasn't deeply insecure, someone would only act that way if they were, but she was an individual, separate from Theo.'

'Sometimes I think you have a better memory of her than I do.'

'It's easier for me, it's just a small part of my childhood, not the defining feature of it.'

Celeste's parents were still together, had been for thirty-five years.

'It's just that, even now, a lifetime later, I wish it hadn't happened. I wish she had been stronger. I needed her to be.'

'I know,' she said and reached out to take Elise's hand, which she squeezed with a firmness only a woman could possess. 'Maybe she felt she was, maybe that was her act of resistance, even if it is not one we understand.'

When Celeste left she made Elise promise to call if she needed anything. Elise almost wished she had asked her to stay. Her tiny apartment seemed suddenly too big for one person. In bed she bunched up the duvet and held it tight. If Mathieu had been there, they could have dissected the day together. She could have told him about work, about Theo, about how terrified she was of what was to come, but as it stood he did not even know where she worked, let alone that her father was sick.

Sometimes, it almost felt as if Celeste were on Theo's side, but it was so easy from outside to see him as some benevolent figure, the father who had managed to bring up his daughter alone. No one else had lived with the distance, the space he created around himself that allowed nobody else into the centre, into his heart, not even his daughter. And after everything, he would now be her responsibility, her burden, and people would understand even less because they would see a lonely old man where she saw a person who had cultivated this very way of being purposefully. He had lived within his boundary wall for as long as she could remember and were it not for this illness, they may never have spoken again, and he would have done nothing to rectify this.

In the sickly light that crept in through the curtains from the street lamps outside, she saw the glimmer of the plastic packages containing the clothes she had bought for Theo earlier that day. *How dare he need her now*, she thought, as she finally fell into a discomforting dream in which Cantara Bourguiba, the woman she had met in work, was interviewing her at the main entrance to the hospital and telling her she could not enter.

CHAPTER 3

Five years, eight months and twenty-three days. Five years, eight months and twenty-three days. Five years, eight months and twenty-three days. Nebay's feet pounded the tarmac to the beat of the words in his head, or maybe the words in his head were in time with his feet, his broken, second-hand-trainers, big-toe-visible, jeans-fraying-at-the-ankles feet.

Five years, eight months and twenty-three days since he had last seen his sister, Asmeret. She had been in detention in the UK for over four years and now they had turned her down. They wanted to deport her just like they had deported him. His beautiful sister. His closest friend. He had told her to appeal, that he would find the money for a good lawyer, and he hoped more than anything that what he had said to her was true.

'You don't have to look after me, little brother, I can look after myself,' she had said on the phone, but no matter how strong she was she could not fight this battle on her own, one individual against the Home Office. He knew because he had tried already. He had spent two years in a separate facility, damned from the start because he did not want to be detained, hid too long and worked too much. Cleaner. Labourer. Sous-chef. Waiter. He had done every single unskilled black-market job there was.

When he was deported from the UK to Eritrea, a country where he knew he would die, he left immediately without even seeing his family, without even looking upon the faces of his parents one last time. It was a miracle they did not arrest him at the airport, he had probably been saved by some tiny admin error, some misplaced paperwork, somebody else's bad day at work. Just as it was another person's job to reduce the number of Eritrean asylum applications that were approved in the UK. Another person trying to get ahead in the workplace.

One family did not get that kind of luck twice.

And yes, maybe he should have told the asylum service the truth, given them all of himself, offered up Emmanuel's murder like a bargaining chip, told them why he had really left the army. It was what Emmanuel would have wanted. He would have begged him to do it. Nebay knew it in his bones. But Emmanuel was his. Strangers did not deserve to have his name upon their lips. His name was all that was left of him.

Enough. This would get him nowhere. Sometimes the past had to be done away with, locked up until later or maybe forever, just so one could live, and if possible, live well. He stopped walking and sat on a bench by the Seine. On the bridge nearest to him two people were fastening padlocks onto the grid work. He watched as they threw the keys in the river. In his mind he did the same. He threw his history into the water and hurled his heart in after it. Taking out a cigarette, he lit it and finally smiled. The sun was beginning to set, and the water reflected it in a shimmering brilliance.

He held onto the image of his sister when they had first stepped onto British soil, that radiant grin that made the worst day bearable, could break up clouds and lift souls. She had laughed out loud to be safe, to be free, to be at the end of the journey that had cost them so much, dragged their faces down to the floor, painted their eyes black. He had to believe in this moment, that what they had felt at that time could still become a reality, at least for her. His cousin in London could find the lawyer, he just had to find the money.

This was his life for now, and he could accept it. He had a bed to sleep in, a job and friends. And he had this view of the water, of one of the oldest cities in Europe, whenever he wanted or needed it. There was something about this river that set his mind at ease. Its continuous flow, regardless of all the human activity around it. It showed its many faces, only dependant on the light which shone upon it and the eyes that viewed it.

Tomorrow he would have to start looking for more work, a day job that left his nights free for the metro. He hated the fact that all he could offer his sister was money, but at least it was something. He had to concentrate on the day at hand. Every day he survived brought him closer to her, even if he could not see where the path led, or when that day would come. He stubbed out his cigarette, bid farewell to the river, and made his way home.

CHAPTER 4

Theo woke to discover himself in a large white room, in a strange white bed, wearing something that was not quite clothes. He had a vision of his daughter's face, but she was not here now. In some ways he was glad, he did not want her to see him like this. There were other people though, other old people in other white beds. Too far to reach. He was, essentially, alone. Surrounded, yet isolated. In pain but numb to it. His mind tipped back into sleep as easily as if sleeping rather than waking were his natural state. His world had become upside down.

Upside down, the whole city had been turned on its head. The port of Algiers was exploding, the *pied-noirs* were leaving, whole families, taking everything with them. They crowded towards the ferry as it docked as if they could not get on it quick enough. Despite their brutal fight to stay, to keep French Algeria alive, Theo felt sorry for them, especially the children. They reminded him of himself as a child, leaving Paris in the exodus, not knowing if they would ever return.

It was July 1962, Algeria was free, and Theo had given up waiting for Marianne to come home and had forced himself to follow the same route his letters had taken before him and return to this damned country. A place he had avoided for the last three years, since the end of his conscription, a place he had wished never to see again. Yet, even now, he could not deny the beauty of it, the gleaming white of the buildings, lit by a cautious sun.

On shore his legs shook slightly as they adjusted to dry land. He paused for a moment, sitting on his rucksack, to run his fingers through his hair and reorder his thoughts, but he could not concentrate, not with all these bodies moving around him. Reaching into the side pocket of his bag he found his hip flask and drank a few sips of whisky. Next he pulled out a cigarette, lit it, inhaled and looked around him for an idea of how to proceed. The first thing was to get away from all these people. He stood again, hoisting his bag onto his back with renewed strength, and walked towards the town. Knowing a little of what had happened in these streets, the protests, their brutal repressions, the bodies and the bombs, weighed him down. He could almost feel the heaviness of his uniform. He looked down at his feet and expected to see his old black army boots. A noise startled him and instinctively he reached for his gun but found instead his rucksack.

The heat of the day landed on him like a rock slide, but once he had found a tap and doused himself with water he felt a little refreshed. As he drew nearer to her house he passed through several abandoned checkpoints, the sandbags still stacked neatly either side of the street, but no officers in sight. As he continued, people began to eye him suspiciously – there was no reason for a European to be in this part of the casbah. Locals avoided his gaze. He began walking faster. Some of the houses around him appeared battered, their brickwork crumbling, signs of recent explosions flowering up walls scarred by curls of blackened smoke, bullet holes like trelliswork drew patterns in the windows and doors. Theo's breathing felt constricted. He was reminded of a recurring dream he had experienced while serving in the army, of being chased through narrower and narrower streets, until he was crawling on his belly in total darkness, knowing that his pursuer was grabbing at his feet.

Further up the street he saw a thin line of smoke rising from one of the buildings. He was close to Marianne's now. Her place could not be more than a few metres from him, yet he could not find it. At first he thought it was the attractive old building with high arched windows, then its slightly dilapidated neighbour with geraniums by the front door, but no, it was none of these.

Eventually, he stopped an old woman. She did not speak French but understood the address and pointed, her face creased with memories, towards the smoking ruin in front of him. He shook his head in disbelief. She must be wrong. He walked further up and asked a teenage boy leaning languidly in the shade.

'Yes, that is it. Everybody dead. Last night. Everybody dead.'

Theo could not move. He had an urge to cuff the young man round the head.

'How?'

'OAS.'

Theo walked back to the house that had once been Marianne's home and started to poke around in the rubble, looking for some sign of her escape, or at least of the fact that she had existed here, in this place, but there was nothing. Ash, burnt timber, a lingering scent he recognised as seared flesh. He threw up under what had once been a stairwell and was now a mangled heap of broken stone and twisted metal. Men not so different to him had done this, the Organisation Armée Secrète. He sat down on the last step and stared at the destruction around him, a bitter farewell from the OAS to the country that had given them their painful birth, a desecration.

When Theo woke, he expected to see the burning buildings of Algiers, to hear the clatter and boom of war, but instead it was just this bleached white room, and the quiet beep of the little machines that were attached to everyone. The man opposite him began to cough, the mask on his face getting in his way, he started struggling to remove it, his old arms waving around helplessly. It was awful, Theo could not watch.

Regardless of what people said, nobody ever died for a reason, reason was only attributed afterwards. Reason was a way for the living to survive. He had seen enough of war to know this, to hold it in his heart as fact. He wiped away his tears as best he could, willing Marianne to have lived long enough for him to find her again. He had thought her dead once already, he could not live through it twice.

CHAPTER 5

That day at work, Elise felt only half-conscious, half-present, a half-being in a half-self. Had she made the right decisions for the people that sat opposite her in the interview room? She did not know. Perhaps Celeste was right after all, she had never managed to dislike her father to the extent that she professed and now, according to the conversation she had had with his doctor that morning, though stable, he was still high risk. The man who had given her life was mortal and fragile. It was not that he was about to die now, not immediately, but they could give no clear prognosis. There was the stroke, there was the Alzheimer's and associated possibilities of infection, the fact that he had not been looking after himself, and then there was his heart. The doctors were not happy with his heart.

Despite everything, all of her feelings of resentment, this fact caused an ache in her chest so profound that she felt as if she may stop breathing. As soon as she finished she headed back to the hospital to deliver his clothes. The night before they had seemed to her a symbol of her lost independence and her inability to say no to this man to whom she owed nothing but genes. Now, they had become instead a form of comfort. On the metro she held them close to her and then told herself off for being foolish, childish. Yet still, they were proof of life, a baseline from which maybe something new could grow. Another childish thought to be chased away.

The ward nurse cornered her as soon as she entered and told her he was ready to come home. They needed the bed. Elise had not expected this. How could someone be dying one minute, and set lose to fend for themselves the next? She had thought they would give them both more time. Hastily, she handed the nurse his clothes. She was not ready to see him. How would they cope with this sudden intimacy?

She waited for him in the corridor while the nurse helped him to dress, but the knowledge that this may be her last true moment of independence brought an overwhelming sense of claustrophobia. Maybe she had got it all wrong, she should find him an old people's home to go to, somewhere where other people held the responsibility. She looked around her as if for an escape route, but she was trapped in this building, in this life, in her skin. She wished she could slough it all off and start again, allow her atoms to reorganise into some other lifeform. As a nurse wheeled her father towards her she could almost see it, the endless jumping and shifting, the unstoppable transformation which every object, living or inanimate, was constantly undergoing. As she stood to meet him she felt dizzy and had to grab the back of the chair for support to prevent her from collapsing right back onto it. Nothing was solid and there was nothing she could do about it. His face, a lopsided silence, greeted her without smiling.

In the taxi on the way back to the apartment they did not speak. Her father stared out of the window; his expression blank. She tried to think of something to say but nothing came to her. The void between them seemed too vast. Theo was, as he had been most of his life, elsewhere. In an attempt to bridge the gap she reached out her hand and he took it without meeting her eyes.

The doctor had explained it all to her again, briefly. The stroke Theo had experienced was minor, but he had been suffering from undiagnosed Alzheimer's for some time. She had been asked to imagine a filing cabinet.

'…when your brain is working normally you can go to the drawer you need for the memory, or word, or idea you are searching for. With Alzheimer's patients, the drawers become muddled, their contents get mixed up, eventually some of them begin to disappear. Your father is in the early stages. A lot of the mental confusion he will suffer in the next few days is actually a result of the stroke. He will get better, probably almost back to his old self, but this will be temporary and given his age and the state of his heart…'

She looked across at her father and wondered how much he understood of what was going on.

'I'll stay at the apartment for now,' she said quietly, and he nodded in response but still did not turn towards her.

When they arrived, she carried his bags up for him. There was no lift and it was painful watching him take one step at a time, as if each one was a decision he had to make which required careful deliberation. When they finally made it to the front door he walked straight through to his bedroom and lay on top of the bedcovers without removing his clothes. When she asked if he needed help he waved her away.

She left him as he was, closing the door behind her. If he did not want her help then she could not force it upon him. Instead she tried to untangle the mess of his life. She filled plastic bags with junk mail and discarded bills. She collected dirty plates and cups until there was no room in the kitchen. She soaked them all until even the memory of what was stuck to them had gone. Her hands became red and cracked. She bleached the bathroom and it stung where the skin was broken. The fumes of it made her eyes water. She sat on the side of the bath and blinked until she felt less light-headed. She stacked and hoovered, dusted and sorted, reorganised and labelled until, in her complete exhaustion, she could begin to think clearly. What was abundantly obvious was that she could not do this on her own, that perhaps he did not even want her to, would not let her, in which case he would need a full-time carer.

That night she slept in her childhood bedroom for the first

time in nearly ten years. It was almost just as she had left it, fading floral wallpaper, a collection of Frida Kahlo sketches she had cut from a magazine, concert posters, and a wardrobe full of dresses she could no longer imagine wearing. She and her father had lived two such different lives while inhabiting the same space, but maybe this was how all families were.

In the morning, she called Simon and told him she would not be able to come into work until they had found a solution. His response was blunt, she had one week to get back to the office if she wanted to keep her job. After she put down the phone she went to check on Theo. He had managed to get his clothes off, they were in a crumpled pile on the floor, and had worked his way under the blankets. She woke him to give his medication, but still he barely looked at her, so she left him to sleep.

In the kitchen, she made herself a small salad with a few limp vegetables she found in the fridge and sat alone at the table to eat. This would be her life for now and she wondered if she could bear it, her father, her inevitable return to work after only a week. Unbelievable that they should give so short a time, and yet she knew she was replaceable, that Simon thought she didn't fit in. He'd likely be happy for an excuse to dismiss her. The thought of it all, combined with the cleaning chemicals from earlier, made her head hurt. She abandoned her meagre dinner half-eaten and poured herself a glass of water. She drank it while leaning against the counter to steady herself. To think she had returned to this place after all these years. Even though she knew the reason was her father's illness, it still felt like a failure.

She imagined her mother standing here on nights like this, alone, her daughter in bed, her husband unavailable in his office or at work. How had she felt? Angry? Abandoned? Both? She would definitely have been drinking something stronger, chasing away whatever emotion she felt. How was a person brought up by these two people supposed to survive? It was as if they had spent their lives intent on hurting each other, until one of them was too exhausted by it to continue. Elise shivered at the thought of it, and quickly left the room.

In the days that followed, while her father slept his time away, Elise tried to organise this new life they had landed in. Celeste and Laila brought some more clothes from her apartment – a space she realised she may soon have to give up – and kept her sane with wine and their inability to take anything in life too seriously. She advertised for a carer, held interviews, and showed these strangers into the apartment. She sat them on the sofa. She offered them coffee. She ushered them into her father's room, hoping to bring him out of this hole he seemed to have fallen into. They all had one thing in common. He hated them, and the better he got the more he hated them. At one point he took her hand as if to apologise.

'Elise,' he said, 'I'm sorry.'

'For what?' she asked.

'Everything.'

She had waited for him to continue, but he turned his face away from her, closing the door to himself as quickly as he had opened it.

'We'll talk when you feel better,' she had said, only half-believing it, and walked into the sitting room to the mantelpiece where the framed picture of her mother was kept. She took the frame in her hands and stared into Monique's eyes. Even now, she wanted to ask her, 'Why?' But the dead could not give her any answers and of the living there was only Theo.

The night before she had to return to work she went into his office, opening the door tentatively as if he would hear her in his sleep, as if he would still care about the sanctity of his workplace. The room smelled of him, of how he used to smell, a whisper of pipe smoke, cologne, and old paper. She switched on the light. On his desk was a copy of Suttel's 1940s map. Paris existed on layers of maps. As she stood in her father's office she knew that below her were three floors above street level, then a basement, under that were the amenity supply lines with their works accesses, under that the metro, and under everything the catacombs. There was nothing solid about Paris. If you thought about it too much it felt as if you were hovering on thin air, and maybe for her mother that had been enough of a reason, the hollowness at the heart of everything.

CHAPTER 6

Outside, the day had withered, curled up in on itself, becoming a tumble of waste; old fruit crates, plastic wrap (in France, everything was covered in plastic wrap), cigarette ends, the dead brown leaves of chestnut trees. Everybody else was walking home or going to dance in some sweaty backstreet. The mouth of the metro spat them out to their separate fates as if they tasted bad. Nebay was headed down into the snakelike caverns of Paris's underground. Between twelve thirty and five thirty in the morning, the darkened train lines belonged to him. He fixed what was broken so that these workers and revellers would never realise there had been anything to fix in the first place. His labour was as invisible as he was.

At the top of the steps, the Doctor and the Lawyer greeted him, slapping his shoulders, laughing in their throats, a constrained and rasping noise. Nebay extended his arm theatrically towards the entrance, 'Shall we, gentlemen?'

They showed their work cards and slipped through the barriers as the last customers slithered out. They made their way to Châtelet and from there to Line 4 to continue their maintenance check in the direction of Porte d'Orléans. The journey was automatic, they barely spoke. This was a transition from one world to another. A rite of passage. It felt sacred in some way. Their matching boiler suits were their ceremonial robes.

Armed with their torches and tool belts, they waded into the darkness. The tunnel whispered to them, breaking the silence. The transformation was complete. Each of them had now taken the night inside of himself. Their shadows loomed up the walls. They were giants among men. They were free.

'Who will begin?' asked the Doctor.

'Tonight we will walk under the Seine and Notre-Dame,' replied Nebay.

'Correct, Professor. The most famous church in Paris.'

'It makes me glad we do this job at night, otherwise fat American tourists could collapse the whole thing and crush us,' the Lawyer added.

'I feel it important to note that not all American tourists are fat...' replied the Doctor.

'Just most of them.'

'The most famous church, but not the oldest,' Nebay brought them to order.

'However, given that the oldest was largely destroyed in the French Revolution and only the pillars remain from the original sixth-century building, this could be considered a moot point,' stated the Doctor.

'Which brings us to the Cult of Reason,' replied Nebay.

'The death of God,' said the Lawyer in a booming voice that echoed off the tunnel walls.

'Man cannot kill God.' The Doctor had retained his faith.

They shone their torches around the tunnel as they spoke, bending to pick up rubbish and check the rails. It felt unnatural to be under so much water. Nebay could feel the weight of it crushing him, pursuing the air out of his lungs.

'Yet God can kill man,' said Nebay.

'But never the ones I want him to...' the Lawyer replied.

'Ours is not to reason why...' said the Doctor.

'Hébert would have disagreed,' Nebay countered.

'Robespierre would not, however,' the Doctor informed him.

'Which brings us to the Cult of the Supreme Being,' said Nebay.

'A movement that not only resurrected an impotent God, but also had far less interesting art.'

'Since when, Mr Lawyer, have you been an aficionado of art?'

'I like *The Jungle Book*.'

'He's lying,' said Nebay, 'he's been to Rousseau's house. If his parents had not made him study law he would have been an artist.'

'Is this true?' asked the Doctor in mock-seriousness.

The Lawyer looked at the ground and knelt to examine the rail. 'Maybe.'

'Then there is hope for you after all.'

They had come to the platform of Cité and sat on the edge with their feet dangling into the tunnel to have a cigarette. While Paris slept they tarried in her intestines. Nebay wondered if anybody above ground was dreaming of them.

'Any word on your sister?' asked the Doctor.

'Yes,' Nebay replied, looking down at his muddy work boots. 'But it is not good news, they turned her down and now she needs money for a lawyer.'

'I'm sorry, brother,' said the Doctor, clapping him on the back. 'Let us know if we can help.'

'It's good to have your support, my middle-class friends, but down here in the working classes the only thing that can help is an extra job.'

'I'll ask my contacts,' said the Lawyer, laughing.

'If only I was living my delightful middle-class life,' said the Doctor, 'I would give you all the money I had. Alas, as you can see, this is not the case.'

'Tell me,' said Nebay, 'what was it like to grow up like that?'

The Doctor and the Lawyer looked at each other.

'For me,' said the Doctor, 'it was a kind of bliss. I did not worry. I did not know hunger. I did not know I would end up here.'

He looked sad after he had said it, as if the memory of joy was painful to him, as indeed it was for all of them.

'Well, Mr Doctor, it sounds like you were one of the lucky ones. I felt pressured my whole life, to succeed, to study law, to work with my father, and as you can see, I have failed at most of these.'

'But you have great friends,' said Nebay, slapping him on the back, 'and hopefully myself and the Doctor will shine so brightly that others will not see your flaws.'

The Lawyer laughed and shook his head, 'I hope this too,' he said.

'And what of you, Professor?' the Doctor asked.

'A different story,' was all Nebay said in reply, not because he was embarrassed by his past, though there were aspects of it which would have been challenging for his friends, but because it weighed too heavily upon him for easy words.

'Another time, perhaps,' said the Lawyer a little awkwardly, sensing the tension in Nebay.

The Doctor stood and the two others followed suit. Soon the metro would open again, and they must disappear once more.

'It's time, my friends,' he said, as the rumble of the first train reached them.

Standing back from the edge of the platform they waited, their transformation taking place even as they stood still. Invisibility fell upon them like a cloak and though the metro stopped, and they climbed aboard, not one of their fellow commuters lifted their gaze to meet them.

At Odéon, Nebay left the Doctor and the Lawyer. He would see them at home later, but for now he needed to breathe above ground. It was still dark, but slowly the city was rubbing the sleep from her eyes. He wound his way up into the Latin Quarter. At a bookshop he paused, imagining his own work positioned in the window, a thought that sent a shiver through him. So many writers had pounded these streets, filling the air with their words. Who was to say that he would not someday be one of them? Lives could change quickly; the Doctor and the Lawyer were proof of this. Surely if people could fall from such heights then they could also rise to places they never thought possible.

He made his way to a cheap Turkish café that opened early and ordered a coffee, watching through the window as the street woke up and the night faded. The people of the day, the visible, seen and listened to, were emerging slowly into the light, carrying the breakfasts they did not have time to eat at home, talking on their phones in hurried voices at odds with their languorous movements. The lighter it got, the faster they moved, the louder they talked. This was no longer his city.

He roused himself as the fullness of the day finally approached and continued his walk, but a cold rain began to fall. He stopped to take cover in the doorway to an old apartment building. A young woman came out on her way to work. He smiled at her and moved towards the door, she held it ajar as he walked through. In the entrance hall he shook himself like a stray dog and only then did he notice the intricate staircase. He walked over to place his hand on the rail. A field of flowers grew out of the metal. He almost laughed. On this wet Autumn day, he had found summer.

CHAPTER 7

Hospital had left Theo weak. He could not understand it. He had been fine before he woke up there. Now he had to take pills every day and his daughter would not leave him alone, which he should be happy about, she had been gone for so long, but by now he was used to living on his own. It meant you did not have to explain yourself to anyone, something he had never been very good at anyway. Elise was the same, at least this is what he had always thought. She had never really needed him, which made it even worse that he now needed her. What would she think of him, this needy old man that he seemed to have become?

And this morning she had finally gone, something he had thought he wanted: for her to get on with her own life, not to be stuck here looking after him, wasting her time, bothering him. Yet suddenly, he was terrified of the opposite, that she would not come back, and along with this, the fear that, if she did disappear, he could no longer get by on his own, the knowledge that there was no one else he could call on.

When she had left, she had kissed him on the cheek and told him he had to cope. It was shaming, to become this, a burden. And to make it worse she kept bringing strangers to stare at him, witnesses; women with face moles, fat men who groaned when they stood up, young men who should have something better to do. He could not even look at them, any of them.

His primary functions would come back, the doctors had said, but only if he took the pills. And he had taken the pills, and now they said that he had all the functions he needed, the doctors were very happy about it. But Theo did not even know what his primary functions were anymore – he had been a son, a husband, a father, he had worked very hard at it, sacrificed everything for it, but what was he now? It was enough to make you tired, all this medical talk. It was enough to make you want to go to bed and not get up again, to place a book over your eyes to keep the light out. Words like 'Stroke' and 'Alzheimer's' were too much for him right now.

And yet, in the mirror in the hall he did not look that different. In fact, he looked just the same, apart from some strange sloping on the left side of his face, like he couldn't make up his mind about something. And a little unkempt, maybe. A little ancient, definitely. But not too bad, considering. If he had not seen his last MRI scan, he would think not too much had changed. He peered into his own eyes. There were no answers there. He put the thing on his head, the felt thing, and quietly let himself out of the front door. He needed air, to clear his head and to work out the next step in his search for Marianne.

On the MRI scan his brain was a map. Once he would have found comfort in that. He would have sought meaning in its complex topography. The orbital view reminded him of the medieval tripartite design. Asia took the position of his frontal and temporal lobes, his occipital lobe was Africa, and the continents were shifting, everything was shrinking. Just like the *mappa mundi*, the information was becoming more concentrated, more selective, less accurate. He gripped the hand rail on the stairs. At some point in the future he knew he would not be able to climb these steps. On the third from last he stumbled and lost his balance. He grabbed the banister as he fell and stopped himself just in time before hitting the floor. He stood for a moment before dizziness overcame him and he sank to the ground to sit. In front of him was the blurred outline of a wrought iron poppy.

When they had finally returned to Paris after the exodus, the months of hiding from the Germans they had done, in the summer of 1940, this staircase was the first thing that had made him feel at home. The streets outside had changed, ugly flags hung from windows, angry-looking men walked the streets.

His parents did not often talk to him about what was going on, but when he started school he heard everything he needed to from the other kids. He heard them calling each other names, he heard the rumours about people disappearing, he noticed when some of his classmates followed them into this seeming abyss which sucked people in but never spat them out again. Even his grandmother left him to live out the war in some home for the elderly in Switzerland. When anybody asked his mother about her parents, she said they were both dead, and it was true of her father, he had died in the last war.

Theo grew up during these years of German occupation, he learnt what it meant to be a refugee, he learnt what it meant to return home and live with hunger in his belly. Both his parents worked, but even with money there was no food to buy. His father's job as a doctor and their French surname were just enough to keep his mother and her ancestral Jewishness safe. She worked at the telephone exchange but in the evenings she was something else entirely, a forger of documents. She drew fake ID cards at the kitchen table by hand, ink marked her fingers like blue blood. Her sewing machine worked to perforate the new stamps. A bottle of lactic acid helped to remove the old. Blotting paper was stacked to one side of her, people's lives to the other. Later the new or altered cards would be collected, ferried out through the back exit to the apartment building, a little-used door that opened onto a small yard and then out into the alley. The only other thing that went out that door were the men and women his father fixed up in the middle of the night, and the bins.

He could remember so clearly the feeling of running down these steps two at a time, his hand bouncing off the railing, making a cold metal thud, thud, thud, his legs limber, ready for anything, eager for adventure. He had snuck out once, when his parents were at work. He had run out into the street. The whole block had been quiet. It had felt as if he might be the only person alive, apart from the machine gun that rattled on in the distance.

At the corner of the street, Theo had hovered, pulling out his imaginary revolver, holding it up to his chest like a Resistance fighter. Taking a deep breath, he had peered around the corner. All clear, but he could not be too careful. After another pause he ran for it, shooting at a horde of imaginary German soldiers as he went. They were getting closer, but he was cutting them down quicker than they could raise their guns.

As he reached the edge of the large square surrounding the Pantheon he saw an old lady making her way to a cluster of pigeons. He aimed his revolver at her head, being careful to take his time. She placed her bony old hand into the deep pocket of her skirt and as she was about to remove it he sensed danger. For all he knew she had an Italian grenade hidden in those folds of old cloth. She could be a German in disguise, or a collaborator come to blow up an ancient monument and break the Parisian spirit. He brought his revolver up to eye level once again and aimed it at her temple. As she was about to withdraw her hand he drew back the trigger and then fired. The force hit her almost instantly. The crumbs splaying from her hand onto the floor. The pigeons rising in a mass that momentarily hid her falling form. Theo looked down at his hand, almost expecting to see a real gun clutched in his fingers. He moved them around just to make sure. Another shot was fired, and he ducked as it ricocheted off the wall above him. He could see the woman clearly now. She had fallen facing him, her grey hair smeared across her face, a pool of blood forming from the hole in her skull. He breathed heavily; sweat prickled his skin, making him itchy. Suddenly, the streets around him seemed terrifying. He leant his head against the cold safety of stone and placed his hands on the rough cobbles. As the earth vibrated once again, he clutched his knees to his chest.

'Are you okay?' A voice came to him, yet he could not understand from where. He did not recognise it other than that it was a man's voice whose French had an Italian lilt with something else mixed in which he could not identify. He realised he had drawn up his legs to his body, his hands held his shins. His back was rested on the coolness of the wall. A hand touched his forehead gently as if to check something.

'Can you talk?'

Theo tried to focus on the face before him.

'Do you need to go to hospital?'

'No, no, just a slip, nothing to worry about.' He tried to get up, but all the strength seemed to have left his body. He looked tentatively at the man in front of him, another witness to his shame, but he was smiling amicably and offering Theo his hand.

Theo got to his feet slowly and took hold of the banister. His hand shook as he did so, and he placed his other upon it to hold it still.

'It's a terrible thing, you know,' he said, 'growing old.'

'Ah, but it is much worse to not see old age at all. Now, let me help you upstairs.'

The young man put one arm around Theo's waist and climbed with him. At the door of the apartment they paused as Theo's shaking fingers worked the key in the lock.

'Please come in and I'll put some coffee on.'

The young man smiled. 'Thank you, but I will make the coffee. You should sit for a while.'

In the kitchen, the man followed the labels on the cupboards which Elise had left for Theo and soon the room filled with the smell of fresh coffee.

'Forgive me, but you do not seem well enough to go out alone.'

'Just because a man takes a fall, just because he's a little older, doesn't mean he shouldn't be allowed outside.'

'Of course, but maybe a slightly older gentleman should go out with a friend.'

'Maybe.' Theo looked more closely at this stranger; he was still smiling. 'What's your name?'

'Nebay.'

'Theo.' He reached across the table to shake Nebay's hand. 'I'm not decrepit, you know.'

'I can see that.'

'I'm sorry,' Theo sighed deeply, 'I've been through rather a lot lately. My daughter says I need a carer, and the truth is, I can't think of anything worse.'

'Understandable, they would probably do terrible things, like help you up the stairs and make you coffee.'

Theo laughed, 'Okay, maybe it's not so bad.'

Nebay looked at the clock on the kitchen wall.

'I should go, will your wife be home soon?'

'I don't have one,' Theo forgot he still wore his wedding ring, it was a habit he had never shaken off, he looked down at it now and spun it around his finger with his thumb, 'but my daughter won't be long.'

'Sorry, I didn't mean to upset you.'

'You haven't, it's been good to meet you. Will you come again?'

Nebay paused and Theo felt sure he would say no, why would he say yes?

'Next week?'

They shook on it and exchanged numbers. After Nebay

left, Theo sat once again in the silence of the apartment. In a notebook on the kitchen table he wrote 'Nebay.' He must not forget. Memory was a slippery thing. On another piece of paper he wrote, 'Marianne, Mayor's Office, Marriage?' Maybe he could find some answers there and avoid having to contact any of their old and equally decrepit friends.

All those years ago, he would never have imagined that they would lose touch. He had met her in his first year at university after completing his National Service. Her mother was Algerian, her father French. She expressed her ideas with a force that suggested she had thought deeply before speaking. He admired her in a way that he had never thought possible. She was better than him. He knew it from the start.

When he tried his usual lines about Camus she criticised him loudly.

'Algerian? He thinks Algeria belongs to him. He might as well be French.' As if being French was in itself a crime or deviation.

She outstripped him intellectually without even trying. He was never cosy with her, never comfortable. When they went climbing she was always ahead of him. He was fit but following her made him pant like a dog. She had fire in her soul, something he recognised from his parents in their youth. Politics was visceral to her. She believed it was her duty to intervene. She had refused to go on holiday with him to Switzerland because they had been neutral during the war and had suspended entry to Jewish refugees.

'They can't even decide what side of the fence they want to sit on. I will not give their fat hoteliers one centime of my money!'

He was in awe of her certainties.

On their first date, Marianne had worn a plain black dress that was loosely cut at the front, exposing her collar bone and the delicate ribs beneath it.

'Have you ever thought of leaving France?' she had asked him over their second glass of wine.

'In what sense? A holiday?'

'An escape.'

'Of course.'

'Here, in Paris,' she continued, as if she had not heard him but sensed he would understand, 'I feel as if all the buildings are leaning in towards me, crushing me, squeezing my bones and maybe even the marrow of my bones.' She held his eyes with her own while she continued. 'And the people, they are watching me and judging me. They are looking at the colour of my skin, my shape and size, they are weighing me up as if to consume me.'

He had been unable to respond, could find no words to match hers.

'If I go, I will take you with me.'

And in that moment, as they had kissed over their abandoned dinner plates, he had truly believed that she would.

Theo went into his room and emptied out all of Marianne's letters onto the bed, among them their photos lay scattered, moments from his life. He picked them up and examined them as if they were clues to some great mystery. This time, when he found her picture, he tucked it into his shirt pocket to keep it safe.

CHAPTER 8

Elise was half running towards the station when she heard a familiar voice.

'Elise!'

She turned.

'Mathieu?'

They hovered. Maybe she could turn away, pretend she had not heard, and focus instead on the picture postcards of the Eiffel Tower in the souvenir shop she stood next to. They were in grainy black-and-white and read *Exposition Universelle 1889*.

'Elise,' he said again, quieter now as he made his way towards her through the early morning crowd of workers, tourists and students.

'Hi,' she finally replied.

'I've been trying to phone you.'

'Oh.'

'I've left messages.'

'I've been staying with Theo so I wouldn't have picked them up.'

'I heard he was sick. How are you both coping?'

Elise paused. 'It's difficult. Look, I'm late for work. I've got to go.'

'Elise, wait. Come out on Saturday, everyone will be there. We haven't seen you for so long that people joke that you are either dead or have eloped with a secret lover. They've even named the lover. You want to know his name?'

She gave in a little and nodded.

'Francois,' he told her, 'and you have gone to live in Florence.'

'Well, you've caught me out,' she replied. 'He's waiting for me now. I have to go.' She turned, walked quickly to the entrance of the metro and rushed down the steps, the sound of her footsteps echoing off the walls.

As she reached the platform, the metro left. She would be late for work. She thought of running back up the stairs to Mathieu, of allowing herself to be held, but instead she huddled her coat around her and chewed at a nail as she watched the interminable minutes tick by, her life slowly disappearing, for the sake a of job she did not even like, for her father. It would be good to go out at the weekend, but she would make sure Celeste and Laila were there as well. She did not trust herself to be alone with Mathieu, not now, and she did not trust their other friends to turn up. The strength she had felt in the moment of leaving him had long since passed, only emptiness was left in its wake.

Simon was standing in the centre of the office when she arrived, his hands clasped in front of him as if he were about to give a sermon. He gave her one of his looks, which she guessed he thought was intimidating.

'Right, everyone, word from on high, there's still too many people coming through our doors, heading off to the UK with happy little smiles on their faces, and never bloody leaving. In the words of the Home Secretary, we want to create a "hostile environment",' at this point he gave Elise another look. 'Got it? We are the front line, guys, we are the first line of defence and if we fail and some asshole with a chip on his shoulder blows up something pretty in London, or even something ugly, and God forbid there's people there, then it will be our heads on the block. So we're going to cut it by a quarter, okay?

We're going to keep the terrorists and the over-stayers and the people who just don't need to be there out. If someone just needs a holiday, unless they are water-bloody-"I've got three million in my bank account"-tight, then they can go elsewhere. Are we clear now? Good.'

Elise went to her desk and logged in, feeling the heat of Simon's stare as she did so, that horrible little man. They were not supposed to have quotas. People were not supposed to be numbers. And these people 'on high' who wanted to keep terrorists out should surely do so themselves, they were the ones with the capability to tap phones and download email accounts. It was nothing to do with her.

When she got home her father was sitting by the long unused fireplace, staring at it idly, as if he could still see the flames and was hypnotised by them.

'Are you okay?' she asked him, when he failed to respond to the fact that she had walked into the room.

He turned to her and smiled sadly. 'Of course.'

She took a seat opposite him, placing herself on the faded sofa. He was holding the photo she had seen in his bedroom; in it he was wearing an army uniform.

'You never told me you completed National Service.'

'It's not something I am proud of,' he said, finally meeting her gaze.

'Where did you fight?'

'Algeria.'

'In the fifties?' Elise was reminded of the woman who she had interviewed a few weeks ago. She must have been born during the war.

'I suppose. You know, your grandmother cried when my call-up papers came, they arrived a few days before my acceptance letter to university, but by then it was too late to delay it. I couldn't believe it.'

'I guess she'd had enough of war already.'

'It changed her, what happened in her war, and I didn't want it to change me.'

'And did it?'

'I think it has to, there's no way it can't.'

'What was Algeria like?'

'I'd rather not talk about it.'

'Why?'

'Because it disgusted me, and what I did still disgusts me, and you know the worst thing about it? When the Germans left France, you know who got them out? Algerians. I remembered seeing the soldiers in the streets when I was a boy, and that's how I thanked them.'

'It's not your fault, Theo.'

'Isn't it? They took war away from my country and I brought it to theirs.'

'It wasn't you. It was the government.'

'And what do we do in France when the government misbehaves? We fight for equality. That's what I should have done.' Theo stared back into the long dead flames, lost to her once again.

'It must have been difficult,' she said to him, but he did not appear to hear, and her inadequate words fell to the floor and stayed there. There must be so much she did not know about this man's life, this man who happened to be her father, but had also been so many other things. She felt a type of grief swell within her and sat back with the weight of it. They stayed there for a long time in silence. She watched him as he stared out into a history she did not know and wondered if they had enough time left to fix this fragile bond of blood.

'We need someone to help us,' she said as she stood, already exhausted, to cook for them.

'Don't worry,' he replied, back with her for another moment, 'I will find somebody suitable. I will do it myself,' and he came to the kitchen with her to lay the table. His old hands moved slowly, as if he were painstakingly re-enacting a task he remembered from long ago, with no knowledge of its relevance to the present.

CHAPTER 9

The tinned music ended and as Nebay approached the worn laminate shop counter, the news began. Hollande was speaking about LGBT rights, there had been a riot in a banlieue, two hundred and forty migrants had died in the Mediterranean.

Nebay imagined their faces dropping beneath the waves. The man at the counter was asking for money. Nebay handed over the change. It made him feel dizzy, this void between experiences, how he had once been a statistic on the radio, 'Two thousand migrants land in Lampedusa in one day', and how he was now on the other side, buying orange juice while others died with no names. The Mediterranean seemed to him a non-consecrated graveyard; religion, nationality, family lineage (the ancestors stretching for generations that allowed you to know where you belonged in the world and who you belonged to), meant nothing to the waves. They died with all the weight of life in them, it was this that dragged them down.

Leaving the shop, he walked slowly back towards the room he shared with the Doctor and the Lawyer. They had been asleep when he left, and he did not want to wake them. Street lamps splashed pools of light along Rue de Belleville and every time he reached one it felt as if he was surfacing, becoming visible like a hand raised above the water. He leant against one of the street lamps to light a cigarette and watched as the working girls outside the Vietnamese restaurant opposite shuffled from foot to foot trying to keep warm.

At home, Nebay lit another cigarette and silently opened the window. There was still an hour before his friends had to wake for work. They lived four storeys up and, from above, Paris looked like a complicated constellation. It was as if the city was the inverse of the night skies he remembered from Eritrea. Out on the Front, during his National Service, far from any major town or city, the sky had appeared more populated than the Earth. There had been more satellites than headlights, more shooting stars than flares. Emmanuel had pointed up one night and quietly said, 'Sometimes a trip to the moon seems more achievable than a world which would accept us.' Nebay had thought that he had been right, especially after what happened, and yet now he stood in a country where it might be possible for them to marry. He stubbed out his cigarette and started to warm water on their small stove to make coffee for his friends when they woke. The simple actions helped him to think of other things.

In his home it had always been his grandmother who would make the coffee, first roasting the beans, then crushing them, the aroma intoxicating. Finally, she would add sugar to the small cups and pour the syrupy liquid over it. Her actions had carried a ritualistic weight. As a child he would watch her, fascinated, as she dished out at least three servings to each visitor before they left. Coffee, he had soon learnt, was one of the most disappointing aspects of Europe. Even in Italy, though they enjoyed it as he did, thick and sweet, they did not roast the beans correctly. It was an industrial process far removed from human hands.

Nebay wondered how sensible it would be for him to visit Theo. Forming any friendships when you had no papers was tricky. There was always the question of how much you told someone, how honest you could be, how honest they would want you to be. Also, there were potential legal repercussions. Harbouring illegal migrants was a crime.

Could he get somebody into trouble just by going over for a coffee? He thought of Theo's shaking hands as they made their way up the stairs, the look in his eyes when he asked Nebay to come back and see him. There was no way he could let him down this time, but he should explain that he would not be able to come over again, say something about work or family commitments.

He looked over to the two sleeping men, the closest thing he had to a family in France. Ateef, the doctor from Sudan, and Sylvestre, the lawyer from Chad. Had they not all made the journey to Paris they may never have met, and in their attempts to move forward with their lives they had all been forced to regress. To work the jobs that others pretended did not even exist. Their skills languished.

The water boiled, Nebay added it to the waiting cups and bellowed, 'Man is born free but everywhere he is in chains!'

'Rousseau!' answered the Lawyer correctly and reached to receive his prize of coffee while still wiping the sleep from his eyes.

'To work,' said the Doctor as they finished their cups and pulled on their boiler suits.

They walked the lines, their feet heavy in the airless tunnel, the silence intimidating. It spoke of everything they could not see or hear.

'Tonight, gentlemen, Saint-Germain-des-Prés. Professor, we are in the land of writers, this is your territory, you may begin,' invited the Doctor.

'Les Deux Magots. I have never been because the coffee now costs five euros,' Nebay replied.

'Yes, home, when it was more economically priced, of Balzac, Baudelaire, Proust...' the Doctor continued.

'Rimbaud, Verlaine, Camus...' Nebay took up the list.
'Queers.'

'Yes, dear Lawyer, I believe that many were, but not all. Isn't that correct, Professor?'

'I would not disagree. Now, Doctor, can you tell us where Rimbaud ended his days?'

'I can. France. But what I think you meant was, where did he settle in the last years of his life?'

'Correct.'

'Harar,' the Doctor answered, clearly enjoying the game.

'What was he doing in Ethiopia?' asked the Lawyer.

'Business. He is supposedly the third white man ever to enter Harar,' the Doctor replied.

'I'm not surprised, terrible city,' the Lawyer grimaced.

'Have you ever been there?'

The Lawyer paused and eyed the Doctor with mock consideration. 'No.'

'He was clearly a man who could not make his mind up; poet/not poet, women/men, black/white,' the Doctor said with a considered tone.

'Maybe he realised he didn't have to.'

'How understanding of you, Professor.'

'Well, it's hardly surprising given that he's a—'

'Yes, Mr Lawyer, as we have already pointed out, he is a writer but, as far as I am aware, not a poet. Are you?'

'No, not a poet.'

'Proust,' the Lawyer chipped in.

'What?' asked the Doctor.

'We didn't mention Proust.'

'When will you learn to listen?'

'When will you say something interesting?'

'*In Search of Lost Time*. Written above our heads and in some ways a rather appropriate title for our endeavours.' Nebay tried to bring them back into line.

'Proust, was he—?'

'Not all nineteenth-century French writers were gay,' the Doctor replied.

'Just most of them.' Nebay laughed at the disapproving look he got from the Doctor. 'It's time for a cigarette break.'

They sat on a step leading into a maintenance hatch. Nebay passed a can of cola around. For a moment they allowed the silence to engulf them until all the sounds within the silence became too much.

'Have you decided what to do about your sister?' the Doctor asked Nebay.

'No, but sending her this money is a start. Have you decided what to do about your wife?'

'No.'

'Just in case you're wondering, I have an uncle I am undecided on…' added the Lawyer.

'Shut up.' The Doctor's face had become serious.

'I think of humour as a survival skill.'

'Well, on that you are right,' the Doctor admitted.

Nebay thought about his time in the army, how young men and women would talk about anything that was not the war; how they would make jokes and tell stories hours after losing a friend, not because they did not care, but because they cared so much that the emotion had to be saved up until there was room for it, and there was never room for it on the Front.

'What are you thinking about, Professor?'

'I am thinking that if we do not stand up soon we will still be here when the trains start.'

'Good point.' The Doctor stood, but the Lawyer stayed seated.

'Has it ever occurred to you that no one would notice if we did nothing, if we came down here, smoked some cigarettes and went home?' asked the Lawyer.

'They would notice if the trains failed, my friend.' Nebay held out his hand to help the Lawyer up.

'And would anything terrible happen if the trains failed? Some of the stops are so close to each other that it's quicker to walk,' the Lawyer continued.

'They would stop paying us the little they do, and some people would be late for work,' Nebay replied.

'And if they stopped paying us then how would you buy the cigarettes? In fact, maybe you are on to something, we should all give up anyway,' the Doctor laughed.

'Okay, you're right. That is serious.' The Lawyer finally took Nebay's hand and stood.

By the time they finished, Nebay was exhausted. He fell asleep on the metro home, the Doctor had to wake him with a gentle shake.

'Emmanuel?' asked Nebay, still dreaming.

'It is Ateef. Come on, you need some rest. Who is Emmanuel?'

'No one. Emmanuel is no one. You are right, I need more sleep.'

In a stupor, Nebay made it back to their lodgings. At twenty-nine, he sometimes felt as ancient as Paris. He only had a few hours before going to visit the old man. He wished now that he had said no when he had the chance.

CHAPTER 10

Theo sat in the flickering dark/light of the metro. An old film reel played across the tunnel walls. He had met Monique at a party his mother had thrown. Alice had been relentless, pestering him ever since he had arrived home from Ecuador where he had been working for the Institut Géographique National. His father had been ill, but for his mother this seemed nothing in comparison to getting Theo to settle down. In fact, he had begun to wonder whether she had forced his father to fake a heart attack just to get him to come home.

Since the end of their war, both of his parents had hardened and withdrawn. Antoine had become distant and spent more and more time at work. He no longer practised as a doctor, but ran a company selling medical supplies instead. Theo believed that the injuries he had been forced to treat under the Germans and after the war as the camps emptied out had been too much for him to bear. His steady hands now shook; he drank a little too much. Alice had gradually become involved with a very different group of friends: the wives of his father's business associates. Women trying to rebuild their lives and reimagine their futures. Over the years she had become unrecognisable to him as the young woman who had risked her life for the future of her country. Her desires and pursuits, dinner parties and dances, seemed alien to him. She had thrown in her lot with the other side.

'Have you ever met Sofia, Pavlov's daughter?'

'No, Ma.'

'What about Katerina, such a pretty name, and just back from a research trip to Chile.'

'I don't need you to find me a date.'

'Then prove it to me by finding one yourself.'

'You don't understand. I'm not interested.'

'I understand very well that you're still sulking after that Algerian girl, but it has been too long. You need to move on. You need to think about the future.'

'I don't want to, and I couldn't even if I did.' As he said the words, he knew that she was right, it had been over ten years, and although there had been other women none of those relationships had lasted. He could not live in the shadow of the dead forever.

'If you ask me, that girl and her little revolution are best forgotten. I'm having a party next weekend, come here instead of going out with those horrible friends of yours. There is somebody I would like you to meet.'

His parents had never supported the Algerians in their fight for independence, and even though they had now won that fight, Alice and Antoine could not accept it. Together they had fought for France against the Germans. They could not stomach the idea that people had then fought against France for the Algerians, when Algeria had been an integral part of the country. They may not have wanted Theo to go to war, but this was because they had rejected the idea of war entirely, it had cost them too much. All they wanted was to put the past behind them and leave it there to rest.

Monique was the daughter of one of his mother's friends. He had walked into Alice's little soirée and seen her dancing, twirling on the spot, her knee-length dress billowing out, a young man's hand holding her up on her high heels. As she spun she had seen him and smiled as if she knew him already. It was disconcerting. He was sure that he had never met her before. Later she had leant into him in the doorway to the kitchen.

'Cartography? How fascinating,' she had whispered, even though it was not a secret, forcing him to move closer to her just to hear the words.

His mother had brushed passed them.

'Oh, good,' she had said, 'I'm glad you two have met.'

He was sure that he had seen a look pass between them, as if a bargain had been sealed, and later his father had patted him on the back, congratulatory, man-to-man. Yet, he had not taken her number, in fact it had not occurred to him that he would see her again, but the following weekend his mother had invited him to lunch and there she was drinking a cold glass of Chablis as if she already lived there.

'She's a very interesting young woman,' his mother had said in the kitchen while they were clearing plates.

'Is she?'

In his blindness he could not see the fullness of her, her intelligence or her wit. He was in love with someone else. He always had been. And try as he might, he could not forget her. The fact that she was lost to him was immaterial.

The pale early morning sun greeted Theo as he exited the metro and brought him back to the present. He walked towards the crossing in a mass of tourists. Maybe this had not been such a good idea. He paused at the entrance way to the Mayor's office, uncertain of how he would react to what he discovered. They also registered deaths. He would have to check that too. For a moment he wished that he had waited for Nebay to arrive, they could have come here together. He would much prefer not to do this alone, and he could never ask Elise. She might see it as a betrayal of Monique, or even worse, of herself. If Marianne had never left him, if he had not married Monique, Elise would never have been born. She would not exist. As difficult as it had been, he could not regret it. Fathering Elise was one of the only truly good things he had ever done, even if he had not done it all that well.

How had it happened, his marriage to the wrong woman, which had led to the birth of the right daughter? All these years later it seemed like a mystery to him as if he had been drugged and his memory was fogged as a result and, in the end, maybe it had been a kind of drug; the glamour and allure of Monique, the will of his mother. Or maybe, in truth, he had just been ready for a different kind of life, any kind of life. He shook his head. He had been foolish, and his foolishness had hurt them both. He knew that now.

His mother had continued her campaign for months, going as far as renting a cottage and inviting Monique along with them before disappearing into the village for long hours at a time, leaving them alone and unattended. Monique had played her part well, rising late and slipping into the kitchen in semi-states of undress, adorning herself in the evening so that every head turned as they entered a restaurant. He recognised the temptation to own something that others wanted. She had beguiled him slowly and he had been too stupid to say no.

The final part of their plan, for he saw it now for what it was, had been a work of art in itself. After months of fawning over him and getting nowhere, Monique suddenly became uninterested. She still came to family dinner parties but now with a succession of young men at her side, each one more beautiful and successful than the last. It began to torment him daily until he could stand it no longer.

It had been more of a test than anything when he finally caught her alone and decided to kiss her. Could he feel anything for another woman? Could he force himself to live, actually live, without Marianne? Foolishly, he had thought the look in Monique's eyes when they parted was love. He had thought he owed her something right from the beginning. He did not realise she was as stuck as he was; an unwilling participant in a game neither of them had set the rules for.

Yet still, their daughter, a combination of both him and her, became a joining far more real than their marriage. He had not planned to be in Paris for the birth, but it just so happened that he had returned for a conference that weekend. Monique rang the Sorbonne and got his secretary. It had taken her a while to track him down to a bar round the corner. As soon as she said the words, something changed in him. He ran from the bar to find a taxi.

'I'm having a baby!' he had said triumphantly.

'Congratulations,' the taxi driver had said into the rear-view mirror. 'You never forget your first.'

At the hospital he had nearly collided with a nurse on his way to the maternity ward. The baby had already been delivered by the time he got there and for the first time he had looked at his wife with real affection, something close to love. She had looked beautiful, bare of make-up, her cheeks flushed, a tiny human held to her breast. He had kissed her forehead, her cheeks, and finally her mouth.

'What shall we call her?' she had asked in a small voice.

'It's a girl?'

'Yes.'

'You decide. You are both so perfect I would only ruin it.'

'What about Elise?'

'Hello, Elise.'

He had kissed his daughter on the soft down of her head.

Births, Deaths and Marriages. The door was so heavy he thought he might not be able to open it. In the entrance hall he followed the signs to the correct office.

'Can I help you?' she asked in a tone of voice which suggested she did not want to.

'Yes, I'm looking for a friend of mine. I'm not sure exactly what the procedure is, but I wanted to look up her marriage.'

'You will need the date and place of the marriage and the names of those involved.'

'I only have her name.'

'I'm afraid, sir, that that is not enough information.'

Theo stalled; he did not want to ask his next question.

'What about her death?' he asked quietly.

'Sorry?'

'Could you look to see if her death has been registered?'

The woman eyed him for some time.

'It is not usual procedure, there are issues of confidentiality.'

Theo could not understand how the matter of whether someone was dead or alive could have repercussions for confidentiality codes.

'Madam, please, I have not seen this person for a very long time but once she was extremely important to me. In fact, she still is. All I wish to know is whether or not my search will be futile.'

She sighed.

'Okay, what is the lady's name?'

'Marianne Anouar.'

'Date of birth?'

'I'm sorry…'

'Place of birth?'

'Paris, I think, but maybe, maybe… Is there any way you can just look under her name? It is not such a usual name. She is a couple of years younger than me. Maybe 1938 or 1939 and her birthday is in the summer, in August I think. I'm sorry, but it has been such a long time. So much has happened…'

'One moment, please,' the woman retreated through a door into a back office.

Theo paced along the length of the dark, hardwood desk. He considered leaving. Maybe he would rather not know. He was just about to exit when the woman returned.

'We have no record of her marriage or her death in Paris. Was she definitely French?'

'Yes, well, half.'

'And what was her other half?'

'Algerian.'

'Well, maybe you should check there.'

Outside he took deep breaths, tried to concentrate, as if through calming his mind he could call her to him. He whispered her name to the crowds on the streets, but they carried on walking. He was no more than an ant trying to crawl up a pillar of sand. The ground kept falling away from him and in the end he could only return to the earth and become one with the dust. Before his eyes, Paris crumbled. It seemed to him that the world he had lived in was constantly at war and for the briefest moment he longed for his inevitable release.

He remembered walking through the debris after the liberation of Paris; the piles of furniture or sandbags, the holes where cobblestones should be, the tree stumps and barbed wire. They had been to see de Gaulle arrive. The war was over, but his parents were not happy. 'Thief,' Theo's father had muttered under his breath and Theo had wanted to ask what it all meant. How could de Gaulle be a thief? He had come to save them just like he promised. He had brought the smiling Americans, the young men from England, the French-speaking North Africans. One of them had given Theo a sweet. His name was Bret. He had been carrying a Michelin Guide as if he were on holiday.

They had walked past the Grand Palais on the way home, smoke still rose from the rubble. As they rounded the corner onto their own street they saw a crowd gathered further down the road. A crying woman with a shaven head was being pushed out of a door and a man was shoved out behind her. A group of men with Resistance armbands that Theo did not recognise were shouting a word he did not understand over and over again.

'Collaborator! Collaborator! Collaborator!'

Theo had suddenly felt unsafe. The ground was tilting up towards him and the walls of the buildings were bending down to crush him. His father had waved to the men and ushered Theo and his mother inside.

Theo had needed something solid to hold on to and pulled out his grandfather's old Michelin Map of France, it looked almost identical to Bret's. He traced the roads that Bret would have taken from Normandy to Paris. Then he reached for the World Atlas and looked for Utah, the state where Bret was from. It had amazed him, that he could have the whole world in his hands like this.

CHAPTER 11

Mathieu, maker of things. Small, delicate things. Big, beautiful things. Component parts, that when put together made magical theatre shows, that expressed the wonder he felt at the world.

'Isn't it amazing,' he would ask when she went to visit him at the theatre, 'that when you pull this lever here,' he would point to the lever and Elise would pull it, 'that this happens?' And with a flourish, the drapes would fall over the stage, a dizzying nightscape of stars spread across them, the backdrop would run along its rails, revealing the next intricately painted scene, lights would spring to life, highlighting some contraption he had built for a show, a piano you could pedal to make it move while you played, a bird of paradise that sang as if it was truly alive, a plywood house whose entire front wall opened like a doll's house, displaying the two floors and four rooms, fully furnished, in which the play would take place, the list went on and on.

'Imagine,' he would say, 'if no one ever pulled the lever.'

Interventionist art shows. Social experiments. He pulled the world apart and put it back together again to see how it worked.

'If you shake society up you get to see where things fall. Often they don't fall where you think they will.'

He lived in an enchanted world, and for a while she had lived there with him. On the night that Elise had ended their relationship they had been to a friend's art performance.

A disaster. There were only six people in the audience including them. Their friend had fallen from the stage during a held pose – his body uncomfortably contorted – which attempted to express our inability to escape from past trauma; a rumination on his childhood in Cuba. After a minute of standing on only one leg, his other limbs wrapped snakelike around his torso, his face a mask of anguish, he had lost his balance and collided with the empty table and chairs closest to the stage. They had tried to console him afterwards, but it was useless. He had sent them home, promising to put ice on his swelling ankle.

'Marry me,' Mathieu had whispered as they had sat idling on a bench by the river afterwards, laughing gently at their friend's misfortune.

The suddenness of it had stolen her words, filled her with panic. She had looked at his beautiful face, a face she loved.

'Marriage does not work out well in my family.'

'But you are not your family.'

'But I am *of* them.'

'So, it's a no?' he asked, as if he already knew the answer. He leant forward, cupped his head in his hands, sighed. 'I should have known.'

Elise had looked out over the dark water, unsure of how to respond. It was a no, categorically, but what did that mean? She reached out a hand to hold his, felt the rough skin of his callouses.

'So…' he had said again, emptiness pouring into the space where words should be, filling up the growing void between them. 'How about you forget I asked?'

A stone of a heart beat within her chest, slow but oh so heavy. They had always existed lightly, her and Mathieu, they had never asked too much of one another, never questioned each other's independence. There had always been space for a door with an exit sign on it, and now Elise was taking it. She stood and started to walk away. He followed.

'Elise, wait.'

'I'm sorry,' she called again, her pace increasing.

She looked back, his shoulders were hunched, his face crumpled. At the door of her apartment she had let herself in without looking around in case he had followed. She knew she only had the strength of will to say no once, but the answer had to be no. And now, against her better judgement, she was about to meet him.

The bar, when she reached it, was on a quiet backstreet and lit cautiously as if scared of discovery. Mathieu was seated alone when she arrived and as she entered he called for another glass to be brought. He looked relieved as if he had not expected her to come and when he stood to kiss her he held her for slightly longer than required for a brief greeting between friends.

Elise pulled away first. She felt suddenly nervous and gladly took the wine he offered her.

'Who else is coming?' she asked.

'I'm sad to say they all cancelled,' he said with a smile that suggested the opposite.

'Well, I invited Laila and Celeste; they'll be here any minute.'

'Great,' he said, although the look on his face did not match the sentiment.

On the other side of the small bar a couple of guys laughed loudly at a joke she could not hear. Elise stared down at her glass at a loss for conversation.

'It's been months,' Mathieu began.

Elise looked up and met his eyes.

'I know we joked about it the other day, but we've been worried about you. I've been worried about you.'

She ran a finger along the tabletop. The wood was warm and smooth. Old candle wax trailed across its surface in red and white, sometimes merging into pink. A line of three drops looked like Orion's Belt and she imagined it to be a map of the stars scrawled over by the Milky Way.

'Elise?'

She looked up from the spread of constellations and tried to focus on the present. Outside, it had begun to rain. She wondered how long it would take for Celeste and Laila to arrive.

'I know,' she managed. 'I needed the space.'

They sat in silence. She had missed him. She wished it was not true, but it was. Celeste walked in, shaking the rain from her hair and smiling broadly.

'Am I interrupting?'

'No, of course not.' Elise pulled a chair out for her.

Mathieu smiled an awkward greeting. 'So, where are you working?' he asked Elise.

'My latest triumph? I work in a visa office with some crazy racists.'

'Sounds wonderful,' he said in mock seriousness, 'which visa office?'

'The UK Border Agency.'

'Why?'

'That's a good question... I need the money.'

'Well, I guess it's more interesting than waitressing.'

'Actually, I met some crazy racists while I was waitressing,' added Celeste.

'This week we got told we had to reduce the number of visas we give out by a quarter. They say we're sending Muslim terrorists to England, though of course they don't say Muslim.'

'Can they do that?' asked Mathieu.

'I guess so, they are, and actually, when they're not saying Muslim, what they're really not saying is brown people and black people.'

'The problem is, you make this about race when it's not, it's about citizenship,' said Celeste.

'But aren't they related? Doesn't one affect the other? Think about the French Jews when the Nazis came – my grandmother for example.'

'Or the fact that the Algerians were not given citizenship even when they were living in the department of France, a department of France which was also their country,' added Mathieu.

'True, but this is modern France. I might have dark skin, but I have lived here all my life, my parents were born here, and their parents were born on French territory. France and Senegal grew up together and made kids. I might be a descendant of that fucked-up union, but I am definitely 100% French, and more than that, I'm Parisian in the same way that Laila is even though her mother is Swedish, and you are even though your grandmother was originally whatever she was.'

'Polish.'

'Exactly.'

'Then why do I feel so terrible about doing my job?'

'Well, for a start, your boss sounds like an asshole.'

'True.'

'And for the very reason that it is about citizenship, it's about where you were born, it's not a fair lottery.'

Laila came in and sat with them, her blue eyes red rimmed from the cold outside.

'What are you all talking about?'

'French guilt,' replied Celeste, kissing her warmly on both cheeks, 'and citizenship.'

'And my terrible job,' Elise added, also rising to greet their friend.

'And what we're not talking about is why your friend abandoned her perfectly wonderful partner,' said Mathieu, smiling even though he was obviously hurt. 'It's been good to see you all, but I think I should go.'

'Please don't leave already,' said Elise, 'it's been good to see you.'

'I think it's for the best. I'm sorry I dragged you out here when none of the people you wanted to see showed up,' he leant down to kiss her briefly, 'I'll call in and see you and Theo sometime,' he said as he walked away.

'Fuck. I wish I was more like you,' Elise said to Laila.

'How?'

'You make love look easy.'

'Love's never easy, but falling in love is, so I don't see why I shouldn't enjoy it as often as possible,' Laila smiled.

'Sounds fair to me,' said Celeste, laughing.

'For me the falling part is the most terrifying, and then the staying part is quite difficult too, and then there's the future part. Actually, I think that's the worst.'

'That's because you're a control freak,' said Celeste, still laughing. 'You need to learn to let go, even if just a tiny, little bit. Me and Laila love you, but I intend to grow old with someone I can have sex with.'

'Mathieu seemed a bit upset,' said Laila.

'I know.'

'Because of the marriage thing?'

'Yes, and because he wants us to get back together.'

'And?' Laila was going to keep pushing this.

'The truth is,' she paused, 'I think I still have feelings for him.'

'Oh, really? We never would have guessed. Would you have guessed, Laila?'

'Never.'

Elise noted the look they gave each other.

'You two think you're very clever, don't you?'

'We are very clever though, and that is precisely why you love us. We know you at least ten times better than you know yourself,' said Celeste.

'Remember when I made that sketch of you in college? I called it *The Unknowable*. It was when that Spanish guy had just left you because his study abroad year had finished,' said Laila.

'And you wouldn't even cry.'

'Even though you were so very, very sad. It looks like you haven't changed.'

'And maybe it's time you did something about it. You're a good person, Elise, you deserve happiness just like the rest of us. Talk to him, take him back, marry him or don't marry him, but please, for once, do what makes you happy. We will not decry you as an antifeminist for having feelings or for wanting the security of a loving relationship.'

'It is time to liberate yourself,' said Laila, though when she heard her words out loud, she began to laugh. 'Sometimes I sound like a walking manifesto.'

'And I don't think we can all aspire to the standards of a bisexual, Swedish love goddess,' said Celeste, also laughing.

'Well, thank you for finally calling me by my full title.'

By this point even Elise had joined in, their laughter banishing her fears for a moment, allowing her to think that maybe other things were possible, good things.

CHAPTER 12

Nebay sat in the window seat of Theo's lounge where he had a good view of the room. It was a whole different life to the one he shared with the Doctor and Lawyer. He could feel the presence of an entire family, generations, still connected through this space which they had all inhabited. He longed for such solidity, such permanence. It had been too long.

Theo sat opposite him in a large chair by the empty fireplace. They had barely spoken since he had arrived. The old man seemed a little upset, not the exuberantly defensive gentleman he had met only a few days before.

'You have a lot of maps,' said Nebay, rubbing his tired eyes.

'Yes, I was a cartographer for many years but I'm afraid my mind's not quite what it used to be. The doctors say I have Alzheimer's.'

'Ah, my grandmother had this. I am sorry for you.'

'Thank you. I am quite sorry for me too.' Something in Theo's tone of voice suggested that he was worried about more than just his health.

'Are you okay?'

'You're not going to give me a psychiatric evaluation, are you? I've had enough of them already.'

Nebay laughed, this was the man he had come to see.

'I promise not to, if you promise to cheer up.'

'Deal. I just have days where everything seems rather difficult. The past feels like it's catching up with me, sometimes I don't know if I'm here or there.'

'Well, even I have days like that, and I am not yet an old man.'

'Give it time…'

'I would rather not.'

'Look, I know this may seem sudden, but I was wondering, would you like to take up the position of carer?'

'A job?'

'Yes, a sort of au pair for old people. You can spend the days with me, keep me out of trouble. I'd pay, of course.'

Nebay looked at this man before him, his tufty hair, wire-rimmed glasses and watery eyes. It was true that he needed more work, but this was not exactly what he had had in mind. He had thought of doing construction or getting another restaurant job.

'Can I think about it?'

'You can, or you can just say yes now, and worry about it later.'

'Okay, but give me a few days,' the words were out of his mouth before he had a chance to think about it. After all, he needed the money and it was not every day that a job was just offered to you.

When he had left he called his sister.

'Hire the lawyer, I will pay,' he could hear her tears down the telephone.

'Thank you, brother, you are my North Star, but please take care of yourself as well.'

At the Western Union he paid in all that he had saved up to this point, money for the next plan, a plan he had never managed to formulate, but now at least his sister had a chance. This fact made him happier than all else.

CHAPTER 13

Theo breathed in the familiar smell of the reading room at the Sorbonne; old books and wood polish. As he had entered the library the woman behind the desk had waved and smiled at him, but he had not recognised her. She must be new. This was for the best. He did not want to make idle chit-chat or pretend to be excited by the success of others; in truth it depressed him.

Running his finger down the index he found the entry he was looking for: Aloysius Alzheimer.

'There you are,' he whispered to his adversary.

He turned to the correct page and scanned the first few paragraphs. He felt he knew much of this already, his birth and death date, the universities he had attended; Theo wanted something more, to understand the man who had discovered and given his name to the illness that plagued him. There should be a meeting point between two members of the academy, two scientists of sorts, a way to think himself out of this problem. They had both spent some time at the University of Berlin, a grand building which Theo had always felt to be somewhat austere in comparison to the Sorbonne. Would Aloysius have agreed, he wondered, or being Bavarian, would he have stuck up for his Germanic brothers? The accompanying photograph did him no favours: he peered out of his spectacles, his balding head round like an egg, his moustache brusque.

Theo felt a hand on his shoulder and turned to see the

librarian, the woman who had waved at him as he came in. She was attractive, with neatly pinned dark brown hair and a warm smile.

'Hi, Theo, how are you and Elise? It's been such a long time! We've missed you round here.'

The woman smiled at him as she said this. There was something overly familiar in her attention towards him, the way her hand lingered on his shoulder. Maybe she was a friend of Elise's. He should be polite.

'Oh, we're well. She works a lot and I, well, I just...'

'She always was a hard worker, you're lucky to have her.'

The woman's face seemed to be registering concern. Theo was beginning to feel very tired.

'Yes, well.' He stood. 'Actually I must go and meet her now. She hates it when I'm late to a lunch date.' He started walking away, towards the door and fresh air where he might be able to think more clearly.

'Well, tell her we're thinking of her.'

'Yes, yes, I will,' replied Theo, slightly unsure as to what he was supposed to do.

As he hurried away he heard her calling his name, but he kept on walking. What did this woman want from him? It was not until he was at the far end of the square, breathing heavily, that he realised he still had the book clutched to his chest. He could not face returning now and being further hounded by that woman. Who was she anyway? And why had he lied about meeting Elise?

Theo sat down at a café table well hidden from the library entrance. The waitress brought him coffee and a lunch menu and suddenly everything felt a little better. Was this the café in which Marianne had worked? He could not remember. He knew that he had met her while he was at university and that she had worked in a café with little tables outside that caught the sun, but was it this one? He could not tell.

He would sit there and smoke, and watch her work, and order coffee, and daydream about what it would be like to hold her. He missed a lecture one day just because of a dress she was wearing, red and low-cut with little flowers. It was loose fitting and he had to wait for each new movement to reveal the shape of her. She had caught him staring and instead of turning away had stared right back until he could no longer hold her gaze. They had made love that night with her red dressed hitched up, the front buttons undone, in the sitting room of the small apartment where he was living alone.

His croque monsieur arrived and he remembered the book he had with him. He turned it once again to the page he had been reading and placed it open in front of him so that he could continue to read while he ate. Aloysius had worked at the Frankfurt Asylum, known locally as the Castle of the Insane, the German for which was *Irrenschloss*. A horrible word. He pushed the book away from him again and continued with his sandwich.

'I am not ready for the nuthouse yet, Aloysius, my dear.'

To think that if he had been born in an earlier time he would have been discarded in a place like that. He ordered more coffee to chase the thought away and watched the waitress weave her path through the mess of chairs and tables.

Marianne had not attended university formally. Instead she would sneak into lectures that she thought sounded interesting and buy second-hand books on topics that caught her imagination. To support herself she waitressed in cafés like this one and in her spare time she edited a small left-wing newspaper. What Theo had not known at the time was that she was working with the National Liberation Front long before she had met him. Some of her late-night waitressing jobs had turned out to be clandestine meetings with Algerian freedom fighters. He should have guessed, but he had tried to force Algeria from his mind ever since he had finished his conscription. He was happy to live a quiet life, safely away from bullets and bombs, but he often worried that he was not enough for her. When he asked her to live with him, she turned him down.

'I'm not domesticated,' she had proclaimed, 'I am feral, like a cat, and I might bite.'

He had laughed through his hurt.

How had he ever been lucky enough to spend time with such a woman? What good had he done to deserve it? None that he could think of, and maybe this was why it had ended the way it did. He could still feel it now, in the depths of himself, the pain of it. Theo felt a tear edge out of his eye.

'What is wrong with you now, old man?' he asked out loud, causing a couple at a nearby table to stare. He raised his hand for the bill. He needed to get home. He would write Marianne a letter and post it to the last address he had for her in Algiers. The place where she had been living the last time he had seen her. The house in which he could have lived with her, if it had not already been too late. It would not work, but it no longer mattered. He just needed to feel he was doing something, moving towards her inch by inch. The waitress appeared not to have seen him, so he placed some notes upon the table, knowing that they were more than adequate for his small bill, but not caring because she had reminded him of Marianne.

He began his walk home as lectures ended for the day. Suddenly, he was surrounded by youth. They all seemed so incredibly young that he could hardly believe they were old enough to fend for themselves, let alone take up serious academic study. A man in his early twenties eyed him with mistrust. Theo stared back at him, taking in his strangely elongated ear piercings. He wondered what these young people saw when they looked at him. He felt the same as he had always done, apart from this forgetting, this losing illness he had, but what did he look like to others? What could still be seen?

When he got back to the apartment, Elise was waiting for him.

'How was your day?' she asked as she started to prepare supper.

'I think I saw a friend of yours at the library, middle-aged woman, brown hair, couldn't remember her name.'

'The woman that works at the front desk?'

'Yes.'

'Theo, she's not my friend, she's yours. You've known her since you started at the university. Mum was convinced you'd had an affair with her for an entire year until she came to the apartment in person with her partner, a woman. Susie and Claire I think.'

'Susie? Well, I'm sure it will all come back to me.' He could not think clearly. His mind was on the letter, trying to find the words.

'Did you ever wonder, Theo, how Mum felt?'

What would he say? Sorry? I miss you? Come back? All of those things? But it had been so long, and the letter would most likely be read by a stranger who had never heard of her.

'Sorry?' he said. His daughter had asked him something.

'Never mind.' She looked sad again.

'Tell me.'

'It doesn't matter.'

He went to his office, found his best writing paper, his best pen, and wrote simply, 'Please contact me to let me know you are well. I fear I am running out of time. Forever yours, Theo.' He made sure to put a return address. He held it in his hands. It was so light and inadequate. There was so much more to say and to ask and so little time before she was taken from him forever by this illness, but he had to try. He went back out into the street to the post box. His hand shook as he held the letter to the opening. He took a deep breath, closed his eyes, and dropped it in.

When he got back to the apartment he realised he still had not told Elise about Nebay.

'I've found someone for the job, you'll like him,' he said, expecting her to be pleased, but for some reason she just nodded, and went off to bed. She must be tired from work.

That night he slept well for the first time in weeks. He had taken another step towards Marianne and, if he was honest, he was relieved by the possibility that she had not married. That it was not that she had rejected him necessarily, but the institution itself.

CHAPTER 14

It was late, but it had been dark all day, the heavy clouds pushing down upon the city as if to crush it. The snow had turned to slush under the churn of commuters' feet, slipping, sliding, but rushing forwards nonetheless. Elise's own feet were cold, her shoes soaked through, her head bent low. A couple walked past her laughing at some private joke, she looked up at their smiling faces, two planets populating their own little cosmos, disrupting the physics of the universe by spinning around each other and ignoring the pull of the cloud-covered sun.

Her father was moving on with his life once again, distracted by some private project, and had announced at breakfast, with a certain level of pomp, that he was intent on employing a person he had only just met to care for him. Nebay. A total stranger, but her father's choice. Of course it was. She had tried to dissuade him but it was impossible, and she had limited energy for the endeavour after these last weeks. And what did this mean for her? She had sublet her apartment for six months. There was no going back for now, and surely she would still have to be with Theo during the nights anyway. She thought about calling Celeste and Laila, but she needed a little time alone to think. When she reached the apartment she let herself in quietly and went straight to her room.

This bedroom and all the memories crowded into this apartment depressed her. Not so long ago, she had been happy. Maybe she could be again. She thought of Mathieu, of all the times they had spent together, of how much they had laughed. Why had she forced herself to destroy what they had instead of seeking a compromise? She opened the window to let in the night air. The cold blast calmed her. She used to sit here and smoke, half her body dangling from the window, weightless over the dark streets below.

Once, her and Mathieu had slipped beneath these city streets through a disused entrance to the catacombs. They had taken a bottle of wine with them and a dodgy flashlight which kept turning itself off. Urban explorers, they had called themselves, though many people had been there before them and scrawled their names across the damp walls. Some had even created underground works of art. Japanese landscapes spread like mould and merged into the faces of beautiful women written over with political slogans and declarations of love. Mathieu had suggested that she should take photos, but she had not wanted to. The impermanence, the knowledge that in time these momentary expressions would disappear, was the point, but now she wished she did have a concrete memory of the moment, and of the kiss that followed it. If she was ever going to move on from the past, she needed to open herself up, dig up all of her feelings, excavate. Under everything, she knew herself to be in need of love.

CHAPTER 15

Nebay had not meant to say yes. He sat by the canal watching the mud-brown water and wondering if he had done the right thing. If it were not for his sister, he would have refused, but Theo had left little room for objections. He was a determined old man and reminded Nebay of his grandfather, a storyteller with an eye for the ladies, but only an eye. Nebay had spent a lot of time with his grandparents while he was growing up. His parents had both worked so he had spent long hours listening to his grandfather's stories or watching his grandmother cook. They had both died after he left. He had not been able to attend their funerals. The thought of his parents dying before he could see them again made his chest tight. To take his mind from this he stood and continued the walk home.

The Doctor and the Lawyer were awake when he returned.

'Professor! Why do you never sleep?' asked the Doctor, rising onto one elbow.

'How can anyone sleep when you snore like a birthing goat?' the Lawyer questioned with the blanket still pulled up over his head.

'I have had a small nasal problem since I was born. It is unfair to mock the afflicted.'

'You're a doctor, fix it.'

'I am glad you have both woken up in such fine moods. I

cannot wait to be trapped underground with only the pair of you for company.'

'It's not as if you have any other friends.'

'Actually, I went to meet with someone this week.'

'Is she nice?'

Nebay ignored the Lawyer and turned to the Doctor for the chance of a sensible conversation. 'He offered me a new job.'

'You mean you're going to leave all this?' asked the Lawyer, waving his hands around their small shared room. 'How could you?'

'Be sensible for one moment, would you? Congratulations, Professor. What is the job?'

'I would be a kind of carer for an old man.'

'Does he know you have no papers?'

'No, I do not know whether to tell him. I do not know what he would say.'

'It could be dangerous for both of you…'

'Is he rich?'

'No, Mr Lawyer, he is not rich. He used to teach at the university. He was a cartographer.'

'I have had a lot of problems with maps, we should meet.'

'I do not know if he will ever be ready for the privilege… and I do not think he drew the maps you have a problem with.'

'Well, some Frenchman did.' The Lawyer had an edge of seriousness to his voice that was unusual to him.

'But not the Professor's Frenchman. Someone seems to have got out of bed on the wrong side.'

'Well, if you would ever let me sleep…'

Nebay handed out cigarettes.

'Anyway, I took it. I did not mean to, but I did. He is very persuasive and, I think, very lonely.'

'When will you finish on the metro? They will no doubt put some cretin with us.'

'Do not worry, for now I will stay. I need all the money I can get so I can send it to my sister.'

'You're crazy, when will you sleep?'
'When I am dead, my friend.'

In the half-light of dawn, after a long night at work, they made their way home. Nebay could see a group of figures gathered by their front door. He gently pulled the Doctor and Lawyer to a halt.

'Look,' he whispered.

The others looked up and saw the men. They were about to turn, but it was too late. The police had already seen them. They began to run.

CHAPTER 16

Theo skulked around the kitchen. A burning smell reached his nostrils and he discovered a dishcloth left on the hob. Who had left it there and why was the hob on? He saw the espresso pot on the side, looked down at his coffee, and realised.

'You stupid old fool,' he said to the walls. 'What use are you? Why don't you work anymore?'

There was a persistent knocking from somewhere nearby. It took Theo some moments to realise that it was the front door.

'Sorry I am late, Theo,' Nebay said breathlessly. He looked like he had been running. 'I had a difficult morning.'

'Join the party, no that's wrong, join the gang, no, no, no,' Theo gesticulated in the direction of the lightly smoking, burnt-brown cloth cooling in the sink.

Nebay smiled. 'Join the club? This is an unusual breakfast.'

'Someone let a stupid old man in, and he burnt everything,' he finally smiled. 'So, what happened to you?'

'A long story, Theo,' Nebay said, and then looked around the room for a moment as if to distract himself. Theo found himself following his gaze, taking in the maps and notes and last smears of dust. 'Is there any of that coffee left?'

Theo poured him a cup and Nebay held it to himself for some time without speaking.

'So?'

Nebay leant against the counter and ran his hand across his brow as if deciding something. He looked more than tired, he looked drained of everything.

'Can I trust you?'

Theo nodded and Nebay pulled out a crumpled cigarette, carefully straightening it before asking, 'Do you mind?'

'Of course not,' Theo replied. In this suddenly changed situation, he felt clearer.

'I should quit really. My doctor friend tells me it is bad for the health, but then he smokes too so maybe I should not listen to him.' With this last comment, Nebay gave an odd half-smile as if the thought that such a small roll of paper could in any way be a danger to his health was ridiculous. Theo did not smile with him. As Nebay lit the cigarette he inhaled deeply, drawing every last bit of smoke into himself, his hands shaking slightly as he took another sip of coffee.

'Sorry. I will get to the point. I am Eritrean, as I said, and my name is Nebay, but this is not the whole truth.' He paused again, tapping the cigarette rhythmically on the saucer Theo had provided as an ashtray, before resuming what he was saying. 'I have no status in this country, Theo. I am out of breath because I have been running from the police.'

Theo took a moment to take in this information, but at the same time he was relieved. He had imagined something much worse and now felt guilty as a result. There was even an excitement about it, a newness, and a chance for one last act of resistance.

'Did you apply for asylum?'

'Yes, and I was turned down. I have also tried England because I have family there, but I was deported. I made my way back here but I can go no further.'

'And if you went home?'

'It is not possible.'

Theo took some moments to consider all the reasons why this may be the case. What could prevent a man from returning home? So many things.

'Are you in trouble with the police in Eritrea?'

'Not as such.'

'A woman then?'

'No, Theo, not a woman. It is more complicated than that.'

'Okay. Well, what then?'

'I am sorry, but I cannot talk about it. You deserve an explanation but I cannot give you one,' he said with a small, hard smile. 'I had better go.'

'What do you mean?' The thought of his new friend exiting his life as suddenly as he had arrived in it was terrible. Theo had not met anyone this interesting for years, decades perhaps, and now it occurred to him that they could in fact help each other. In different ways, they were both in sticky situations.

'Now you know the truth there is no way that I can stay.'

'Nebay,' Theo looked him directly in the eye as he spoke, 'I don't care what your legal status is. Obviously, I wish you could tell me more, but we are friends, at least I hope that is what we are becoming.'

Nebay returned his gaze with a long straight stare and Theo sensed him running through his options, weighing things up.

'Theo, I am a *sans-papiers*. If you have me in your house you are breaking the law.'

'I am aware of the law.' *And for much of my life I have been too scared to break it*, he thought to himself, *but not now.* At this age, with this illness, there was nothing left to fear apart from loss, the loss of everything, of the past, of life itself.

'I do not know…'

'It is my choice,' Theo replied. 'But maybe we should keep this to ourselves.'

'Surely we should tell your daughter.'

'If she knows nothing, she can be accused of nothing. Like you said, I will be committing an offence by having you here but that's my choice.' He thought it best not to mention Elise's job, it would only complicate matters further, and by now he was sure this was the person he wanted to spend his days with.

'I do not know, Theo, my job would be to look after you, putting you in danger of arrest is not that…'

'But imagine if I died from boredom while being looked after by one of the people that has replied to Elise's ad, then you would feel terrible.'

Nebay laughed, 'I think you are good at getting what you want.'

'If only that were true.'

'Okay, I will say nothing, and I will still take the job.'

'Thank you,' Theo replied, relaxing again. He thought he should lighten the mood somehow, change the subject. 'Do you play backgammon?'

He went to his office and brought out an ornate folding board that doubled as a box. The dark wood was carved with a pattern of interlocking flowers and edged with brass filigree.

'It is very beautiful.'

'Yes, I bought it on one of my travels. I forget where now.'

He set the board down, opened it, and began to lay out the pieces. It took him a few minutes to be satisfied as he swapped their positions, stared at the board and then changed them slightly.

'Yes, that's it,' he said finally, 'and I remember now, I bought it in India. I'd been mapping a section of the lower Himalayas, and this reminded me of home. The flowers on the outside like the staircase.'

'I can see the resemblance…' Nebay began but Theo continued, chasing the thought while he had it.

'I'd been away for months and when I came across this in a small shop it brought me close to tears, silly really, but Elise was only a baby, and I missed her. The young shopkeeper had made it himself. That night we played for hours, drinking that sweet tea they like. For a simple game it can be quite addictive.' Theo came back to the present and smiled at Nebay. 'I must have had this board for over thirty years.'

Theo explained the rules and they began chasing each other around the board, Nebay clearly winning.

'Beginner's luck,' Theo suggested as they finished the first game. They were still playing when the sound of Elise's key in the door interrupted them.

Elise walked into the sitting room and threw herself onto the sofa. She looked exhausted and grey as if covered with the evening smog.

'How was your day?' asked Theo, after introducing her to Nebay.

'Not great,' she said quietly before dragging herself off to her bedroom.

'Well, Nebay, thank you very much for today. Same time tomorrow?'

Nebay looked a little confused as Theo ushered him out, they were still in the middle of a game, but Theo was anxious to have him leave before his daughter re-emerged. Best not to have any awkward questions and let things settle.

When Elise came back out she had changed and looked more relaxed.

'Has Nebay gone?' she asked, looking around the room as if expecting to see him there.

'Yes, there seemed no point in holding him up now you're home.'

'It would be nice to meet him properly.'

'There's plenty of time for that.'

Theo brought her in a glass of wine.

'Thank you, Elise, for all that you have done for me up until now.'

She gave him a look he could not read.

'That's okay. I'm your daughter, Theo, it's kind of my job.'

'I never asked you to.'

'That's not what I'm saying, Theo.'

'But you had to give up your life.'

'The truth is, I didn't really have one. I'd already given it up.'

'You don't have to say things like that just to make me feel better. I'm not a child, I can take it.'

'I'm not, and I don't know if you've noticed but you've grown rather defensive in your old age – that's supposed to be my role in the family, you know?'

Theo could not help but smile.

CHAPTER 17

Saturday, thank fuck, thank fuck, thank fuck. Elise was still in bed when the doorbell rang. She opened the door to Mathieu who breezed in before she had a chance to say anything. Under his arm he carried a bag full of freshly baked pastries which he presented to Theo.

'Your favourite, if I remember correctly.'

'Mathieu! How good to see you. It's been, well, how long has it been?'

'Too long, Theo.'

Elise still stood in the doorway.

'Good morning,' she said, to his back, while he embraced her father. 'This is unexpected.'

'Well, if I had asked, you would have said no.'

'You're right, I would have.'

She could hear them talking while she made breakfast, the rumble of her father's voice, Mathieu's quiet responses. It felt suddenly as if he had always been there. And yet, sitting at the table waiting for the kettle to boil, she thought of her mother's letter to her. 'The world is full of difficult choices, try to make better ones than I did.' And so she had made her choices – never settle down, never marry, never be beholden to another. The letter had probably been written right here. She ran her hand along the smooth pine.

'Are you okay?'

Mathieu had come into the room without her noticing, the kettle was boiling and she had not heard it.

'Yes, of course. I'm fine.'

He helped her carry through the plates and cups. She sat down next to him. Theo continued to bombard him with questions, clearly happy that he had come, but she could not concentrate on the flow of conversation. Mathieu's hand was near hers on the sofa, but this was not the reason why. Opposite her, in his old grey cardigan and his worn carpet slippers, was the man she had always blamed for her mother's death. The death that had necessitated the letter, the letter upon which Elise had based so much. This tired, old guy who had donated his DNA to her creation. She watched as he charmed Mathieu, saw the easy way they smiled at one another, laughed at each other's jokes. If Monique had died because of a man, it had not been this man, in fact it seemed unlikely that it could have been a man at all. It had been bigger than that. It had been chemistry, biology, brain function. She had seen it all her life. Her mother was happy one minute, sad the next. Elise had woken every morning never knowing exactly who she would meet over the breakfast table, the happy person, or the sad one, and when school ended, she never knew who she would come home to. She had given herself parameters to live between even then, she could not expect too much, and she could not give too much in return. As a child she had known that she must keep herself safe from her mother's extremes.

Before she knew it, Mathieu was standing to leave.

'I'll see you soon,' he said as he left, but she had not paid enough attention to know exactly what he meant.

The next day, for the first time in months, she felt the need to paint. She woke up with an image already in her head, dressed quickly, made coffee, and tried to begin. White, the beginning of everything; innocence. Yet for some white meant death, the end of everything; white lilies at a funeral. The paintbrush lolled in Elise's hand, the paint hardening on the bristles. Blue, flowers and bruises. Her head was tilted to the side, her hair up in an untidy heap, her second-hand jogging bottoms tucked into her socks and the sleeves of her Pink Floyd T-shirt rolled up, exposing her shoulders.

It did not feel right. Black, a shade with too much history, the dark dog of depression which curled up at her feet, the look on the Algerian woman's face when she walked out of the interview, the dying areas of her father's brain, the loss of love.

She had met Mathieu twelve years ago nearly to the day in the first year of her undergraduate degree. She and Celeste had recently met Laila, and it was one of their first nights out together. They had gone to an old fancy-dress shop which played music late. The place was full of pink wigs and gilded mirrors. They had been greeted by a guy in a corset and bustle who took their money as they went in. Mathieu had been sitting on his own when they arrived, he looked a little out of place in his chunky woollen sweater and glasses, but when his friends arrived they were dressed in every colour imaginable, as if he were surrounded by peacock feathers, which on closer inspection, he was. She had walked up to him, her drink in hand, and asked if she could perch on the bench next to him. He had assented and began to tell her about the theatre where he worked. He had a quiet voice, but loud hands. He waved them around to explain his points as if drawing in the air.

At the moment that they may have kissed the music had stopped. They had walked back to his apartment hand in hand but while he went into the kitchen to pour more drinks she had fallen asleep on his sofa. The following day she had woken with a terrible hangover, surrounded by theatre posters from the *Belle Époque*. On that first day he had taken her for a drink at the bar that would become their regular and as the evening slipped into night his hand had found its way to her thigh.

She put down the paintbrush again and leant back on her chair to stare further into the whiteness. It occurred to her that in its own way the canvas was already perfect, that any mark she made on it would be an intrusion of some kind, a transgression, a certain kind of violation.

She picked up the paintbrush again, examining the feel of the stiff dry bristles on the palm of her hand. The blue was wrong. She mixed white and black, allowed a bleed from the rejected blue, and began. With this warm grey, she found her starting point.

CHAPTER 18

After leaving Theo's, Nebay went to Belleville Park to meet the Doctor. He arrived and walked up through the trees and dog walkers to the bench at the top. The Doctor was not there. Nebay took out a cigarette, lit it, inhaled. This was definitely the time they had agreed to meet, and this was definitely the place. Having lost the police in the streets that morning, they had hunkered down in the back of a small café and decided on this plan. The Doctor was never late.

Nebay was beginning to feel the strain of not sleeping. His eyes itched and his concentration wandered. He lit another cigarette, stared out over Belleville as the light abandoned her, and hoped that his friends were safe. He wondered if somehow this could be his fault. There was something about Theo's daughter he did not trust, or rather, felt he did not understand. The way the old man had shoved him out of the door when she returned was odd. Could she be police? He did not think so, but still, there was something.

A man approached from the bottom of the hill. It was getting dark now and Nebay could not make out his features, but he was sure it must be the Doctor by now. The man drew closer. It was not him. Nebay's cigarette packet was empty. He threw it towards the bin and missed. It was too dark. He should go, but hope kept him seated.

Nebay knew this feeling all too well. The knowledge that

someone could be snatched from you without your permission. Life could take people away from you and not even inform you. He may never see either of them again. Anything could have happened. When you lived an invisible life you could die an invisible death. You could be deported to an invisible country and murdered for reasons that officially did not exist. You could end up in a Parisian mortuary with a Jean Dupont toe tag. To be invisible you had to have disappeared from somewhere already. It made it easy to disappear again.

The Doctor and the Lawyer were all that kept him sane in this city; he could not lose them now. He thought of the many other people he had met on his journeys who had moved on elsewhere, or more often had got stuck somewhere far behind in Greece or Italy or Spain, or further back still in Libya, Tunisia or Turkey. Or, people who had not made it out at all, the kid with the big wide-open smile who fell overboard, the pregnant woman who collapsed at the Italian/French border and got pushed back, never to be heard of again. A map of missing things, broken connections, lost people. There was nothing more dangerous to the journey than the human tendency to care too much. Travellers must remain strangers if they are to survive each other's loss.

He was exhausted by it. Compared to the constant running from one authority or another, the lack of sleep was nothing. The Doctor and the Lawyer were his only physical and present connections to life, without them there was nothing, just a man-shaped hole in the universe. A being made entirely of what was now absent. Emmanuel, his family, his country and language, his life.

He lit a cigarette and breathed in the smoke until his hands stopped shaking. He debated over whether to go to work. Losing his metro job would make it much harder to save money for his sister, but he had not slept for forty-eight hours and, more importantly, the police may have got the address from his employers. He decided to discreetly check their meeting spot at the entrance to the metro. Through the park and the ill-lit roads that followed, he kept his hands in his pockets and his hood up. Across the street from the metro he stopped and went into a shop to buy cigarettes. While the man behind the counter picked out his brand, Nebay checked out the street. There was no one. Not his friends. Not the police.

Outside the shop he waited a little longer. Could he go to their room? Was it safe? Would he ever again have the luxury of keeping his possessions in one stable place he could call home?

He could go to the Jungle. Lose himself for a while. Perhaps that was what the Doctor and the Lawyer had done. He may even find them there. He imagined it; walking up to a campfire and hearing the Lawyer's voice, 'What took you so long?', and feeling the supportive hand of the Doctor on his shoulder, 'We made it! Once again, we escaped the guillotine.'

'I would rather be guillotined than live like this,' the Lawyer would say. It was always worse when he became despondent. His role was to lighten the mood not destroy it. And they would look into the fire and contemplate their fates.

Nebay roused himself. He had fallen asleep on the bench outside the shop. Two policemen now stood at the entrance to the metro. He pulled his hood down further and walked towards his quarters. He would be able to see from the street if the light was on. Again he waited, watching for movement. The light was off. They had either not returned or had snuck in and were laying low. He could not risk it. He thought about going to Theo's, but he had probably shocked the old man enough for one day. Also, his daughter would be there. Not a good idea. Regardless of how he felt about her, he was pretty sure she did not trust him either.

It was cold. He hugged his jacket closer and walked until he found a bar. He wanted a beer, but it would send him to sleep. He ordered two coffees, downed the first and sipped the second tentatively. In the future he would write all this down. It would be nothing more than a story, hopefully one that sold well, and he would not have to live these words anymore.

Money brought options. If you had enough you did not even need a backstreet passport, regardless of where you were from. If you had money people welcomed you, encouraged you, supported you.

He whiled away the hours of the night convincing himself he had a future and that the Doctor and Lawyer were alive, well, and would turn up at any moment to tell him how stupid he was to spend his time worrying.

'We're invincible,' the Lawyer had once stated after a similar escape, and at that time, and in that moment, it had felt true.

CHAPTER 19

Outside, the sky was scowling. Theo was restless. He moved from one room to another unsure of why he had entered. In his office he shuffled the paper on the desk. An unfinished article on the development of cartographic practice in Southeast Asia fell to the floor. He left it there and stepped on it as he walked out of the room. He walked back into his office. There was a paper on the floor. Who would knock something so important over and just leave it there? People should not be touching his things. He walked towards the kitchen thinking to broach the subject with Nebay, but by the time he got there he had forgotten.

'We need to go out,' he stated firmly.

'Theo, the weather is bad, and you do not seem well. Maybe it is not such a good idea.'

Nebay was cooking dinner, adding the final touches to a lasagne. The tomato sauce smelled good, but it did not sway Theo's resolve.

'If I stay here I will go mad. There is so much to do, so many unfinished things. They are driving me crazy. I need to get out. I need a drink.'

'Elise was very clear that drinking is not good for you.'

'A daughter cannot tell a father what to do. A little drink will not kill me. A hangover will not wipe me off this earth. I am already dying. I want to have some fun.'

'I really do not think it is a good idea.'

'Well, I do.'

Theo left the room and went to get his coat. Nebay could come or stay, but he guessed he would follow him. He stopped at the front door.

'Okay then. I'm leaving!'

Nebay came into the corridor looking defeated.

'Okay, okay. Let me get my things. I guess we can eat dinner when we get back.'

Minutes later they were in the street. The rain made the paving stones seem opaque under their feet. Theo imagined he could see all the way down, forty-five million years down into the heart of the old quarries. What sort of people took the ground from under them to build the houses above? He was not an architect or an engineer, but he understood the need for foundations, the requirement of living things to have something solid under their feet.

'Take me to a place you know.'

'What sort of place?'

'A bar, maybe a bar with dancing.'

'You are not well enough to go dancing.'

'I am a dying man. If I don't dance now, when will I?'

'There is something different about you today.'

Theo remained silent. He could not express how he felt. He had still not received a reply to his letter. Inside he felt like his heart was jumping as if it was on a bouncing thing, a trampoline. How would he survive the passing of time until a reply came? What would he do when it did? Would he be able to find her, finally, would he be able to see her again? Just once more would be enough. Just once.

They had arrived at the entrance to the metro. The rain was getting heavier. He called the wet stuff a bastard under his breath, drawing a look from Nebay. Without discussing it they started down the steps. It was only sensible to escape the rain and the further down they went the more solid the ground became. Theo's pace quickened. As they strode on together he felt the years fall from him. He bought the metro tickets from the machine, feeling confident in his mastery of such technology, and handed one to Nebay.

'Where to?' asked Theo.

'I know a place in Belleville but I am not sure it is the sort of place…'

'Sounds perfect.'

'You have to understand, I do not really go out often.'

'All the more reason.'

'If you are sure.'

'I'm sure.'

There were no seats on the metro, so they stood, holding onto the hanging things. Strange, he felt no pain in his legs or back. He almost felt good. He felt alive! But then he caught sight of his reflection in the window glass.

'Tomorrow I think I need to buy a new hat.'

Nebay looked at him quizzically. 'If that is what you want, then that is what we will do.'

When the metro regurgitated them onto the streets of Belleville, Theo felt as if he were in a different city. How long had it been since he was last here, a place that had once been so familiar to him? He could not remember. It was dark and the lights of Chinese supermarkets illuminated the pavements. The owner of a café called out a greeting to Nebay which he returned. A restaurant with a rotisserie by the front door piled with roasted chickens made Theo momentarily hungry, but that was not why they were here. There were more important experiences to be had.

He was enjoying the night air and light breeze. It reminded him of the mountains at this time of year. There was a certain scent; a combination of leaf mulch and wet bark, the suggestion of frost. It brought back to him an image of Marianne on skis sitting on the wooden steps of a chalet they had rented. After he had taken the photo he had carried her inside and removed the complicated salopettes from her body.

Nebay lit a cigarette and offered one to Theo who declined.

'We are nearly there.'

'Good,' Theo said but suddenly he felt like lingering in the outside air a little longer. 'I will have a cigarette after all. It's been a long time, and this is probably the right time to take it back up.'

He coughed on his first inhale. The smoke tasted bitter and chemical, but by the third pull he had remembered the old magic. Marianne had always smoked when she was driving. They would escape to the countryside in her beaten-up old car. Theo would hold the map, find a road that looked interesting and direct them to it. As night fell they would find a small guest house or a place to pitch the tent. In the evenings, Theo would stare into his lover's eyes and wonder what his life had been without her. What had been its point before she arrived?

She would write an account of their day in her notebook and read it back to him.

'Irresponsible male gave driver wrong directions to beach and thus beach café could not be reached for lunch. Day ruined until ingenious *female* driver found solution: due to inclement weather conditions, traditional car picnic was organised in picturesque layby.'

She could be like that. She could be relaxed and funny. The fact that most of the time she was not, and had her head buried in some book describing an endless assault of injustices, had made him love those moments even more.

They had reached the bar. It sat on a corner, back from the street, with a scattering of chairs and small tables along the pavement. There was a crowd of young people outside, smoking and drinking. Music could be heard through the open doors. It was fast paced, and he could see people dancing.

'Are you ready?'

Theo nodded, bracing himself. The crush of people was overwhelming. They weaved through the crowd to the bar.

'What would you like to drink?' Theo asked.

'What are you having?'

'Whisky.'

'I'll join you, no ice.'

There was no room to breathe let alone sit inside so they took their drinks to one of the little pavement tables. Theo was beginning to feel foolish.

'I'm sorry I made you take me out. Dinner looked good.'

'You were right though. It's good to get out. I am glad we came.'

'So am I. The truth is, I'm not feeling quite myself. I'm waiting for a reply to a letter I sent to an old girlfriend. Every day I wait drives me a little more crazy.'

'Love's like that,' Nebay replied as two men walked passed holding hands.

'Have you ever found someone to…?'

'Love?'

'Yes.'

'I have known love. I have known it very well.'

'Where is she now?'

'Nowhere, he is nowhere now. Maybe we should be getting back soon.'

Theo did not know how to respond and Nebay's tone did not invite questions.

The following morning he awoke with a headache and a feeling of anticipation. He wrapped his dressing gown around him and made his way slowly down the stairs to the mail box. He turned the key and looked inside. There was a letter with an Algerian stamp. He stared at it until he heard someone coming. As if he had something to hide, he placed it quickly in his pocket and raced, as fast as his old legs could carry him, back to his bedroom. He needed privacy.

The letter looked small held between Theo's large fingers. His hand shook slightly. Part of him wanted to rip it open immediately, while a small voice cautioned against disappointment, said hide it, never look at it again, better to know nothing than to know the worst.

He ripped it open.

Dear Mr Demarais,

I am afraid to say that although your friend did once stay here, and is remembered by some of our neighbours, I myself was not born until after her departure. My parents, God bless them, have both passed away and would have been the only ones who may have known of a forwarding address. However, knowing of her role in the Resistance, I have tried to do what little I can. We have a lot to thank her for.

The only possible lead that I can offer you is that my aunt, my mother's younger sister, who also boarded with us at the time, believes that she departed for France in order to have medical treatment during the summer of 1981. Do not worry, I believe the matter was non-urgent.

I wish you the best of luck in your search but am afraid I can be of no further use.

Yours sincerely,

Mr Boudjedra

Theo folded the paper and put it on the arm of his chair. She had left Algeria not long after they had last seen each other and not long before Elise was born. Could it be that she had been in France all along? Would she have returned to Paris? He stood, his legs stiff, and walked to the table in the hall where the phone was. On the shelf under the phone was a rather dusty directory. Why had he not thought of it before? He took it back to his chair with him. It seemed unlikely that somebody with no internet presence would have their phone number so obviously listed, but then maybe she was a traditionalist after all. He flicked through pages until he reached the end of the A section. Nothing. He rested his head on the high-backed chair. An emotion he was familiar with, a sense of failure mixed with helplessness, returned to him. He closed his eyes and tried to think. Tried to untie all the knots in his head, ease a thought out. One clear thought.

Surely, there must be someone, some old acquaintance

from university who would have her address or know someone who did. Of course, these old connections were dwindling, falling into the ground faster than you could say their names, and for this reason he had avoided it thus far. He was, after all, just a few rows behind them, balancing on the grave's edge. He shook his head, listening to the rattle of everything shifting and falling, and made his way to the office to find his old address book.

He flicked through the pages, uncertain of exactly who he was looking for. After five phone calls he had discovered that two more of his friends were dead, one had emigrated to the south of Spain, one had been locked up by her loving family in a care home and the last one had no memory of Marianne ever existing. He was exhausted. He remembered the two men who had died so clearly, Pierre especially, they used to go climbing together. They had travelled to Portugal and spent three days hiking in the Serra de Estrela. He had been so strong and yet in the end it meant nothing. They had been together in Algeria – one of the few friends Theo had kept from the army – and had met in the Paris barracks. Pierre had been recalled after serving in Indochina.

'I only married her two months ago,' he had confided in Theo on his first night. 'She's pregnant and I just had to leave her. She hates my mother, but her own parents live in the South. I'm worried that when I get back she'll be gone.'

'I'm sure she'll wait for you,' Theo had said, not believing it.

'I thought I was free of all this. I thought I could finally build a life.'

That night, Theo had lain in his narrow bunk and heard objections reverberate throughout the room.

'I bought the bloody thing on hire purchase. Who's going to pay for it now?'

'My father's in hospital, I won't see him again.'

He fell asleep with the sound of his new companions' complaints in his ears.

When it was finally time for them to board the train to

Marseille, they were taken to country stations just outside Paris. Many refused to cooperate. Riot police were brought in. By the end of the day the trains were filled, and the new recruits were even more disillusioned. As darkness fell and the train pulled away, the conscripts banged on the sides.

'Send us home!'

'Down with war!'

Theo sat next to Pierre as they travelled through the countryside of France, and the villages and fields fell away. When they finally arrived in the port of Algiers, one thing was clear to him – Algeria was only French in the imagination of the government and on the maps adorning the classroom walls of his youth.

CHAPTER 20

Λ scarred face. A mutilation. Elise's reflection in the glass of a framed world map in the kitchen of the apartment caught her off guard. The lines of continents fragmented her features, deep set wrinkles formed by valley beds made her look prematurely ancient, borders disfigured her cheeks with trails of varicose veins, mountains erupted like burst blood vessels. She stared fifty years into her future. Her life momentarily compacted. She had the sense of running out of time.

Back in her room, she put on a short flowery dress. As she pulled on tights she heard the door. Mathieu was here. Theo had invited him for dinner. She could hear him talking to her father and Nebay. For a while she considered staying were she was and leaving them to it. She was sitting on the edge of her bed, her knees bent up and her arms resting on them. Her hair was still loosely tied in a ponytail. There was a knock on the door and as she stood it opened.

'Theo? You should wait until I answer before coming in.'

Her father was staring at her.

'Are you okay?' she asked.

He did not move so she walked towards him.

'What's wrong?'

He shook his head as if clearing his vision. 'Sorry, Elise, you shocked me that's all.'

'You just walked into my bedroom and yet you say I shocked you?'

He still looked confused. 'I know, I know. I'm sorry. It's just…'

'What?'

'You just reminded me of someone. That's all.'

'Of who?'

'No matter. Come through. Mathieu is here.'

'Okay, I'm coming now.'

Elise closed the door again as her father retreated. She took her hair down and briefly checked it in the mirror. What had he been talking about? For a moment she had thought he did not recognise her.

'Did you know that Nebay is a writer?' asked Mathieu as she walked into the sitting room.

'No,' she smiled at them both sitting side by side on the sofa. She still felt she did not really know Nebay. They hardly saw each other apart from first thing in the morning and as she got home from work. 'What do you write?'

'Nothing really, I should not have said anything.'

'That's what all writers say,' said Mathieu. 'Just like Elise, when she says she's not an artist, even when she's covered in paint.'

'I did not know you painted.'

'Well, I don't much anymore.'

'Elise started painting when she was just a child. If you left her alone for more than two minutes she'd be drawing on the walls. I came into my office one day and there she was, drawing all over my paperwork.'

'That's not true,' she said, but as the words came out of her mouth she remembered.

'It is. You said, "Papa, I've drawn you a map, so you always know how to get home," in a very serious voice.'

She had snuck into his office with her felt-tips. When he caught her she had worried he would tell her off, but instead he came to admire her work. Funny how she had forgotten all the good memories and stored up all the bad ones instead.

'You do have a tendency to be serious,' said Mathieu as he went to check on the dinner he had made with Nebay, leaving her no time to reply. 'It's ready!' he called moments later.

They sat down to eat, carbonara heaped on their plates.

'Last time I ate this was with an old girlfriend of mine. She thought it was vegetarian and spat out the first piece of ham she found, it landed right in my wine,' Theo laughed to himself.

Elise wondered whether this girlfriend had been before, after or during his marriage, but did not ask.

'The last time I cooked this was for Elise on our tenth anniversary. Do you remember?'

'Yes, and do you admit that I am not always serious?' For dinner they had dressed in each other's clothes, Mathieu wearing a stretchy black dress with red leggings while she opted for a tweed suit he had bought in a second-hand shop.

'Okay, you are not always serious.'

'Well, the last time I ate this was in Italy,' said Nebay.

'You win. Did you get the chance to go to Florence? I've always wanted to,' said Mathieu.

'No, but it's likely I'll visit again.'

A look passed between her father and Nebay.

'Let's hope not,' said Theo quietly.

'But, Theo, you love Italy,' said Elise.

He looked at her for a moment before replying, 'Ah, yes, of course. Sorry, I'm rather tired.'

Mathieu began clearing the plates and Elise got up to help him. After the dishes were done, they sat alone at the kitchen table.

'Why did you do it?' she finally asked. 'You must have known what I would say.'

'It was impulsive. If I had thought about it properly I would never have had the courage.'

'To ask me to be chained to the kitchen sink for the rest of my days?' Elise laughed. 'Sorry.'

'I think we have a very different understanding of what it was that I was asking, as you've just proven.'

'Okay, what were you asking?'

'Well, for me, because my parents were never together, I have a very romantic idea, I guess. It seems, to me, very cosy, very warm. I was asking you if we could share our lives, for all of our lives. I was asking you if we could build a life together.'

'It sounds beautiful.' She paused. 'I suppose to me marriage seems like a kind of death, not in the literal sense, not because of what my mum did in the end, but more because of what it meant for her while she was alive.'

'But don't you see? You are suggesting she was in some way made by her marriage, that she was not her own person over and above that.'

'You're saying I'm an antifeminist.'

'No, you have to stop misinterpreting me, sometimes I think you do it on purpose. I'm saying that you are a person who has spent most of her life grieving, and trying to explain that grief, and the death that led to it, in a way which makes it comprehensible. To make it logical in some way, so that it can be tidied away.'

Elise was silent for some time.

'I hate to admit it, but maybe, in part, you are right.'

'See, it's good to talk.'

'I should be getting to bed.'

Mathieu got up to leave. 'Think about what I have said.'

'I will, I'll sleep on it.'

'Okay, okay, I'm going.'

CHAPTER 21

For a week, Nebay stayed at Theo's. The old man needed him, and he had nowhere else to go. In the evenings he went to a café over the road to write, not wanting to crowd the small apartment. He had heard nothing from the Doctor or the Lawyer. It was time to try the Jungle. Elise and Theo had plans for the weekend, so it was easy to slip away without being asked any questions. He did not want to worry them.

On the way, he went to the Western Union and made a second transfer to Asmeret. It was not as much as he had wanted to send her, just under a thousand euros, but it would pay for a little more time with Ms Sykes, the lawyer. When they had last spoken, his sister had told him that Ms Sykes was very positive and believed that she should have been granted asylum the first time around. They could have an answer in just a few weeks. He hoped that he would see her soon, but hope was a tricky thing for people like him, so he pushed the thought from his mind. If in this life he saw her again, he would be grateful, better to leave it at that.

The Parisian Jungle looked much like any other shanty town, but even less permanent; a mismatched array of tents and a few small shacks built with other people's leftovers, constructed hurriedly and destroyed just as quickly by the police. There was something universal in the design that was almost comforting. And just like any city there were divisions and boundaries. Different nationalities lived separately with few crossovers. Countries who had long been at war did not live next to each other. Eritrea and Ethiopia kept their distance, living on opposite sides of the canal. It was a complicated line, one built on brotherhood and hatred, and so many years of struggle that the beginnings and ends of wars had become as blurred as their border.

He walked through the muddy alleyways, avoiding guy ropes and misplaced timber. A few people looked familiar, but he saw nobody he knew well. He stopped to ask a man with whom he had once shared the back of a truck, along with thirty others, if he had seen the Doctor or the Lawyer but he had no recollection of them. A man was selling tea from the front of his tent. Nebay bought a cup and sat in the dust to work out where to go from here. Their mobile phones had been off since he last saw them. This suggested they were in police custody – it would be unusual for them both to lose them at the same time – in which case he would just have to wait until they were released. The Parisian police had limited holding cells so he would probably not be waiting for long.

The tent opposite him, the sort you could buy in the supermarket, had the flap open and rolled back. Inside, everything was immaculate; all the person's possessions remained in one small bag for a fast getaway when the police next came to clear the area. The sleeping bag, with no roll mat underneath, was laid out neatly like a well-made bed, the only comfort this person allowed themselves. Beside it, a bottle of water, nothing more. When the young woman who lived there came back she carefully removed her shoes before entering and then brought them in once she had seated herself, placing them neatly on a plastic bag out of the reach of hungry hands.

Nebay nodded to her when she looked in his direction and she smiled cautiously back, before zipping up the tent. What would she lie there and think about, he wondered, with no books or radio to keep her company? Did she have friends? Was she as lucky as him in this regard? Or was she lonely and afraid? Did she sleep at night, or during the day only, to keep herself safe? He had often asked himself these questions about his sister, even now, in the detention centre where she was held in the UK, he knew she did not feel safe. He hung his head, helplessness washing over him like the muddy brown water of the canal.

What would Emmanuel think if he could see him now? What sort of life was this? Definitely not the one they had dreamed up together. When they had spoken once about Paris they had imagined sipping espresso together and walking through the streets hand in hand. It was not even a grand imagining, just small and simple acts of love.

'In Europe,' Emmanuel had said, 'we could be a real family.'

Oh, but we were, thought Nebay, *we always were*.

Emmanuel's face stayed in his mind, along with the ragged edge of his optimism. A group of children ran past Nebay, one carrying a baby who looked only a few months old. They kicked up mud as they passed, laughing, and made him smile. Maybe it was okay to hope after all.

CHAPTER 22

His hands hurt as he desperately searched through his address book. Rheumatoid arthritis: another annotation to the name that had once belonged to him, Theo Demarais. Too much climbing as a young man, the doctor had said gleefully through his shiny, young teeth.

He had worked his way through to 'S', Sebastian, an old friend from university who had gone on to teach secondary school in the suburbs. He rang the number. No answer. He hung up, ignoring the polite woman's request to leave a message. The idea of recording a voicemail intimidated him. What would he say? He rang again, but now he felt foolish. Previously he had only managed to get as far as 'Do you remember a woman called Marianne?' before the recipient of the call had said 'No'. But if Sebastian answered he would want to know more. Why after all this time? Still in love with her are you? And it felt stupid and clichéd to say, 'I'm lonely, I have been since I lost her and my last girlfriend left me for a man eighteen years my junior', at his age, when he should know better or be more interested in stamp collecting or slapping young waitresses' bottoms in cafés, because once you were old you could get away with anything, and this had been one of their jokes. A million years ago he and Sebastian had laughed at themselves as old men, never believing it would happen.

Eventually he found the phone in his hand again and his fingers on the dial. His message would be short and to the point. His intended greeting was running through his head when the phone was answered.

'Hello?'

Theo knew Sebastian's voice immediately. Strange, what stayed and what left, it was as if he had heard it only yesterday.

'It's Theo. I'm sorry to call out of the blue but...'

'Theo?'

'Yes! How are you?'

'Good, how are you? Is everything alright? An unexpected call is generally not good news. It's not another funeral, is it? I don't think I can take another.'

'Don't worry, it's not a funeral. How did we get so old?'

'Old? I'm not old. I'm a rather fit seventy-seven.'

'Well, I'll leave that for your wife to judge.'

'Unfortunately, Saber is no longer with us to pass comment.'

'Oh, Sebastian, I'm sorry. I shouldn't have...'

'Don't worry, it's been three years, I've got a girlfriend of eighty-one. She calls me her toy boy. Now, what are you after you old rascal if it's not to tell me another of our number has succumbed?'

'Do you remember Marianne?'

'The firecracker? Of course, never met another like her.'

'Are you still in touch?'

'Not since Saber died,' the tone of his voice had changed. Theo became nervous.

'Sorry, I didn't mean to...'

If it was three years since Saber had died, what did that mean for Marianne?

'No, Theo, don't worry...' His voice was hesitant, hanging lost like a broken wire after a storm.

'Hello?'

'I'm still here. It's just that I don't know if she'd want to see you.' This last bit was rushed, too serious and too awkward for their broken, young-man friendship.

After a moment, Theo realised he was holding his breath, as if to suck in the moment. She had to be alive to still be angry, and an angry alive person could be apologised to. His heart felt as if it were truly beating for the first time in years, pumping the blood around his body, keeping him alive until he saw her.

'I see,' he managed.

'You didn't leave her in the best of circumstances.'

But I can explain, he thought, *I can explain it all to her now. It's not too late.*

'Of course, yes, you're right. I shouldn't have called,' he said, wishing that Sebastian would just give him the number so he could hang up and get on with ringing her.

'No, Theo, it's good to hear from you. I'll try and track her down. Let her know you want to talk.'

Theo could only whisper his thank-you and his hands shook as he placed the receiver down. Sebastian did not have her number or would not give it to him. Maybe she had even asked him expressly not to. What a fool he had been to think she would still care for him now after all he had done. He had failed her over and over again. He thought of that day in 1961, 17 October, the day that changed everything. Clear and crisp and more present than his own reflection in the mirror above the hall table where the telephone lived, had always lived, since there had first been a phone in the apartment.

They had been smoking, jammed around a tiny table, at the back of a café packed with fellow students. Dinner lay destroyed around them. Theo picked up the crossword – it was only half-finished – and dusted off the crumbs. Marianne had doodled a series of interlocking lines in the margins of the newspaper. He traced the indentations of her pen with his finger and sighed at all the unanswered questions. He had been thinking of the day that de Gaulle walked into Paris, how it felt as if he had come to rescue them, how his parents had looked so defeated in the midst of it all. He finally understood. De Gaulle was not a man to be trusted. He had betrayed the values that his father had fought for and now Marianne wanted to join the fight against him.

'I am going to go. The curfew is an affront to our basic human rights.'

Theo took her hands in his.

'They are my people,' she said.

'You are French.'

'But I am also half-Algerian and that is all that matters to the police and to de Gaulle. You have seen the posters, Papon is a pig, and I would think he was a pig even if I wasn't Algerian. He is using torture in Paris, Theo, in Paris. Where is our equality, fraternity and liberty?'

Theo thought of the dead policemen, killed by the FLN, and their families. He thought of the slaughtered Algerians, killed by the French Army, and their families. He thought of the war that had birthed him, of the dead woman sprawled on the ground with life oozing from her, of the Jewish families rounded up by the same policemen that still patrolled the streets of Paris.

'Are you sure?'

'Yes.'

'Then I'll come.'

They paid their bill and walked out into the street. It was already getting dark. At the Odéon they decided to take the metro.

'I'm sorry, madam, but you cannot pass,' stated an officer at the entrance.

'What do you mean?'

'No Algerians on the metro, madam.'

'You're crazy, she's not Algerian, she's Italian.'

'Sir, I'm afraid it doesn't matter. She cannot access the metro today.'

Marianne spat at the policeman's feet. 'You disgust me,' she said in Arabic as Theo gently took her arm.

'My love, there is no point.'

'There is always a point when you are confronted by a fascist pig.'

The officer made to move towards them.

'Look, this isn't worth it. Let's go and find everyone else.'

Marianne turned reluctantly and they began the long walk to the Right Bank.

As they reached the Grande Boulevards they fell in line with the marchers. People were dressed in their Sunday best, suited and with straight backs, proud. Theo watched as Marianne raised her head a little higher. She reached for his hand.

'It is beautiful.'

In the distance they heard the sound of sirens, but it seemed unimportant when there was such a feeling of strength. Theo began to relax. He smiled at the people around him. Whole families walked together; men, women and children. The street was wide, but they filled it, it felt like they owned it. A grandmother walked beside them, her grandchild in a flowery frock in her arms. Theo saw the wide smile Marianne gave to them. She looked happier than he had ever seen her.

Towards Opéra they began to hear the sound of the first lines meeting the police. He had been wrong to let down his guard. The faces around them changed, some full of fear, others overflowing with anger. Theo felt the ground tilt up towards him, his breathing quickened. As the crowd started running they were forced to run with them. On the edge of his vision he saw people being picked off and dragged away by the police to be taken to waiting buses. Shots were fired nearby. He felt the urge to duck, to curl up into a small ball, to disappear. The air around them had changed and their numbers had dwindled. Theo pulled Marianne to a halt. Others stopped with them as if to take a last great collective breath. On the exhale they saw the police line that had formed in front of them, batons raised. Theo's grip on Marianne's hand tightened. Their exits were blocked. The floor was scattered with bowler hats. Some Sunday suits were ripped.

'I think it might be time to leave.'

'You want to run away? You want to let them win?'

'Marianne, they are armed, they will win.'

Theo realised for the first time just how far Marianne was willing to go, but he had already seen war, in Paris and Algeria. He wanted to protect her from herself.

The crowd around them surged forward again, nearly knocking them both to the ground. The shots continued.

'My love, listen to me,' he turned towards her again. 'It is not safe. We have to leave.'

They pushed sideways out of the crowd and headed towards the Saint-Michel Bridge. Others followed. The police lined the roads and met them at the bridge, blocking their way. As people tried to cross they beat them. The body of a young man, no older than them, was thrown, carelessly, into the water. The policeman who had done so then resumed his attack with no trace of his action on his face. Theo looked down just in time to see the body disappear under the bridge, partly covered by the dark brown water of the Seine. They clambered out through the press of people, clawing their way along the cold stone in order to stay upright. When they finally reached the road they stopped again, unsure of which way to head.

Theo took Marianne's hand, trying to make it look as if they were merely innocent bystanders, hoping, and hating himself for doing it, that his white skin and Marianne's relatively fair complexion would get them out of this situation.

Police cars were already careering up the street to block the exit of those still on the bridge. As they began to walk back towards home, the ominous truth of the day's events stripping them of conversation, a police officer approached them.

'You look to be a long way from home, sir,' he said, addressing Theo and ignoring Marianne. 'I hope you haven't been involved with this lot,' he continued, with a nod of his head towards the bridge where in the darkness all that could be seen were shadows.

'Just trying to go out for a stroll, Officer, but there's all these fucking Arabs in the way. I don't know what has become of Paris.'

The policeman smiled.

'Well, that's something we're working on. You might want to think a little more about your route next time, not to mention the company you keep,' he added with a sneer.

Theo tried hard to keep his cool. It would be pointless to lose it now, when they were so nearly safe.

'Of course,' he managed to growl out between his teeth. 'Thank you, Officer.'

They walked on.

'Fucking Arabs?!' Marianne spat as soon as the policeman was out of earshot.

'You know what I was doing.'

'Do I?'

'I was just trying to get us away safely.'

'You were trying get yourself away safely!'

'Marianne, that's not the case, you know that's not…'

She had dropped his hand and started walking off down the street at twice the pace. He caught up with her and she turned to him in fury.

'They're murdering them! They're hacking people up in broad daylight as if this was some backstreet in Algiers and it is bad enough they do it there! Nowhere is safe.'

'Marianne,' he said gently, trying to take her hand, but she would not let him.

'No!' She raised her fists and shook them at the air as if taking on the god she did not believe in. 'No! No! No!'

CHAPTER 23

They would link arms, Elise matching her mother's longer stride. She remembered staring up at her beautiful face in awe of the glamorous woman at her side. After Elise had told her about her day at school, recounted what she had learnt, her mother would fill in the gaps. This was how she had learnt of the night when Marie Antoinette had wandered lost in Paris looking for her husband's carriage in a desperate attempt to flee from their fate. She had imagined, through her mother's words, the desperate fear of a woman lost in her own city, unaware of its slums and alleyways, unable to negotiate her way even a few metres in the mist. She had felt the claustrophobia of winding lanes narrower than the Queen's corridors, the temporary relief when the destination was reached, the crushing reality of capture and the inevitability of the guillotine. Days like this were the good days, the ones Elise liked to remember.

It was the anniversary of her mother's death. She had woken early to the bells from Saint-Sulpice. In the bathroom, she removed a coffee cup from the sink and searched for a towel. She still did not know where Nebay put things. After a shower she went into the kitchen and tidied a pile of books and paperwork from the draining board. Theo must have been up in the night. There was a copy of Kafka's *The Trial* among the debris.

She had been twelve when her mother died, and an image of that night – the bright light through an open door, a reflection of her own face in the bathroom mirror, the beautiful face of her mother, swollen and distorted – had stayed with her, etched into some dark recess of her retina, and with it, buried even deeper, was the fear that her mother's illness had been passed on to her, that she too would one day feel as if there was no longer any point in going forward, until all that was left was the inevitable and long-awaited end.

Elise and Theo used to mark this day almost every year; it was a day of truce between them. There had, of course, been some that he had forgotten. When she was young he had tried to do something that Elise would enjoy like a trip to the zoo or a picnic in the park. Later they had started going for lunch at her mother's favourite restaurant, Valerie's. It was an elegant place with high-backed chairs and silver candlesticks on the tables. Monique and Theo had sometimes come for dinner here when he returned from one of his trips. Unfortunately, Valerie's had recently closed, leaving black holes where lit windows used to be.

Elise and Theo left the apartment together. She supported him as he walked down the stairs. He paused as they reached the door onto the street.

'You look lovely, my dear,' he said patting her arm.

Elise gave a small smile in response. She was wearing a short black dress her mother would have liked. She may even have had one similar. As soon as Elise had seen it there had been something strangely familiar about the cut of the fabric and even its smell. She felt the cotton now between her fingers, comforting.

'Where shall we go today?' he asked. 'Why not take me to one of your favourites.'

'I'm afraid I don't eat out enough to have a favourite. You choose.'

Elise cut into the soft pink flesh of the salmon. They were seated in a small café by the Seine that Theo had chosen. Her father stared vacantly out of the window as if looking into another time. The salmon was dry in Elise's throat and she took a large sip of wine to wash it down.

'Who did I remind you of the other day, when Mathieu came for dinner?'

'Sorry?'

'You walked into my bedroom and said I reminded you of someone else.'

'Oh, just an old friend from university, someone I was very close to.'

'Someone you met before Mum?'

'Yes, she was very special, you would have liked her.'

'Why did you marry Monique? You must have had other options, and you never seemed happy together.'

Theo put down his knife and fork and sat back in his chair.

'The most honest answer I can give you is that I don't really know. I thought for a moment that we were in love, it turned out that we were not. I'm sorry, it's probably not what you want to hear.'

'At least it's the truth.' Elise paused, unsure if she should ask her next question, one that she had always avoided up until now, but who knew how long they had left. 'Why do you think she ended it the way she did?'

'I don't know, Elise, she wasn't happy, she'd never really been happy with me and I don't think she was very happy with herself either. I just wish you hadn't found her like that.'

'I've blamed you, you know, for most of my life.'

'I know. I have blamed me too.'

She reached out her hand to him and he took it.

'It was just her illness, I always knew it really, but you were a more tangible target. It was not your fault,' she said to her father who seemed on the edge of tears.

'Yes, well, enough of all of this silliness. Let's go home, shall we?'

Elise paid the bill and went to use the bathroom, when she got back to their table Theo had gone.

CHAPTER 24

A young Asian guy pointed towards a computer and Nebay went to take his place at the screen. The rest of the internet café was filled with the usual assortment of non-native French. Legals or semi-legals. You could tell by the way they sat, relaxed, their headset giving them partial privacy as they talked to their families on Skype or connected to their friends on Facebook. Nebay did not have Facebook. He avoided anything that could be so easily monitored by the state.

He logged into his email account, hoping for an update from his sister, and saw a message from the Lawyer.

Professor!
Don't panic. The Doctor's being held for a few days. Just another little game to play. My phone got lost during the chase – police chases are never as exciting as American movies suggest. I think we might all need new jobs... Maybe your old man needs some more carers? Don't worry, I don't think I could stomach a French mapmaker.

Meet me tonight if you get this. I'll be at home. I think it's safe for now.

Nebay logged out immediately, threw some change in the direction of the counter and walked as quickly as he could back to Belleville. When he arrived in their room, the Lawyer looked tired but okay. He was drinking a beer on his own.

'Glad you could join us!' he said, passing Nebay a bottle.

'It seems I have already missed the party,' Nebay replied, taking the bottle and embracing his friend.

'Yes, a shame, there was a whole crowd here, dancing girls… maybe not your thing.'

'Maybe not, but even I can appreciate dancing.'

'In Paris they do not dance.'

The Lawyer seemed downhearted and Nebay did not know how to raise his spirits. For now he was just glad that he was safe and that they were together again, but he knew that without work he would have nothing to do but sit and think about the past. One thing they all had in common was that they were in Paris because they had pasts that it was best to forget.

'That's not true, there's a bar just round the corner where they dance.'

'The music is terrible. It sounds like someone rattling a can while someone else bangs a drum out of time.'

'You are being difficult to please.'

'We are living in difficult times.'

Nebay realised that they seldom spent time alone together without the Doctor. It seemed wrong. The rhythm they were used to faltered. He finished his beer and lit a cigarette while thinking of a way to cheer up the Lawyer.

'When I was young my sister once tried to dress me up in her clothes. She was older than me. She had always wanted a little sister to play with, but she got me instead and I was the last.'

Finally the Lawyer laughed. 'Is that why you're…?'

'No, Mr Lawyer. Being put in a dress when you are five does not make you gay.'

The Lawyer smiled but looked to the floor. They never discussed Nebay's sexuality. It was generally acknowledged only in the light of comedy, but it was accepted, just. He knew that the Doctor and the Lawyer had both found it difficult at first, in their own ways, and the fact that they had got this far meant a lot to him. To be accepted for who he was among his friends and family was all that he had ever wanted.

He had come out to his sister when he was fourteen. She had laughed at him. She had always known. Her smile and love on that day had been everything he needed. He knew he could not tell the world, but to have told one person and to have been accepted was enough in that moment.

'What will you do for work?' Nebay asked to fill the silence.

'Construction, maybe. Whatever I can find. Or maybe it is time to leave. To try something different.'

'Well, do not make any rash decisions without your doctor present…'

The Lawyer laughed again. 'You're right, he would disapprove. He would say, "Sleep on it."'

'He would, and he would remind you of all that you would leave behind, isn't that what you told me the other day?'

'Ah, Professor, I fear that you two intellectuals would fare just fine without me.'

'Well, that's where you are wrong, because without you we would surely die of grieving!'

The Lawyer laughed. 'A big responsibility to place upon my shoulders!'

'I'm just telling you the simple truth,' Nebay laughed. 'If you stay you won't have to worry about it.'

'I'll sleep on it, I will. No rash decisions tonight, I promise.'

'Good,' said Nebay, relieved. He imagined waking up alone in their room, a note of goodbye pinned to the door, the only proof of their lives together.

'Now let's talk about something more cheerful,' said the Lawyer, finally coming back to himself. 'Did you hear the score in the Inter Milan game?'

'I did! A great victory!' replied Nebay and they brought their beer bottles together with a loud clank to celebrate.

It was only the small things in life that could be guaranteed to bring you joy.

CHAPTER 25

Theo was sitting alone in a strange restaurant that looked as if it was for tourists. Why would he have come here? Why would he have come here alone? He touched his face, there were tears there, he was crying again, he felt terribly sad. Why was he crying? Why was he sad? He stood up to leave. A man could not just sit on his own in a restaurant crying, especially when he did not even know why. What if someone saw him? What if someone asked him what all this crying was about? What would he tell them?

He left and walked towards the river. It was cold and he hugged himself as he paused at one of the small stalls to look at books. The titles danced before his eyes. He picked up one that looked familiar and opened it. The pages of Camus's *A Happy Death* were well worn and gave off the comforting smell of an old book. He recognised it now, of course he did, but the individual words refused to stay in their sentences. As soon as he pinned one down the previous one escaped. It was no good. He replaced it, feeling grumpy, and walked away. What was it that that man had said? That happiness was a long patience? Was that it? It certainly felt that way.

Had he been happy? Had he ever really been happy since he lost Marianne? The question hung in the air around him and he looked up towards the tall buildings, the Paris stone and pigeons. There was so much beauty here that one became unable to see it. Was that the way with happiness also?

Taking a street he did not recognise, he walked away from the water. Strange that such a small city could still hold secrets after a lifetime's relationship. The idea of exploration made him feel elated, his sadness lifted. This was what it was all about: new places, new people and experiences. To discover, to map, to move on. This had been the life of the first cartographers. He paused outside a small bar and watched the families eating their late lunches; parents hurrying food into their children's mouths, waiters frowning in impatience. Theo strained to recall similar experiences in his own life. He created a picture of himself having a family meal with his daughter and her mother, their names were on the tip of his tongue, right at the edge of it, but he could not quite find them, and the image he had imagined felt like a falsehood. He continued hastily up the narrow street, an ache beginning in his legs as he trudged along the cobbled pavement.

At a crossroads he stopped. Which way to go now? He still did not recognise a single landmark. Could it really be that he had never walked these streets before, or had they simply fallen off his map like everything else? Like a globe, things curved away from him. A whisper of fear crept in. To be lost in your own city seemed like too much of a cruelty. He turned left, intending to turn left again, surely that would take him back to the river? Anybody could find their direction from the Seine. The first left took him past an old record shop, a delicatessen, a hair stylist's. He had never seen any of them before. By the time he came to take the second left he could no longer be sure that he had wanted to take a left and not a right, but he did it anyway. He was beginning to panic. How could he have let this happen?

Theo's walk had become a run, but his old legs still moved too slowly and then there was the pain that began in his feet and seemed to end somewhere in his lower back. He could feel sweat beginning to gather on his forehead, his armpits, his groin. He disgusted himself; an old man sweating and lurching. He reached for grace, for a place of redemption, and Marianne's face appeared before him with her sharp eyes and her soft smile. Collapsing on a bench, he was only barely aware of the sound of the Seine. Marianne's face was all that mattered and when two men in uniform approached him it seemed only right that they had come to bring him to her. There would be no point to anything else. That was all his life was for.

Arms hooked themselves into his arms. He shook his head in embarrassment, he smelled bad, he did not need help, he did not understand who these men were or what they wanted with him. In the periphery of his vision he saw the river and at least this was right. He had got himself to the right place.

'Have you seen her?' he asked as they searched his pockets. 'Have you seen Marianne?'

She had left in the morning without waking him. As his eyes adjusted to the half-light of dawn he could still make out the indentation of her head upon the pillow. The conversation that had led to this was on repeat. He went through it again and again. He had not realised that it would have such immediate repercussions.

'I have to dedicate myself to the struggle.'

'What do you mean?'

'I'm going to Algiers. I have a friend there. He will help me to make the arrangements.'

'Marianne, no. You can support their work from here. I can help...'

'What? Like you helped today, "fucking Arabs", you call that helping?'

'I call that keeping you safe.'

'You have no idea what happens outside the realm of your pampered little Parisian life.'

'You do not know what I have seen.'

'I know the Nazis came to Paris. I know you had to fight in Algeria. But who are the Nazis now? It is our responsibility to stop this.'

He had already escaped once. He had already survived. He did not know if he would be that lucky again. He could not go. He had not gone. And now he was alone.

CHAPTER 26

The waiter had not noticed Theo leaving. The other customers had not noticed him being there in the first place. Outside, there was no sign of him. Elise called his name and received no answer. He could be anywhere. She ran to the nearest metro station, searching the crowds as she went. On the train she sat nervously on the edge of her seat, picking at the skin around her fingernails. Rain had begun to fall by the time she arrived at the Odéon and she thought of her father lost out there in the cold. She should not have asked him that question. He was ill. She should not have upset him.

There was a police car outside the apartment. He was dead and it was her fault. She ran up the stairs two at a time and found two officers outside their door.

'Are you Miss Elise Demarais?' asked the taller of the officers.

'Yes,' she whispered, her hand still on the banister, her face chalky like the ancient plaster on the walls.

'We found your father.'

Elise waited for further information, but none came.

'And is he okay?' she ventured.

'He was wandering near the river and seemed very confused. We checked his ID and brought him here. He kept talking about a woman called Marianne and asking us if we'd seen her. Is that his wife?'

'No.'

'It's just as well you turned up now or we would have been ringing Social Services.'

Elise released her grip on the banister. 'Thank you, Officers,' she said trying to sound calm. Social Services would no doubt put Theo in a nursing home.

'You might want to keep a closer eye on him in the future.'

'Of course, I'm sorry to have wasted your time.'

'Just make sure it doesn't happen again, Miss,' said the tall one curtly as they turned to leave.

Theo was sitting on the sofa when she entered.

'Hello,' he said cheerily as if nothing had happened. 'When is Nebay coming?'

'Tomorrow, Theo. He will be here tomorrow.' She went to feel her father's forehead. 'How are you feeling?'

'Good, why?'

'No reason, just checking you're okay.'

'I'm okay.' It was as if he had been washed clean of their entire day, there was no trace of it.

Celeste and Laila arrived at the apartment an hour later, Theo was already sleeping, his head leant back against the chair rest.

'You must have been terrified,' said Laila, giving Elise a hug.

'For a second I thought I'd lost him for good. He could have fallen in the river or anything, been run over by a car...'

'He's safe now, time to stop panicking,' Celeste pulled out a chair for her at the kitchen table. 'Sit.'

Elise sat.

'How is it with the new carer? What was his name again?' asked Laila.

'Nebay, I don't see him much, but Theo seems happy.'

'And you?'

'I'd be much happier if none of this was happening.'

'You won't like this, but I think it's good for you. You needed to spend time with him,' said Celeste.

'But the circumstances…'

'In any other circumstances, you would still be in your little flat ignoring his existence.'

'I didn't ignore him.'

'Well, okay, but you didn't see him or call him either.'

Elise did not know how to respond.

'I think you're doing a great job,' said Laila. 'You're doing really well.'

Without expecting it, Elise felt close to tears.

'The thing is, Celeste's right. I didn't spend enough time with him, and now he's slipping away, and I'm not ready to let him go.'

That night, Celeste and Laila stayed on the floor of Elise's bedroom on a pile of old blankets, it was comforting to have them close by even though she struggled to sleep.

The day before her mother had taken her own life she had made pancakes with chocolate sauce, Elise's favourite. Having melted the chocolate, she had dabbed some on Elise's nose and then chased her around the kitchen with a chocolatey finger, threatening to give her war paint. In the end they had collapsed on the floor, weak from laughing. It was a good memory, but it kept her awake nonetheless. Throughout her life, whenever something good had happened, she had expected its exact opposite the following day. The happier she felt, the sadder she knew she would be.

CHAPTER 27

A pile of paper, a stack of books, a heap of clothes. Theo had knocked them all over. He was searching for something but would not tell Nebay what it was.

'It's a surprise,' he said hotly when Nebay asked.

'I could help you look for it.'

'I don't need help.'

'But…'

'It won't be a surprise if you help. If you tell someone then it is not a surprise.'

'Okay.'

The safest place was the window seat in the sitting room. If Nebay picked anything up it would only be knocked over again. He took out his notebook and filled in a short diary entry for the day before. He had decided to commemorate, rather than forget, the past. Watching Theo scrabbling around for memories had made him realise how much he too had already forgotten. The day before, he had written about Emmanuel, about how they had met on the same day that Nebay had moved into the barracks. He had noticed him across the training ground. The long, tall stretch of him, shining in the sunlight. His elegant hand shading his eyes. His thick-rimmed glasses giving him the air of an academic well beyond his years. Nebay had sensed, even then, that it was a moment that would change the course of his life irrevocably.

Eventually, Theo emerged triumphant.

'I have it! I have all of Paris for you!'

He handed Nebay a little red book, the same one that every Parisian carried. Nebay had one in his bag. It was a map of the city. The most popular and the easiest to come by.

'Thank you,' he said, accepting it reverently.

'And now,' announced Theo, 'we can go out.'

They took to the streets, Theo holding the map. He twisted it around in his hands. Moved it closer to his face then further away again. Nebay saw the tears in his eyes.

'I can't...' was all Theo could say.

Instead they went back to the apartment and watched an old black and white movie Nebay did not know the name of. He placed a blanket over Theo's knees and Theo drew it over Nebay's legs as well. It was not long until they both fell asleep. When Nebay woke, Theo's head was resting on his shoulder. He stayed still and let the old man sleep on.

It had been a while since he had spoken to his sister or had any update about her case. The silence worried him. Tomorrow he would try to call her. He had been sending her every cent he could spare, he just hoped that it was enough. He had promised his mother that he would look after Asmeret and he could not let her down.

When Elise came home they supported Theo to bed together. She looked exhausted from work. He knew that he should stay a little while and talk to her about it, give her the opportunity to tell someone about her day, but he was also tired and too wrapped up in his own worries to take on another person's. He felt the guilt of it, but he left nonetheless. Theo had a doctor's appointment in the morning, and Nebay needed some sleep before all of this began again.

CHAPTER 28

They had taken him back to the hospital again, the horrible smelling doctor place. They had said it was for his own good, all the testing and the prodding and the questions, but it felt like he was on trial, a trial to determine whether he was a sane person. It was disturbing, not knowing if you had gotten all the answers right, not knowing what the right answers were anymore. They told him he was dehydrated, had a bladder infection, needed to look after himself better, needed to sleep more, when he already felt like he slept all the time, more than he had ever slept in his life. It was all so boring, this business of getting old.

But, and it was a big but, a big old silver lining and saving grace and all those other things that people said, he seemed to remember a little better for now. But, *the* but again, the one that had given him hope, on the way home from the hospital as they crawled through the Marais in a taxi, his old eyes had caught something, the sight of Marianne's apartment building, a *For Rent* sign hanging from what was once her balcony.

He had wanted to go there immediately, partly just because he had known it, he remembered it as if it were etched into his bones. It was a space they had inhabited together. They had breathed all that air in there. Their feet had walked across those floorboards. Their hands had turned the taps. It was the last place that had been truly theirs. The last place she had lived before leaving for Algeria. In the end he had settled for asking Nebay to find the number and to make an appointment to view it.

Now they were finally standing on the street outside with the estate agent.

'Have you been looking after the gentleman for long?' she asked Nebay.

There were benefits to being old and not existing anymore: people ignored you.

'A while now, yes.'

'And you are thinking of moving to the Right Bank?'

'That's why we're here,' said Nebay with an unconvincing smile.

They were outside the door to the flat. The estate agent turned the key and let them in. Someone had painted the walls a garish yellow, the floorboards were scuffed and heavily marked, some of those marks would be theirs, their map. Theo left Nebay talking to the woman about rising house prices and wandered on, not that there was much ground to cover, the place was tiny. The last night he had stayed here he had drank a lot and slept on the sofa. He stood in the place where the sofa used to be. The morning after, before finally leaving, having waited a week thinking that she would return, he had lain in her bed one last time, inhaled the lingering scent of her. He stood were the bed used to be, he knelt. It was not close enough. He lay on the ground. His eyes were wet. They were always wet these days, for things that were such a long time ago, things that could not really matter anymore and yet they did. It would always matter to him that he lost her. History was all anybody truly had and yet even this could be twisted and turned, stolen, lost and reinterpreted.

Theo could hear footsteps coming. He stood up, dusted himself down and wiped his face. He went to the cupboard in the wall. It was a long shot, but he had left something here the day he went, an intention of sorts. Opening the doors, he bent down to the ground and removed the drawer. Under it there was a loose floorboard. Marianne had joked that it would be a perfect hiding place for information if they had been in the Resistance in the Second World War. He took up the floorboard and reached his hand in. It was there, a black-and-white photograph of Marianne and him outside a coffee shop. He had froth from the coffee on his nose and she was laughing. He had always loved this picture. He turned it around in his hands, wondering at such concrete proof of their love. On the back there was something written. He did not remember writing her a note but perhaps he did.

Dear Theo,

I have come to Paris but of course you are not here. I came to pick up some things that the landlord had stored for me and found this in our little hiding place. I wonder if you will ever see this note. It was difficult in Algeria, but I am glad I did it. It was the right thing to do.

Love always,

Marianne

01.08.62

He had been in Egypt. He had been in bloody Egypt and convinced that she was dead. Not that he would have seen this note here anyway, but if he had been in Paris she would have found him. They could have found each other. The estate agent stood behind him, clearing her throat.

'Sorry,' Nebay said, 'he gets a little confused these days, don't you, Theo. Now let's stand up and let this lady get back to work.'

'Yes, of course,' he muttered as he stood.

They walked back out into the drizzle. The estate agent walked off looking disappointed. She clearly had no faith in them renting the property.

'Thank you, Nebay. You were brilliant.'

'I have always liked the idea of being an actor. Can I just say that you play the role of confused elderly gentleman very well?'

'Can you tell I have been practising?'

'Really? I thought it was natural.'

They walked down the street together like two naughty school boys.

'And how did it feel to be back there?'

'I found this.' He handed Nebay the photograph.

'That's you and her?'

'Yes.'

'You were a very handsome couple.'

'Read the back.'

He turned it over.

'She came to look for you.' Nebay handed the photograph back. 'We will find her, you know. I have a good feeling about it.'

'I hope you're right, Nebay, I really do. And how are you? No more trouble with the police?'

'For now everything is okay, but they are still holding one of my friends.'

'On what charge?'

'Being undocumented, probably, I do not know.'

'I'm sorry, I hope he gets out soon.'

'But I have good news too. I spoke to my sister this morning, she is asking for asylum in the UK, and there is a big campaign for her to stay.' He handed Theo his phone with a picture of a young woman and a newspaper headline. 'This is her.'

Theo looked up at Nebay and back down at the phone, they had the same long straight nose, the same eyes.

'What is her name?'

'Asmeret.'

'And what does the headline say?'

'Set her free.'

When Nebay took the phone back he cradled it gently

and stole one last look at his sister. Theo threaded his arm through Nebay's and they continued to walk, linked like this, their steps at an even pace. Theo could not give him words to replace or conjure up his family, but he could give this freely, he could offer friendship.

CHAPTER 29

Elise was filling in a form on the computer screen when her mobile rang. It was Nebay. He sounded concerned.

'He has gone again.'

'What do you mean gone?'

'I turned around for two seconds and he had left. He disappeared in the crowd. I could not find him anywhere. I am so sorry. What should I do?'

'Okay, Nebay. Where are you? I will come there.'

When she got off the phone, Simon was hovering nearby.

'Who's this Nebay then?' he asked.

Elise tried to ignore him. He must have been listening to her conversation.

'I'm afraid I have to leave. Family emergency.'

Elise walked swiftly up the Rue de Condé from the Odéon metro station, past rows of mopeds and bicycles chained up as if someone was afraid that they would make a break for it. Theo and Nebay had been at a visiting Cezanne exhibition at the Musée de Luxembourg when Theo had gone missing. He could not be too far away; he was slow on his feet these days.

She reached the Jardin du Luxembourg and saw Nebay. As she walked up to him she became nervous. They had never been alone before. She felt unsure of how to greet him or what to say.

'Hi,' she said, standing on her tiptoes to kiss his cheek. The warmth of his skin reassured her.

He returned the greeting.

'How long is it since you saw him?' she asked, trying to sound calm.

'About half an hour. You came very quickly.'

'I ran. Let's start with the gardens.'

'I've already searched them quite thoroughly.'

'I'm sure you have.' She looked him in the eye. 'I just need to see for myself.'

'Okay.'

They began to walk towards the gate near the museum entrance. A sculpture of Hercules met them as they entered. His muscles strained as he fought against the rocks that sought to crush him. The tennis courts were deserted but a loud basketball game was being played, each boy jumping higher than the one before.

After they had completed a circuit of the gardens, there was still no sign. He had seemed so well last night, happy about some outing he had had with Nebay that he would not tell her about. She had not expected this.

'Maybe we should call the police,' suggested Elise.

'He cannot have gone far. I am sure we will find him soon,' replied Nebay swiftly.

'You sound so sure.'

'I am an optimist.'

She decided to leave it a little longer. They walked on. The rows of green metal chairs that lined the gardens had been disturbed by the memory of conversations now past. Had Theo sat in one of these? Some chairs had broken ranks; one sat lonely under a tree, another was upturned by the pond, all were whispers of human activity.

They walked swiftly through the endless rows of chestnut trees, but it was no good. How would they ever find him here?

She directed them to a café they had been to before, but the waiter dozed on his feet in front of the coffee machine. All the tables were vacant.

'It's no good, he's not here.'

They walked back towards the main street and an ambulance with its siren blaring raced passed them, a police car following as if in pursuit. The air around them changed. Sirens seemed to be sounding in all directions.

'Do not worry, it is not for him,' Nebay tried to reassure her.

'How do you know?'

Nebay was quiet. Elise started walking in the direction of the sirens. She was aware of Nebay calling her back but walked on regardless. More emergency vehicles passed them as they headed further away from the river and the Sorbonne. With every siren her pace increased until she was almost running. They reached the back of a large crowd of people. Elise had not been paying attention to the direction she had been travelling and now took a moment to look up. She did not know the street name, but she knew the area. They were above the catacombs and near the theatre where Mathieu worked. Through the crowd of legs she could see a jagged edge of tarmac.

'*Le fontis voit le jour*,' said Elise. It was an expression her mother had taught her.

'Sorry?'

'It's an old Parisian saying. One of the quarry or catacomb pillars must have collapsed. Now everything below will be shown the light of day for the first time. What if Theo was here when it happened?'

'Why would he have been here? He has the whole of Paris. You must try not to worry. We will find him.'

Elise looked at Nebay and took him in. She thought she noted a slight nervousness in his eyes but there was something so solid about his presence that she could not help but believe him.

CHAPTER 30

Something in the tilt of the model's head in *Young Man and Skull* by Cezanne, something inexact that spoke of longing and of loss, had made Nebay's heart stop. There had been a look in the boy's eye that reminded him of Emmanuel, an innocence. It was just a smear of oil paint, the impression of a long distant stranger. Yet, such a thing, a small thing like this, could force you to recall so much, take you so far away that you lost somebody in the present, in real time.

Elise stood by him anxiously, watching the chaos and, as if she were his sister, he put his arm around her. He had known many people like Elise, people who had been hurt by life and built up all kinds of defences, security systems, perimeter boundaries. If you got too close an alarm bell sounded and all the doors closed at once. Her body relaxed almost imperceptibly under his touch. Even these people needed comfort. In fact, they needed it more than most.

She had rushed forward to check the identity of the man who was pulled up, but she had not been allowed through. Now she strained to see more, but the man was already in the ambulance. Nebay doubted that Theo would have walked this far, but Elise's anxiety was contagious.

'Wait here,' he said, 'I will go and talk to them.'

Of course, it was a stupid thing to do. He told himself how stupid it was repeatedly as he forced his way through the crowd. A man in his position did not willingly walk up to a line of police unless there was no choice. But the thought of Theo lying injured forced him right up to the incident tape.

'Excuse me,' he attempted.

The officer ignored him. Often it felt as if the police were the only people who saw him. Now, when he wanted their attention, he could not get it.

He tried a different approach and walked around the crowd to see if he would be able to get a view of the interior of the ambulance. As he got to a point where it may have been possible, they slammed the door. He made his way back to Elise.

'I am sorry. They will not speak to me and I cannot see what is going on. If we do not find Theo soon we will have to phone the hospital.'

'Thank you for trying.'

'You should not thank me. I was supposed to be looking after him and I let him go.'

'It's not your fault. He's hard to keep an eye on. I lost him when we went out to lunch the other day. I came out of the restroom and he wasn't there. When I finally got back to the apartment the police had just brought him home. I felt terrible. I still do.'

'It's a difficult time for you both.'

Elise turned away. 'Let's carry on looking, shall we?'

Nebay nodded and they walked out of the crowd and back onto the pavement.

CHAPTER 31

There had been a woman in the art gallery, an old woman, old like him and familiar in some way he could not explain and did not try to. Theo had begun to follow her without even realising. She was leaving. He stopped in the doorway to see if he could catch a glimpse of her face, but she was looking down and her wispy hair was whipped up by the breeze, making it impossible. She had a flowered head scarf, black with little red poppies, and there was something about the way she wore it that made him think maybe, maybe this was her. Maybe this was Marianne.

His legs had carried him off, down the path after her and onto the road. She walked briskly for her age and Theo had difficulty in keeping up with her. For a while they walked along the wall of the Montparnasse cemetery until they reached the entrance and she turned in. Theo kept up his pursuit, but it was difficult to remain discreet in the low-slung grid work of graves. He fell further back to avoid detection until eventually he almost bumped into the back of her around a corner where she had paused in front of one of the graves. She seemed lost in thought and Theo skirted around her without her noticing. He carried on until she was out of sight and waited in silence. Sitting on a grave to rest his legs, he closed his eyes. If it was true that she did not want to see him, then surprising her here, of all places, would be the worst thing he could do. So he remained where he was, in silence, and thought of all the other silences he had lived through. The silence of his parents after the war, gone the late-night visitors and their conversations about politics, gone the passion, gone the hope and the fight and all the words which went with them.

And the silence of the next war, even greater, even more profound. A lot of his and Marianne's friends had, like Theo, completed National Service, but it was never talked about. Even when they discussed the war they seldom mentioned their personal experiences. How did it help to know that terrible things had been done by both sides? How did it help to have seen them with your own eyes? And people did not tend to ask questions. Apart, obviously, from Marianne. She could not shy away from debate.

'Men of France,' she had addressed them all one evening before she left, 'how did it feel to oppress your colonial subjects as all good Frenchmen should?'

Most of the men were Theo's age or a little older. If they were really unlucky they would have seen Indochina and then been recalled to Algeria.

'Marianne,' Theo had said quietly, 'let it be.'

The other men in the room had looked at the floor. It had become quite clear to them as soon as they had returned home that, regardless of what their generals had said to them, the French people had not been behind them. Many did not even care. Those who did, however, were often more sympathetic to the idea of Algerian liberation than they were to the returnee soldiers.

'Why? Does it make you uncomfortable?'

'No.' He got up to leave. He needed some air.

Outside he drew heavily on his cigarette and watched the exhaled smoke spiral upwards. In Algeria he had watched for curls of smoke in the brush with his binoculars.

'I'm sorry.'

Theo turned and found Marianne standing beside him,

her arms wrapped around herself against the cold. An unlit cigarette in her hand. He lit it for her.

'Don't be. You have a point. But for us there was no politics. Just them and us. The people that want to kill you and the people who don't. Simple.'

Marianne leant back as if to get a better look at him. She brought her hands up to his face.

'You, Theo Demarais, are a good man, but there is always politics.'

He kissed her and said nothing. There were some things that could not be said.

He awoke where he had sat down and struggled to stand, his body now stiff and his calves aching from the long walk. He rushed as best he could to the grave where he had last seen the woman, but she had disappeared, and he could find no trace of her. Instead he looked at the grave she had been so intent on. He read the headstone. A young man whose name he did not recognise. He had been a little older than Elise and had died a few years ago. The cause was not stated. He felt shame at intruding upon a stranger's grief. He was just a stupid old man chasing ghosts. What had he been thinking, that she had appeared before him through the power of his own want? He had tried that before and it had not worked.

A high-pitched wailing sound brought him back to himself. What was it? What made that sound? He wound his way out of the graveyard, eager to leave the dead, and walked in the direction of the noise. The traffic was stationary along the road. An accident of some sort? A collision? Theo was drawn on. Far away, in between the squeal of sirens, he thought he could hear someone crying out as if in pain. He thought of Elise, but she was at work. She was safe. The police were now in view, waving people away. He saw the back end of a car stuck up at a strange angle. A sink hole. Paris was devouring her inhabitants once again like a goddess requiring sacrifice.

No wonder Theo felt so unsteady living in a city in which even the solidity of the earth could not be counted upon.

Then through the crowd he saw Elise's pale and frightened face. At first he thought to call out but could not. He walked towards her, picking his way through the press of people.

Elise and Nebay greeted him as if he was a disobedient child.

'Where have you been? We looked everywhere for you.'

'I am an adult and I can go where I want.' He had not meant to sound so angry. He saw the look they gave each other and ignored it.

They began to walk home together, but Elise had to get the metro back to work.

'Stay safe,' she said as she left.

As they walked on he could feel Nebay's gaze upon him as if he did not dare let him out of his sight. It made him feel uncomfortable. He wanted to make conversation, to change the line of focus, but first he had to apologise.

'I'm sorry, I find it difficult having my own daughter looking after me. It should be the other way around.'

Nebay just nodded and briefly put his hand on Theo's shoulder. He felt understood, that was enough, but Nebay's silences often left him wondering what he was thinking. He, like Theo, had been to war. He, like Theo, had hidden his flesh and bones from bullets, but this idea seemed ridiculous, as all wars do, when viewed from a point of safety. They both lived half-lives. Sometimes they existed in the present and among the living. The rest of the time they spent in the past with the dead and the lost.

From the lookout tower where he had been stationed with Pierre during the war they could see a kilometre of fence in each direction. The fence was actually two fences, ten metres apart, and thirty metres from that was the barbed wire. No man's land, between the outer fence and the wire, was heavily mined. Tunisia sat on the other side of all of this. Every time the fence was cut within seven kilometres in either direction, the alarm would sound, and Theo and his team would be sent out in search of the Algerian rebels. This happened regularly, often in the middle of the night. After an initial inspection at the time of the break, a dawn search party would be organised. They would trace the trail of footsteps and cigarette butts, look for lines of smoke, obvious resting places and car tracks. If they spotted the party, the paratroopers would be called in. The rebels would be dealt with. The process would begin again. Every time they lost the trail, Theo felt a deep sense of relief.

He had fallen into the routine of army life, but his only goal was to survive until the end of his conscription, return home, and take up his studies. He promised himself that once he escaped he would never return. Whenever the alarm sounded in the middle of the night his whole body would tense. Was this the night that he would be ambushed and murdered in some forgotten corner of the Algerian countryside?

As his mind became more focused on the idea of survival his concerns for the people who risked their lives to cross the border waned. He thought he would do anything just to make it through to the end of his two years. He would kill for his freedom if he had to, at least he thought he would, he felt able.

On a night during his sixth month of active service his team were dispatched to a break. When they reached the site it was clear that a mine had exploded. In the dark they could not see far even with their torches, but still they could make out the shape of a body in no man's land.

'The others may be nearby,' his sergeant had whispered.

They fanned out to search the area, always keeping in sight of one another. Theo walked into a wooded copse. He stopped. He was sure he had heard the click of a gun being readied to fire. He tried to keep his breathing calm and glanced about him. To his left he could see a foot protruding from behind a dense bush.

'Don't shoot,' he whispered into the darkness.

He took one step closer towards the individual.

'How do I know you won't shoot me?' came the response.

Theo looked about him again. He had lost sight of the other men in his battalion. The voice he had heard was young. He would try and reason with him. The young man had the upper hand and a clear shot.

'If I walk away now, I will not tell them that I saw you. You can continue on your way and we will not try to follow until dawn. If you shoot me everyone will hear. There will be ten men here in an instant. You will die. I don't want that to happen.'

There was silence from the bush. Theo waited for a short time for the response. Pierre was bound to show up at any minute.

'Are you okay?'

'I was caught by the mine blast. I'm bleeding.'

'I'm going to walk towards you and see if I can help.'

'Okay.'

Theo moved slowly, careful not to make too much noise. Behind the bush the young man lay on his side, his hand over a wound in his stomach. Theo knelt down to offer him his water. The young man took it gratefully.

'How old are you?' Theo asked him.

'Seventeen, and you?'

'Nineteen.'

Theo heard the call of the sergeant.

'I have to go, try to get far away from here before it is too late.'

He left the young man as he found him and walked back towards the group.

At daybreak they set out again, beginning from the point at which they had been the night before. The broken body in no man's land was now easy to see. They began another short search.

'There's another body here, sir,' called one of the other

conscripts from the copse that Theo had stood in only a few hours before.

The heat left Theo's body. The boy to whom he had talked had died, alone and cold. The knowledge that it could just as easily have been him made no difference. He felt the guilt of it as if he had shot him himself.

CHAPTER 32

The sound of her own shoes on the cobblestones filled Elise's mind, she blocked out everything else, all other thoughts, all feelings, and every last desire. It had been another terrible day at work on top of the stress of looking for Theo in the middle of it all. She could feel herself crumbling, pieces of her falling off into the gutter, it was too much.

She missed Mathieu. She missed their shared friends, their good, left-wing coffee and their conversation. It was inescapable. And yet. The image that came to her mind, of herself trapped in an apartment with a baby, of Mathieu coming home late from the theatre, of the resentment slowly boiling, of the life she had wanted and the life she was living colliding, crashing, breaking her just like it broke her mother, was still so strong. But she had to admit that, more than anything else, this image was based upon fear. That she had made the decision to leave Mathieu because she was scared of the consequences, the commitment it would take from her, not because of the question he had asked her. She had been looking for an escape route all along.

Keeping her head down, she moved off the pavement and onto the road to avoid the crowds of tourists and Erasmus students. Her world was finally infiltrated by the loud honk of a car horn and she turned and stepped between two parked cars just in time for an angry BMW driver to speed past her, cursing. Awoken to her surroundings, she spotted a familiar figure at the counter of an open-fronted crêperie.

Mathieu stood resting the firmness of his stomach on the metal surface while ordering something with cheese that was not on the menu. With one hand he gesticulated to expand upon his explanation of what he wanted; the other hand was wrapped in his hair. He looked pale, thin and unhealthy. He loved to cook. He was not cooking.

She wanted to walk in and talk to him, maybe even take him home, apologise, make love. But she could not let herself. Not yet. She walked on. When she reached the apartment she quickly ran her fingers through her hair, took several deep breaths and put a smile in place.

'Hi,' Nebay greeted her cheerily, 'Theo is already in bed. Did you get back to work okay?' He was sat on the sofa with a book in his hand.

She smiled at him for a moment before answering, calming herself.

'Good, and how was he after?'

'Quiet, he was tired. We read Camus.' He stood to leave.

'Do you have to go straight away?'

'I'm in no rush.'

'Great, well, how about I have a quick shower and then pour you a glass of wine?'

'Okay.'

When she re-emerged he had already poured it.

'You take too long in the shower.'

Elise sat down next to him on the sofa, curling her legs up under herself so that she could face him. He had his reading glasses propped halfway down his nose.

'What shall we cheers to?' she asked, holding up her glass.

'Love, always.'

'The problem with writers is that they're always so romantic.'

'I cannot disagree, but I do not think artists are any better.'

'Well, that's where you're wrong. Hearts of stone, every one of us.'

'And on that matter, how is Mathieu?'

'Not you too. My friends, Celeste and Laila, have been pestering me about it for weeks.'

'He loves you.'

'I know.'

'And you love him.'

She looked at him for a moment. 'Yes.'

'So?'

'It's not that simple.'

'Why?'

'Because life is not a storybook where everyone is happy in the end.'

'But you could be. You have the opportunity. You just have to take it.'

'Has Theo told you much about my mother?'

'No.'

'Has he told you that she killed herself in the bathroom of this apartment?'

He shook his head, took two cigarettes out of the packet and offered one to Elise.

'I haven't smoked since college,' she said, taking it.

Nebay handed her his lighter.

'You found her?'

'Yes, how did you know that?'

'The look on your face. In the army you learn that look.'

'You must have lost people too.'

'Yes.'

He was about to say more when they heard Theo's bedroom door open.

'Nebay? Is it time to go out? Should I take something? Should I have the small things, the ones you take with water?'

'I am coming, Theo. Do not worry. It is still night.' Before he left he bent to kiss Elise on the forehead, briefly holding her face in his hands. 'It is a task though, surviving, you have to honour it,' he said to her before walking towards Theo's bedroom.

'Night? Still? But I have been alone for so long.'

'You have only been in bed for two hours,' Nebay replied, now at Theo's doorway. 'You need more sleep, my friend.'

'Sleep? I can't.'

'You can. I'll read to you.'

Nebay disapeared into her father's bedroom and she could hear the soft rumble of his voice as he read. When he finally emerged he looked exhausted.

'I am sorry, it is late, I have to go.' he said from the doorway. 'Theo is back in bed. I will see you in the morning.'

'Your cigarettes…'

'Do not worry, smoke them, I will buy more.'

Elise lit a second cigarette from the burning end of the first and inhaled deeply, drawing the smoke into her body as if it were knowledge, or art, or love. She tried to imagine a happy life, contemplating where she would live, who she would live with, what type of person they would be if she could choose anyone, any place, any life, and then she realised she did not have to. She had already had it all, with Mathieu. Before she went to bed, she checked on Theo, opening his door just enough to see him so she did not wake him up with the light from the hallway. He looked so small curled up under the covers and for the first time in her life she hoped desperately that he had once found happiness too.

CHAPTER 33

He had stopped taking the metro unless he had to. Paris's heart was lost to him, he no longer trawled through her most intimate parts. He hopped on a bus and watched the dark streets. Parisians and tourists in all their guises, instantly recognisable from each other. The natives had ceased to notice the beauty around them while the travellers kept their heads lifted to see the sights and seek what adventure there might be to find.

The old man was worrying him and soon he would have to talk to Elise, tell her the truth. The fact that she did not know about his status made him uncomfortable, but tonight when he had had the opportunity, he had not been prepared. His thoughts kept slipping and sliding away from him. He got off the bus and started walking towards home. Home, though, was not the word, especially not after the police had visited. They would have to clear out pretty soon and he sensed that the other residents would soon do the same. The various rooms in the building were rented to an assortment of immigrants. They did not really mix with them. Everybody was in survival mode. You had to focus on finding enough money, getting enough to eat, keeping your children safe. It was every person for themselves. It had to be.

The landlord must do okay from it. Nebay had only met him once. Usually the Doctor dealt with him. The Doctor. In many ways he had saved Nebay's life. He had got him the job at the metro, found them a room to share with the Lawyer. Before that, Nebay had reached a dead end. He had been deported. He was in mourning for his family, who were still living, yet forever inaccessible to him. And Emmanuel, taken and gone, buried in a place he did not know. He had run out of money and was sleeping rough, curled up on benches and under bridges, getting moved on by the police in the middle of the night. He was avoiding his fellow Eritreans, they reminded him too much of home. He could not bear to watch them move, listen to them talk, it would bring too much back to him. He would see his father's smile on one. His mother's walk in another. He had ached with all his body for his own soil, for the sun he knew. He had even longed for the mist that sat in fat clouds around the mountains, for the people of Asmara too used to looking down on the rest of the world from their mountain city. His mountain city. He had wanted, had felt the deep and simple need, to return home. And yet this was the only thing he could never do.

By the time the Doctor found him he had, essentially, lost hope. A thing he hated to concede. Why? Because despite everything, and although he hated to admit it, he was proud. He was proud to be Eritrean and he was proud of Eritrea, just not of her current politics and politicians. He found it crazy that so many people he had met in Europe were content to hate their members of parliament, that they expected it to be this way. Eritrea was supposed to be a country built by its people, built for its people, and every single person thought it should be run according to their own specifications. It was a country that truly belonged to the men and women who fought for liberation but, as so often happens with power, one man had lost sight of the ideals of the group he had come from.

He felt an affinity with the French, a people who had beheaded their own monarchy to reclaim their freedom, but if the new French ruling elite were treated to the same experience he sensed that modern France would react differently. The poor and the revolution were only glorious in the past, at a safe distance, but close enough to maintain the feeling that liberty had been fought for and won. There was no need to fight again.

These streets had contained all of that strength of feeling, the passion and the rage. He imagined the beautiful young men running to their deaths against royal troops in the knowledge that the risk they took offered a better prospect than living in an unjust world. At what moment did a people reach the tipping point where the wrongs they bore became too great a weight to carry, where the future had to change in order for it to be survived? In Eritrea the decision had been made the moment the UN handed the country over in federation to Ethiopia. It had been confirmed when Haile Selassie took control of their government. Having survived colonisation, Eritrea was not about to be placed back into a position of servitude. But now? Would they reach a point again when things would have to change?

He had arrived at the door to their room and could hear talking from inside. He paused, listening to the voices, checking it was safe. It was.

'Doctor!' A rush of joy filled him as he opened the door and saw the returnee. He took his friend warmly in his arms. 'I have missed you!'

'And I you.'

'Was I not good enough company?' asked the Lawyer.

'I'm sure you were more than adequate,' replied the Doctor, 'but even I can tell you have become a little despondent, and I have only spent an hour in your company.'

'Okay, I admit it, I always feel more confident when my doctor is present.'

Nebay relaxed for the first time in days. With the Doctor home and his sister's case coming along well there was only the old man to worry about.

'We need to celebrate!' he announced and with a little of

his wages from Theo he took his friends to a nearby restaurant for rice and chicken.

'Possibly the finest meal I have ever eaten,' said the Doctor, leaning back on his chair after they had finished and were waiting for their coffees to arrive.

'There's nothing like a few days in a French police cell to make average chicken taste like chicken for kings. If only you had a friend who was a lawyer, we could have got you out sooner,' laughed the Lawyer.

'If only we had a friend who was a lawyer and was legally allowed to work as one,' said Nebay, a little too seriously.

'I have to say,' said the Doctor, 'that on this occasion, having enjoyed this meal and the company so much, and only on this occasion, it might have been worth it.'

'That's only because we can't afford a better meal,' said the Lawyer. 'To make the food we can afford taste good you have to go to prison first…'

As he turned around, about to continue his commentary on the food, the Lawyer realised the waiter had arrived with the coffees.

'It was delicious,' he said in an exaggerated attempt to remove the stain of the words he had just spoken.

'I'll get you gentlemen the bill,' said the waiter and walked swiftly off, leaving them laughing together in his wake.

CHAPTER 34

He felt the water rising, he could smell it, the dampness. He looked down, but there were no visible signs. Still though, it was happening, the water was rising all around him, taking everything he knew and messing it up, bits of paper everywhere, floating, all in a muddle, and his poor head smashing against the hard corners of buildings. He was sinking to the bottom. He would not survive the flood.

She was lost to him.

It had happened again. In the darkness, Theo opened his eyes. This was not his bed. He lifted up his hand to feel the numb side of his face on which he had been lying. Under the growth of stubble were the pockmarks of carpet bristles. His other hand searched around him. He was lying on the floor. He reached further and found the sofa leg. He was in the living room. He placed his hand on his chest. His heart was beating rapidly. In his dream he had been climbing. It had been so vivid. He could still see the colours of the prayer flags; blue, white, red, yellow. It had felt so real. His body had been his again, clinging to a rock face, trying to wipe the sun blindness from his eyes. These were the last seconds before the fall. He always woke when the first stone shifted under his foot, with the sound of its rattling descent in his ears and the empty smell of ice. As he looked up, Marianne was above him. The rope flapped and spun in the air. Would it hold?

His head hurt. He felt for something to rest it on. There was a hard, rectangular thing. It was better than nothing. On that day, all those years ago, the dream day, he had broken his leg in the fall. He remembered the pain as his foot jarred against rock, forcing all his bones up into themselves. He remembered Marianne's panicked face as she had climbed back down to him. She had loved him. She had saved him. And he had not done the same for her.

He breathed deeply and evenly to calm himself. Spread out like Leonardo's Vitruvian Man, he stared into the darkness and into the history that hid there. After he had visited Marianne's destroyed home in Algiers, Theo had gone to the police station. The French police officers had stared at him stiffly as he entered, and he had realised immediately that he could not ask them about her. They were on opposite sides now. If there was any chance she had survived then he would condemn her by informing them that she had been in a house clearly targeted because of its revolutionary occupants. Even if she were truly dead he could put himself in danger by being known as her associate. He backed out into the glare of the day. An officer came to the door to watch him stumble back out the way he had come.

On the ferry home he had taken a bottle of whisky for company. Was she dead or had he just abandoned her? Which was worse? He no longer knew. Twenty-one hours later he arrived in Marseilles having not slept and crawled into a bed in the cheapest hostel he could find, ignoring the late-night returnees to his dorm room. His sheets smelled of someone else's sweat. The acrid scent that wafted in from the communal toilet burnt his eyes and made them water. He rubbed them, but still he did not cry. The boy had told him that everyone was dead. She must be dead. Yet without a body, without proof, it was intangible.

What would he say to their shared acquaintances? He had never met her parents. Should he try to contact them? And if he did, what could he tell them? That he let her leave, that he had followed, but too late, that he had been too scared to stay? If he had nothing concrete to say maybe he should say nothing at all. She had left him. She had not come back. He had gone to her. She had not been there.

If this was a climbing story he would have cut the rope and been sure he had done the right thing. No point in two people dying. But no point in life without her either. Another day had passed in travel, bumping down too many country roads on too many buses. Another day with no sleep. By the time he reached Paris he was near delirium. His trip to Algiers seemed unreal in the midst of Parisian traffic, in the bakery where he hunted for food, only to find that his mouth was too dry to chew. Maybe it had never happened, maybe she was still alive, but in the deepest recesses of himself he had already come to a conclusion.

For the next twenty years, Theo believed that Marianne was dead. Even after his marriage, he had spent as little time as possible in Paris. At first he was trying to escape the memory of her, but later it just became what he did, how he lived. He integrated this pattern into his way of being, until it was simply who he was. He had spent so much time outside in open plains, on mountainsides, always with a view to the horizon, that even the thought of Paris felt as if it would crush him. He remembered that conversation he had held with Marianne an aeon ago when she had told him that she felt the same way and he had agreed. All these years later he realised that at that time he had lied. The feeling he had always had in Paris was a fear of losing control, something that had crept up on him since childhood. It was only now that the concrete and shop signs truly made him feel trapped, that his travels made him feel foreign, that his dark, sun-exposed skin made him stand out. It was only now, having lost her, that he understood the urge to escape, to find some blank canvas on which to create oneself anew.

CHAPTER 35

The interview room was stuffy. Elise rubbed her eyes and yawned. Theo was not sleeping and, as a result, neither was she. When the young man entered she quickly straightened her posture and greeted him cordially, only then did she look at the information in front of her. There was something not quite right about it, but her mind was elsewhere. Nebay wanted to talk to her after work. She levelled her concentration on the applicant.

'What is your name?'

'Mohammed Osman.'

'And your country?'

'Palestine.'

'You are going to the UK to study?'

'Yes.' His voice was deep.

Elise looked at the paperwork in front of her again.

'What institution will you attend, Mohammed?' she asked, biding time. There was something that did not fit.

'Bristol University.'

It was something about his deep voice and the lines under his eyes. Surely you could not have lost that much sleep by his age?

'And I see by your date of birth you are eighteen.'

'Yes.'

She looked at his face as he spoke and there it was, the slight look to the left.

'What are you studying?'

'Medicine, I have a scholarship.'

Mohammed sat straight and defiant. He met her eye. He was daring her to do something, to challenge him, to ruin his life.

'And where is your scholarship from?'

'The university.'

'It must have been hard to get.'

'It was.'

There was a moment of silence during which Elise took in the situation. She had no concrete proof that anything was amiss, but Mohammed would not have been asked to an interview unless there was some suspicion. The study documents seemed genuine; it was his ID which worried her. She looked it over again. It was all there. He wanted to be a doctor. Would she stop him?

'Well,' she said after some time, 'everything seems to be in order. Good luck with your studies.'

Osman stood and shook her hand. He did not let his relief show, but his hand was damp and his handshake firm, as if they had just agreed on something.

Simon pulled her aside as she left the interview room. 'That didn't take you long,' he said pointedly.

'Well, it turned out to be relatively simple. I don't really know why he had to be interviewed. He's just a student.'

'Do you understand, Elise, why we have these interviews?'

'Yes, Simon, I do.'

He took a step towards her and she instinctively moved out of his reach.

'We'll talk about this later. And read your emails will you?'

They could call Mohammed back in and investigate further. They could discover that he was lying about his age and possibly travelling on faked documents. They could sack her. She disliked this job, but she needed it. She logged into her emails. The first was tagged as high importance and entitled 'Fake Documents'. She opened it. The rest of the text informed her that as an employee of the UKBA she had to be particularly vigilant to a new type of counterfeit passport being produced in Paris. Someone had hacked the database, even iris scanners could not be used to check legitimacy. Employees were asked to look for signs in the visa applicants themselves instead. This was what Simon had meant.

She looked around her wondering what response the email had received from her colleagues. What did they expect her to do, give all applicants a lie detector test, question them under torture, threaten their families? She imagined Simon joining her in the interview room, shining a torch into an interviewee's eyes, 'Are you who you say you are?' Was anyone, strictly speaking, exactly who they said they were? It all seemed ridiculous. She was not a private detective. She was just a woman who filled in forms.

When she got back to the apartment, Mathieu was in the kitchen. She did not know what to say. All the words in her head jammed on the way out.

'Sorry I haven't been in touch, it's been crazy at work,' he said.

'That's okay. It's good to see you.'

'Ready?' asked Nebay as he walked in. 'Mathieu is going to look after Theo.'

'Thank you,' she said to Mathieu as they left.

'Where shall we go?' Nebay asked.

'Somewhere close.'

They found a small place a few streets away that Elise had never been to before and sat outside so that they could smoke. After they had ordered coffee they sat in silence. When it arrived they both stirred in one sugar lump. Elise's chair wobbled on the uneven cobblestones.

'Did he seem okay to you?' she asked.

'Who, Theo?'

'No, Mathieu.'

'He seemed fine, why?'

'I haven't heard from him in a while that's all.'

'I thought you were not interested.'

'That's not what I said.'

'No?'

'Sorry, I'm sure you haven't brought me here to talk about Mathieu.'

'You're right,' he said, but stopped before speaking whatever was on his mind.

Elise leant towards him, 'It's okay, whatever it is, you can tell me.'

'I should have told you before.' He paused. 'And I want you to know I'm sorry I didn't. I didn't know if I could trust you.'

'And you trust me now?'

'Yes,' he said, meeting her eyes.

'Okay, good.'

But still he hesitated, and Elise wondered how bad it could possibly be to make him act in this way.

'I have no papers,' he said finally.

Elise thought of the likely undocumented people she saw on the way to work every day on their street corners and benches, of the tent camps she had heard of but never seen. It had never occurred to her that Nebay could be in this situation.

She took out another cigarette. 'Does Theo know?'

'Yes, he wanted to protect you by not telling you. I argued with him about it, but you know how he is.'

Of course her father had known.

'He probably didn't want me to know because of my job,' *and because despite his age, he could still be a strange and controlling man*, she thought, but did not say.

'What is it that you do?'

'I work in the UK Border Agency Visa office. To be honest I didn't want to tell you either.'

'Why?'

'I spend all day making other people's lives harder.'

'There are worse jobs.'

'Maybe.' Elise paused, 'I'm so sorry you're in this situation.'

'There are worse situations, believe me.' He smiled a half-laugh. 'I'm glad I've finally told you. I feel lighter.'

Elise ordered them both another coffee. She needed some time to work out what, if anything, to do.

'Are you worried about my position? It could put you and Theo in danger to have me in your home.'

'It would be far worse for Theo if you left. You seem very close, the two of you.'

'I suppose we are.'

The coffee arrived and Elise stirred in the sugar slowly. She knew she would not be able to cope if it were just her and Theo again, and she knew that he would accept no one else to look after him.

'Well, that's what matters the most. He needs a friend right now. If we come across any problems, we'll deal with them then.'

They sat for a while, smoking and watching all the people who walked by. If work found out, Elise would definitely lose her job, possibly even be arrested. They would have to try and limit the risk of exposure.

'How does he pay you?' she asked.

'In cash.'

'Good.' This was at least difficult to trace.

'You're sure it's okay for me to continue working?'

'Yes.' It was a big risk, but it was not as if they were the only people in Paris to take it, or in the rest of France, or in the world. 'Are you staying in a safe place?'

'Yes, for now I'm living with some friends, it's good.'

'You have to let me know if there's anything I can do to help, or if for any reason you think we're at risk, and I mean all of us, you, me and Theo.'

'Of course.'

'Okay.' This, she felt, was the best she could do.

'And I wanted to say, I am sorry about your mother,' said

Nebay, taking her by surprise. 'I realise I didn't say this when you told me, but I am.'

'Thank you, it was a long time ago. I'm sorry that you lost someone too. Can I ask who it was?'

'You can, but maybe I will answer another day. We have had enough revelations for now I think.'

She agreed and they finished their coffees and walked back to the apartment. Mathieu was waiting for them.

'Elise, why don't you walk me out?'

'Of course.'

They made their way down the steps slowly, Mathieu seemed to be building up to something.

'I wanted you to know I've met someone, someone at the theatre. I'm sure you won't care but I wanted to tell you anyway.'

She stopped on the bottom step. She could not work out how to reply so she smiled and nodded and turned her back on him to climb back up.

CHAPTER 36

Yesterday he had found Theo on the floor, foetal, naked, with tears running silently like tiny rivers across his cheeks and falling in sombre procession onto the atlas under his head. Nebay had spoken soft words and raised him to his feet, carried him to the bathroom, washed him and placed him back into his bed. Elise had come out in a rush, full of the day to come, worry all over her face already. He had said nothing because there was too much to say. He could have mentioned it over coffee, but what good would it do other than to worry her further. The old man had an appointment with the doctor tomorrow, they would no doubt change his medication then, for now he should rest.

Nebay sat by his bedside, watching the rise and fall of his breath, he was still too tired to get up. He wished he had been able to care for Emmanuel in this way in the last hours of his life, that he had been able to wash away the mess that men had made of his skin, to cleanse him. How was it possible that he could be given the grace to care for this man, a recent stranger, when he had not been granted the time to care for his own family, his lover, his friends? Some small voice answered that this was just the balance of the world, that while he cared for Theo someone else cared for the people Nebay had been forced to leave behind. He hoped it was true and knew it may not be.

Theo mumbled in his sleep, repeating the woman's name,

the one he looked for. It seemed he searched for her even in his dreams. As he began to wake, Nebay went to get water so that Theo could take his medication. It was nearly midday already. As soon as he left the room, Theo called for him and he went back.

'I have been having terrible dreams. I was cold and drowning, but now I can see your face I know it's not true. I just had to see your face.'

'It is okay, Theo, I am not going any further than the kitchen. I will get you water and bring it in.'

'Thank you, Nebay. I don't know what I would do without you.'

He brought the water through and placed it on Theo's bedside table next to his pill box.

'I think you sleepwalked yesterday. I found you in the living room. Do you remember anything? Have you been taking your sleeping pills?'

'I can't remember. I don't know. Do I take sleeping pills?'

'Yes, Theo. They are supposed to stop this happening. You might need a higher dose.'

'I think they give me nightmares.'

'They are supposed to help.'

'I don't know.'

'Okay, well do not worry. We will talk to the doctors.'

'Please don't. They'll give me more of the little things. The things that take my mind away.'

'It is not the medication that makes you forget things, Theo, it is your illness.'

'Am I ill?'

'Do you feel well?'

'No, now you mention it. I feel strange.'

'You will feel better after you take your medicine.'

He watched Theo drink, small, cautious sips, a little pill with each. He thought of his father and his mother. Who was with them? Were they well? Did they miss him as much as he missed them?

His father had taught history at Asmara University but was asked to leave when his version of history no longer matched the state's version. After that, when he was lucky enough to have work, he washed plates in restaurants and carried loads on construction sites.

'But I lived through it,' he would say. 'How can they tell me I am wrong when I saw it with my own eyes?'

'Because our eyes only show us what is straight in front of us, but if you close your eyes then you can say anything you want because you saw nothing, which in this country is the same as seeing it all,' his mother had said in response.

Theo dressed slowly. He was shaking and fumbled with the buttons of his shirt. Nebay did them up for him.

'I didn't used to be this old, you know.'

'I know.'

'I used to be young and strong like you. I thought it would last forever.'

'I think everybody does.'

'Then they are stupid.'

'Maybe they are.'

They walked into the living room and Theo sat down with a thump on his chair.

'Can we have music?'

'What would you like?'

'Edith, you know which one. I want that song. I want to get rid of all these… these…'

'Regrets?'

'The things you wished had not happened?'

'Yes.'

'I want them to go away.'

'Okay. I'll put her on.'

The strength of her voice made them both silent for a while. That strange little woman. They had watched a film about her recently, sitting on the sofa under a blanket with a glass of wine. Elise had been out and came in towards the end. She had given them a funny little smile and gone to her bedroom. Nebay wished he had invited her to join them. It had been a sad smile.

'I won't find her, you know,' Theo said at the end of the song. 'It's too late. It has been too long.'

'You do not know that, Theo. You have to have hope.'

'Do you?'

'Do I what?'

'Have hope?'

'I try to.'

Theo had tears in his eyes again.

'I can't stop the water. It's there all the time, the thing that makes you hurt inside.'

'Sadness?'

'Love. I think it is love.'

'I know. I have the same thing.'

'Can we go outside, please? I think I need to see the air.'

'Of course, but are you well enough?'

'I will try to be.'

They stepped outside into the rain. Theo's expression suddenly brightened. He took off his hat and offered his face up to the heavens.

'It's always raining in Paris. I know I'm in Paris when I can feel the rain.'

'It is because you are at home,' Nebay said quietly.

'Yes. I know this place. I have been here before…'

CHAPTER 37

The clock on the wall of his specialist's office showed that it was three fifteen. A minute passed. Dr Chevalier continued to look through his notes. Theo shifted in his chair. He did not like it here. He wanted to go back outside. There was white stuff everywhere. It was pretty.

'So, Mr Demarais, how have you been feeling?'

'Oh, you know, so-so.'

Dr Chevalier looked towards Elise who in turn looked at Theo.

'Actually, I am having some difficulty.'

'Oh, yes? What sort of difficulty?'

'Well,' Theo looked at Elise hoping for support, 'I think there have been some problems.'

'I see, and what sort of problems have there been?'

'Erm…' Theo cleared his throat. He looked back up at the clock. Another minute had passed. How long would this take? What did this damned man want to know?

'You were saying there have been some problems, Mr Demarais?' Dr Chevalier tried again.

'This,' Theo said louder than he had intended, suddenly incensed, 'this is the problem.' Theo poked his finger down at the table. He wanted to stand and leave, push his chair back loudly and slam the door, but he felt he had to stand his ground. He was clearly being interrogated for a reason.

'We could up his dose,' Dr Chevalier said, turning to Elise, 'but there may be side effects.'

Theo stared at his daughter; outrage etched across his face. What sort of conspiracy was this?

'What sort of side effects?'

'Hallucinations, irritability, depression…'

'I think it may be partly stress related. He's not been sleeping, and when he does he sleepwalks, but other than that it has mainly been just forgetfulness and a little confusion.'

Theo's anger subsided as quickly as it had come. It was true that he had felt a little confused of late. He had to trust that Elise would only do what was best for him. It still worried him though, the situation they appeared to be in, the inspection.

'So, you are saying he has become worse only recently?'

'Yes, in the last week we have really noticed a difference.'

'I see.'

What did he see? Theo looked down to check his appearance. He had on his good dark trousers, his grey V-neck, his favourite red jacket. Nebay had picked them out for him, everything was in order.

'I really think I'm not doing too badly,' he concluded out loud.

Elise and Dr Chevalier looked at him. He wished he had not spoken.

'Yes, Theo, you are doing very well,' said the doctor.

Why was his daughter on the side of this stranger? It was not fair.

'What we want to do is help you to do even better,' the doctor continued.

He did not trust this Dr Chevalier. What did he mean? Better than what?

'I think it's time to go.' Theo could stand it no longer. The room was small and stuffy. There was no window.

'If you would prefer, you can wait outside while I talk to your daughter for a little longer.'

This was not what he preferred but he looked at Elise

and discovered she was making no sign of leaving. Without saying anything else he walked out into the corridor. Nebay was waiting for him, but he was not in the mood to loiter. He looked in each direction, unsure of which way to turn. On the wall opposite was a sign with an arrow and the word *cafétéria*. Although the meaning of the word temporarily evaded him, he felt that this was the direction in which he should go.

'I need to…' Theo said to Nebay.

'Okay,' Nebay replied and followed him.

He walked down the corridor, noting the squares of blue linoleum that covered the floor and forgetting to look for further arrows. At the next junction he turned right. His pace was quickening, he was leaving Nebay behind. The linoleum on the floor was now pink. It was ugly. He disliked ugliness. He quickened his pace again. A bend in the corridor sent him left. He continued. The further he got from the small room and man who asked questions the better he felt. He pushed his way through a heavy door that blocked his passage and found himself on a ward. A nurse approached him.

'Are you okay, sir?'

Theo would have answered but his attention was taken by the people who surrounded him, sick people kept alive with drips and tubes. It felt like a vision of his future. He was paralysed by the realisation of it. He was doomed and nothing he could do would change this fact. He could walk as far as he wanted and never outrun it. This would always be where he ended up.

'Sir?' The nurse looked worried.

Nebay caught up with him.

'Sorry, I lost him.'

Theo turned to Nebay.

'I'm in the wrong place.'

'Do not worry, it is nearly time to leave.'

The doors felt heavier on the way out, the pink linoleum seemed even uglier. He was here for an assessment because he was ill, because he was slowly losing his mind. The clarity of this thought shocked him because it highlighted just how deluded he had been moments before. He needed to leave. Trying to retrace his steps, he followed the corridor to the right until he reached the blue linoleum, but by the time he reached it he could not remember which way to turn. Nebay tried to take his hand. The cruelty of it made him want to cry. He leant against the wall and attempted to think, but it was no good. There was nothing, just space and emptiness where knowledge should be. He covered his eyes.

Elise walked towards them and put her hands on his shoulders to focus him.

'How are you feeling?'

Theo shook his head. 'We need to leave.'

'Okay, Theo, we're going now.'

His daughter looked so sad. Everything he did seemed to make her sadder.

'I am sorry, Elise, I am so very sorry about all of this. I am sorry about it all.'

Elise took his hand and led him towards the exit. In the fresh air he felt like he could breathe again. Everything was white, clean. His feet crunched through it, the crunching whiteness on the ground. He realised he was being led like a child and relented. There was nothing he could do now.

'What did the doctor say?' Nebay asked.

'We are going to increase his medication. He should feel a little better for a while. The doctor said he should get lots of sleep and take it easy for a bit. No more drinking. No more late-night bars.' She gave Nebay a look. They were always looking at each other these days and speaking all their words. They had so many.

CHAPTER 38

The stairs up from the metro birthed Elise, Theo and Nebay into the main hall of the Gare du Nord. Their train could go no further. Snow had fallen on the exposed tracks. There was a crush of stranded commuters. At first, Elise assumed that the shouts were coming from angry workers struggling to fight their way through the crowd and hoping to catch their trains home, but as they drew closer it became clear that this was not the case. The air was static with pent-up anger.

Instinctively, Elise took hold of Theo's hand and realised that his other hand was already safely clasped in Nebay's firm grip. She looked up and caught Nebay's eye; something in his gaze prompted further caution. She wedged her handbag between her arm and body, clutching the base of it with her free hand.

'Can you see what's happening?' she shouted over the noise.

Ahead she heard the smash and splinter of glass. The fury around them had found a form in an alternating chant.

'Fuck the police!'

'Fuck France!'

As if these two phrases provided both a question and an answer.

Theo turned to her.

'Who is angry now? If they carry on they'll damage everything.'

'Don't worry, Theo, we'll be out of here soon,' she said,

but it was as if he did not hear her. He looked terrified. 'Theo,' she tried again, but he could not seem to recognise his own name. 'Papa, look at me,' and finally he did. 'It will be okay,' she said, and he nodded and held her hand tighter. She could not remember the last time she had called him this.

Nebay pulled them forward and further into the crowd, heading for the exit. They discovered that there was actually a large space in the centre occupied on one side by riot police hidden behind helmets and shields and on the other by a group of teenagers. One of them called out to Nebay in what Elise recognised as Arabic.

'Do you understand what he said?' Elise asked.

'Only a little, the police have shot another black boy.'

'Jumping the barrier?'

'Yes, jumping.'

The teenagers again called out to Nebay, but this time in French.

'What are you doing, brother? Drop the hand of that white man. Whose side are you on?'

'They are killing us, and you walk with them!' called another.

Elise sensed the increasing danger and tugged them along the edge of the crowd towards the line of police. She looked back to check that Nebay was following, but for a moment he was frozen. She tried to make out the expression on his face, but he had turned his head the other way.

'Nebay,' she called out louder than she had intended, blood rising to her face as she did so. He needed to hurry.

'Where is Marianne? She should be with us.'

'Theo, Papa,' Elise tried to focus on her father and bring him back to them. 'Who is Marianne? You are confused.'

'What do you mean confused! She was just here! We can't lose her! We can't leave her in the crowd with all these people, she won't know how to find us.' He tailed off towards the end. 'That's not right, is it? That's not right.' Theo's face was collapsing in the onslaught of noise and the press of bodies.

'I'm sorry, Papa,' Elise said gently. 'We have to get out of here and then we can talk about it.'

Finally, Elise saw Nebay walking towards them. Without thinking, she took his hand as well. They continued to edge sideways and as they reached the police line the teenagers charged. When the two groups met it sounded like a building falling; an endless tumbling of bricks.

Nebay was leading them through the crush once again. Elise's chest felt restricted, she could barely breathe. A middle-aged woman full of her own private outrage angrily elbowed her in the ribs. The more that the gathered commuters pushed to get free, the closer that their little group came to the flailing batons of the police and the sticks and metal poles of the young people. A final surge brought Nebay face to face with a policeman, his baton already raised for the attack. Elise tried to place her body between them.

'No!' she shouted but it was too late, a trickle of blood ran down Nebay's stunned face. She tried to pull him away, but he would not budge and stood defiantly in front of the policeman, forcing him into eye contact.

'They are children. You are beating and killing children. In my country I would be tempted to shoot you myself.'

The policeman stared back at him, shocked into stillness. Even after Nebay stepped away from him, propelled by the sharp tug of Elise on his arm, it took several seconds for him to regain his composure.

'That was a stupid thing to do. They could have arrested you. They could have found out who you were.'

'No, Elise, it was the only thing to do,' he said quietly, in a tone which suggested he did not want to discuss it further.

'They're at it again,' Theo mumbled as Elise dragged him forward and he stared wide-eyed at the crowd.

'Who is at what, Papa?'

'The men with the sticks, they're breaking things again.'

Exhausted by the last half hour, Elise did not reply to her father and instead turned to Nebay. Now that they were in the safety of the snow-covered street she wanted to check his wound. She placed one hand on his chin and eased his head back, trying to see clearly in the failing light. From her handbag she produced a tissue and was about to reach up to wipe away the blood when Nebay took it from her.

'I have suffered much worse.'

He held it to his forehead. When he removed it he examined the scarlet flower that had appeared on the flimsy white paper before folding it, spitting on it and quickly wiping away the remainder of the blood. He checked the results in a car side mirror, licked a corner to remove the final specks and then stood again, ready to leave. As they walked along hoping to spot a vacant taxi, he absent-mindedly discarded the stained tissue in a bin.

'What shall we have for dinner tonight? I feel like spaghetti,' he said, suddenly cheerful as if the last hour had been wiped away as easily as his blood.

'I have always loved Italy. I've been there, you know. Rome is very, very…' Theo began.

'Beautiful?'

'Diagonal. Very, very diagonal.'

Elise looked from her father to Nebay.

'I think I need a glass of wine,' she stated to the air.

'A Chianti, there's nothing like it. Reminds me of a time… something happened.'

They both looked at Theo, waiting for more, but his eyes had a distant look.

'Chianti it is,' she said to bring him back.

'Good,' and he smiled at her with uncalled-for tenderness as if she had just undertaken an act of great kindness.

Nebay's wound had begun to bleed again, but she said nothing, she understood the need to feel self-sufficient. They stopped outside a shop and as Nebay was about to enter, Elise held him back.

'I think it might be better if I go.'

'Why?' His tone was defensive again.

'Your head is bleeding.' She held out another tissue which he eventually took and held to his wound in silence while several seconds ticked by, his face struggling to find composure. A drop of blood landed on the snow.

'I am sorry, Elise.' He shook his head and looked as if he were about to say more but could not find the words.

'Don't worry, I'll be back in a second,' and she almost added 'watch Theo for me' which she knew was not necessary, but for a brief moment she had wondered if Nebay truly was the person she thought him to be.

CHAPTER 39

The Doctor's face said it all.

'We have to leave. The police have been here again asking for everybody's papers.'

Nebay slumped on his bed. In France, a country that he had come to believe in, there had been young men and women beaten by the police in front of him and now this. The ideals of liberty, fraternity and equality did not extend to all. He said as much to the Doctor.

'But we are not French, my friend.'

'But the people in the train station were.'

'And what was the colour of their skin?'

'Black.'

'Then they have not been French for long enough.'

'We were French once. It didn't do anything good for us,' added the Lawyer.

'You were a colony. Algeria was the only one they really adopted and look what happened to them.'

There was silence for a moment.

'Have you thought about where you will go?' Nebay asked them.

'I was hoping we would go somewhere together,' the Doctor replied.

'I don't think I can leave the old man.'

'What about your sister?'

'For now she is still in detention. Even if I was in the UK, I would not be able to see her.'

'We could go back to the jungle until we find some more work,' suggested the Lawyer.

'I've had enough of the jungle,' said the Doctor. 'I get to Britain or I try for papers somewhere else, but either way I'm running out of time. My children are growing up without me and my wife must have forgotten who I am.'

'How could she ever forget a stallion like you?'

The Doctor smiled, but his heart was not in it.

'You are right. You need to find stability,' said Nebay.

'If not I need to go home.'

'What would happen if you did?'

'That would depend on who knew I was there. We would have to leave again pretty quickly. Maybe even go and live with your brothers, the Ethiopians, anywhere that is not Sudan.'

'Be realistic. Would you even make it back to your family?'

'Why be realistic in a world where real life is so depressing?' The Lawyer had a way of putting things.

'You are right, sorry, but I do not want our friend to go and get shot for no reason.'

'My family is a good enough reason.'

'They would not even know you had died.'

Again, silence. The occasional roar of a passing car, like the tick of a clock, kept time.

'Shit.'

'Don't despair, Mr Lawyer. I will not abandon you,' the Doctor said as he patted his friend warmly on the knee.

Nebay went out to get beer, but really he needed the air. He thought of Theo in the rain with his hat off and smiled as the first flakes of snow fell onto his bare head. There had to be something, even in all of this, to keep you going. He went to the internet café first. It would only take a minute. His sister's face was all over the British media. She was considered a 'genuine' asylum seeker. Her escape from prison, where she had been placed for disobeying an army officer's request for sexual favours during her National Service, was written about in great detail. Nebay closed all the pages at once. They would grant her protection, he knew that now, but to have been confronted by his sister's story all over again was too much. To be unable to protect the people you loved was unbearable. If she was to be released soon, he wanted to be there for her.

'I have been thinking,' he announced to the room when he returned. 'You were right, Mr Lawyer. I should go to the Eritrean part of the Jungle and you should come with me. We can find out what the situation is in Calais and you can take some time to think about your next moves.'

'They won't take us, will they?'

'Of course they will, you are with me, and if not, we will stay on the edge.'

'That's the problem with Eritreans, just because you had your big battle for independence you think you're a step above the rest of us.'

'Not true.'

'A bit true.'

'Okay, a bit true.'

They brought their bottles together and took out cigarettes. Now a plan had been decided on they relaxed a little. Nebay looked around the walls of their small room. He would miss it. He had been happy here even if he had only realised the truth of it now.

'To friendship,' he said, raising his bottle again.

'You've only had one sip and it seems you may be under the influence already.'

'I think you'll find our friend is just celebrating the time we have spent together under this lovely dry roof and maybe you should let him.' The Doctor raised his bottle as well.

Finally, the Lawyer joined in. 'You are right,' he said begrudgingly, 'it has been a strange pleasure.'

Later that night, Nebay could not sleep. In the morning, when he left to go to Theo's, he would take his bag and in it everything he owned in this country. It was the end of something, but maybe also a beginning. He listened to the snoring of the Doctor and the grumbles of the Lawyer and smiled to himself. He had been wrong: it was not where you lived, but who you lived with that made a place home.

CHAPTER 40

Everyone was angry. Why? Why had all those people been shouting? What had it meant? He went to his office, he needed to make sense of it all, everything was wrong, he could not grasp it.

He looked down at his hands, his big wide hands, covered in lines and knobbly bits. The hands he looked at were old, could not be his, but if not his then whose? What about this face? He could see it reflected in the picture of Elise on his desk, Elise when she was happy, a different Elise to the one he lived with now. He touched his cheeks, all rubbery with flapping bits, the eyebrows had gone crazy, trying to escape into the hairline. How had it happened, this face? Where had it come from, what had worried it to give it these wrinkles, what had kept it awake at night to give it these dark holes for eyes? He stuck out the tongue, pale, unhealthy, not his either, he had been transplanted. There had been a terrible mistake. Panic was something he had become familiar with. He felt it now.

He peered out of the window, the street looked wrong, covered in the whiteness that fell everywhere, but he was in his office, it must be right. It was his understanding, his expectation, that was wrong. He picked up a pen, searched for a sheet of paper. In the centre he drew a small square, this was the apartment, everything spread out from this point.

The street curved and split, this was where the market was, the one he had gone to with Elise when she was a child. In the opposite direction he drew the route to the Odéon metro station. He drew the Sorbonne, the square with the coffee shop where he met Marianne. He filled in the grid work of Luxembourg gardens where he had left Nebay. He continued it, sticking a new bit of paper to the first with some sticky tape he found in a drawer. He reached Belleville. He drew the apartment he had lived in with Monique when they were first married. He drew the park where they had walked on weekends. Further again, he drew the hospital where Elise was born, the bridge on which he and Marianne had fought with the police. He reached the outer arrondissements, the *banlieues*. This was where the angry people had come from. Shoved out on the edges, he understood the abandonment they felt on the periphery of the map. They could fall off at any minute. They were vulnerable like him.

On a new piece of paper he changed the scale. He sketched France, Spain, Northern Africa. Algiers was a little dot, but he could see the winding alleyways, he could smell the heat off the stone, the charred scent of lost bodies eaten up by fallen masonry and flame. His eyes were wet with eye water. He felt it with his fingers, rubbed them to dry them, but they just got wetter. He looked down at what he had created, a great sprawling mess, an ugly confusion of lines, and pushed them away from him, only vaguely aware of the sound of falling objects, the crash of something breaking.

There had been no phone call. Marianne did not want to see him. He felt as if he had spent his entire life waiting in vain. If he could tear up all those years he would. He would go back and change it all. There was no other way. Monique had tricked him, and he had let her. But then there was Elise, his daughter, his only good thing. What a mess this life was, what a mess this whole life had been.

On the morning of his wedding day, Theo had drunk a bottle of red and washed it down with a nip of whisky. By the time he had consumed both, his breathing had returned to normal. In the small chapel Monique had chosen, their families had gathered. They stared at him expectantly while they waited for his future wife to appear. He swayed slightly in his tight suit. He had started to put a bit of weight on now that he was not travelling all the time.

As Monique walked down the aisle she smiled coolly at him and it was only after the final vows had been uttered that she leant in to him during their first kiss as man and wife to whisper.

'I only did this for my father. You should know I have a lover whom I do not intend to leave.'

He had leant back, looked into her eyes, smiled as was expected by the crowd, and wondered if he hated her. They had a brief honeymoon planned on the Riviera. Monique had booked them an expensive hotel with his money. He clung to the fact that it was only for a weekend and wondered how soon he could be on a flight out of Paris.

On the first night they shared a bed he could not make love to her. In fact, he was surprised that she wanted him to.

'Come on,' she cajoled. 'We have to make the best of a bad situation. Let's try and enjoy it a little.'

The following day they drank a glass of wine with lunch. They ate slowly but drank fast. Theo could not think of a thing to say so when the waiter came back he ordered a bottle. Monique had smiled at him in approval. He had almost smiled back.

That night, after they had taken all that they could from one another, and lay awkward and awake, she turned to him and drew her finger across his lips.

'Another debt paid,' she said before rolling over to face the wall.

He wondered what she meant but did not ask.

***

Nebay came to give him pills to take. Some to stop the losing, some to take the pain of losing away. Later he would have the ones for sleeping. If he ever woke up it would all begin again in the morning. It was a kind of life, but not one that he had ever thought would belong to him.

CHAPTER 41

Turning on the radio, Elise knocked the glass to the floor. It shattered on the boards and as she went to pick up the dust pan and brush, she cut her foot. At the same moment, Theo walked in.

'Stop!'

He jumped. 'What?'

'There's glass everywhere. I broke a glass.'

Theo watched her sweep up all the little pieces. 'You're getting as bad as me.'

'Funny.'

'What day is it?'

'Saturday.'

'No Nebay then.'

'No Nebay, just me. He said he's doing a writing course. I thought we could go to the market.'

'I'll get my coat.'

'No coffee?'

'We can have it while we're out, a treat, it's good to have a treat now and again.'

The market was busy. The snow had cleared, and scraps of pale blue sky could be seen through the clouds. People jostled up close. Through a particularly tight press she realised she had taken her father's hand. He grimaced at her and she dropped it as quickly as she had taken it. He was obviously feeling a bit better.

They stopped at a fishmongers. Heaps of crab and lobster tried to swim through ice. Elise looked into their beady little eyes. Stolen from the sea, they looked forlorn. Theo moved on towards the neighbouring cheese stall.

'Maybe we should get a little something for after?' He was eyeing up a small goat's cheese.

'Good idea.'

They walked on, Theo carrying the cheese in a paper bag. He seemed happy to be in the market.

'You know, this reminds me of when you were small. Do you remember? We used to come here on Saturdays all the time.'

'Yes, I remember that we came here sometimes, when you were home.'

But Theo seemed not to be listening. He was walking quickly away from her. She could still hear him talking but could not make out the words until she caught up.

'…funny, I thought I saw her this time. I really thought I saw…'

'Who, Papa?'

'Oh, Elise.' He almost sounded surprised to see her. 'Nothing, I thought I saw an old friend, nothing to worry about.'

At the vegetable stall, Elise was examining the courgettes when he did it again. She turned around and he was gone. She ran down the street calling his name. She searched the faces at all the stalls, but none of them were her father's. She returned to the cheese stall, but he was not there either. Just as she was beginning to panic she saw him sitting in a café.

'Theo, what are you doing?'

'I thought we could have coffee.'

'I was shopping. You just walked off.'

'Did I?'

'Yes, Theo, that's exactly what you did.'

'My legs were tired.'

'Well, you should have said.'

'I thought I did.'

There was no point. 'If I go to buy the vegetables will you stay here?'

'Yes.'

She did not believe him, but she had little choice. Without thinking, she bought whatever came to hand. When she got back to the café he was still there, this time eating lunch.

'You could have waited for me.'

He looked at her with a blank expression on his face.

'Did you have your medication this morning?'

'Sorry?'

'Your pills? Did you take your pills?'

'I don't know. Nebay normally sorts that out. He takes care of it.'

'Okay, I'm sorry, I'll give them to you when we get home.'

He looked as if he had lost the thread of conversation once again and just smiled. Elise ordered a coffee and took out a cigarette, she was enjoying her re-found habit. She needed to get him back to the apartment. When they had both finished, they walked slowly towards home.

'Celeste and Laila are coming over later.'

'Who?'

'My friends. You've know Celeste since we went to school together.'

'Have I?'

'And I met Laila at art college.'

'Did you?'

'Never mind.'

'Where is Mathieu? We haven't seen him in such a long time.'

'I don't want to talk about it, and how can you remember him and not Celeste and Laila? We've know them longer.'

'What? It was Mathieu I asked about. Where is Mathieu?' Theo was becoming quite agitated.

'I don't know, Theo, he hasn't phoned. I haven't spoken to him.'

'That's a shame.'

'He has a new girlfriend.'

'Really? Well, if you talk to him, tell him I'd love to see him.'

'Okay, I will, but it might be some time.'

'Time? I don't think I have much of that.'

While Elise put away the shopping, Theo started washing his socks in the kitchen sink. She still had not given him his pill.

'Theo, stop that, come here. I'll get your medication.'

'In the army we washed our clothes in the sink and nobody complained.'

'You're not in the army now.'

'I was.'

'I know.'

'Do you?'

'Yes, you told me a few weeks ago.'

'Did I?'

'Yes.'

She brought the little pill box and the various containers into the kitchen and got him some water.

'I don't like these pills.'

'I know, Papa, but they're good for you.'

'I'm not so sure.'

'Well, the doctors are.'

'But then it is the doctors who think I'm ill.'

'You are ill, Theo.'

'That's your opinion.'

She watched him take the pills, checking that he had swallowed them, and willed the hours to pass.

Celeste and Laila arrived late, after Laila's life modelling class was over. Elise was already exhausted.

'You look terrible,' said Celeste as she kissed her.

'Thanks,' said Elise, she did not even have the energy to laugh.

'How has your day been?' asked Laila, emptying takeaway containers onto four plates.

'I think Theo's asleep. I'll warm it up for him later.'

Laila put the fourth plate back where she had found it.

'So? Your day?'

'I think I might be losing my mind. I don't know how Nebay does it.'

'The carer?'

'Yes, he's off for the weekend. I imagine he just needed a break from this mad house.'

'But you and Theo are getting on okay?' asked Celeste.

'Well, yes, but he's not exactly himself right now. Earlier he started washing his socks in the kitchen sink, he said it's what he did in the army, I didn't even know he'd been in the army until he told me a few weeks ago and now he can't even remember the conversation, and I forgot to give him his medication this morning.'

'National Service?' asked Laila.

'Yes, and then he said he didn't even know who either of you were, and he's become obsessed with Mathieu, who's not coming over anymore because he got himself a new girlfriend.'

'Sounds like you're having a bad week,' said Celeste, a small smile on her face.

'You think?' Elise laughed, but it was a hollow sound, the sort of laugh that might end in tears. 'I don't know how much more of this I can take.'

'If you need us to, we can help out more,' said Laila, placing the plates on the table.

'Thank you, but I wouldn't know where to begin, or what to ask you to do. If he doesn't even know who you are anymore it might just confuse him even more.'

'Oh, I'm sure he would remember us pretty quickly when he saw us. Is there anything the doctors can do?'

'Hopefully. He had an appointment this week. They've altered his medication again, he should feel a bit better soon, but if I'm too tired to remember to give it to him, what use will it be?'

'You've just had a difficult day. Eat, you'll feel better,' said Laila.

'And when Nebay is back, we'll get him to stay over one night and we'll take you out. You need a break too, and we all need an art show with free wine.'

'Art? I think I've forgotten what it is.'

'Well, we're here to remind you. If you want I could give you one of my opening semester lectures on form.'

'Please don't, Celeste, she wants to actually enjoy art again.'

Theo came into the kitchen and stared at the three of them.

'Are you okay, Papa?'

He looked at her as if from a great distance, she was the horizon, but he was blinded by the sun and could not make her out.

'Who are these people?' he asked. 'Why are they here? This is my home. I can't have strangers here. I'm sick. I'm tired. It's too much! Get out, you hear me? Get out!'

CHAPTER 42

Under canvas, the sound of the rain was like the drum of fingers on a tabletop amplified right next to Nebay's head. He rolled over and found himself up against the snoring Doctor. He turned again and discovered the outstretched arm of the Lawyer. He lay on his back.

The day came clean slowly and a pale blue light could be seen through the thin skin of the tent. It was cold. He rubbed his hands together and wondered how long it would take for his friends to wake. In the end he left them and went to find someone with a stove and coffee. Outside, there were still a few patches of tarnished grey snow. He walked over to a newly made fire and sat at the edge, warming as much of his body as he could. A tent was being put up nearby and there were new faces. He would talk to them later, when they had settled in a little and rested. It was one of the most ancient forms of communication, the passing on of information from one nomad to another. And yet it was vital, even now, to those who migrated with the birds to find a new life.

Coffee was handed around and someone brought out a packet of biscuits. Everyone took one, passing the packet around the circle. People who have nothing share everything. Nebay took one and thanked his hosts. The Doctor and the Lawyer joined them and sat on the corner of a wooden pallet.

'Good afternoon,' said Nebay to his friends.

'It's nine o'clock in the morning. I worry for you.'

'If you had slept in between two big snoring men then I think you would have risen early as well.'

'I don't know what you mean,' said the Doctor.

'I do, we've talked about this before. You have a problem,' replied the Lawyer.

'A medical problem.'

'A snoring problem.'

'He is not the only one,' added Nebay.

As it started to rain again the Doctor and the Lawyer went to wash while Nebay went to talk to the people who had arrived in the night. They had travelled up from Italy to Calais but had been unable to cross to England.

'Our friend was injured when they cleared the Jungle again. We have come here to find work instead.'

'How many times did you try to cross?'

'More than I know how to count.'

'Thank you,' he said to the group of young men as he left.

His friends knew from his expression that it had not gone well.

'Well,' said the Lawyer trying to sound cheerful, 'as none of us have work today, maybe we should have a little game of cards.'

'One game of chance in preparation for another,' said the Doctor.

'You two play, I need to walk a bit.' Nebay got out his notebook and wandered in the direction of the city. Writing helped him to clear his head. He thought of the time not so long ago that he had wandered the streets of the Latin Quarter imagining his future book in shop windows. It seemed silly now. How would he ever manage it? Even if he tried to write the book, how would he find the right words? He felt he lived a life that could not fully be expressed or explained. He lived outside of something, everything, and even though so many people shared his experience even more did not.

He was wandering without a destination, lost in some bit of Paris he did not know, a borderland between the outer and the inner cities. Some shopfronts were closed, others broken, but here and there a little café had popped up, as if grown from the destruction around it. When he finally stopped to get his bearings, his sister called.

'I have won, brother, I have finally won!'

Nebay had tears in his eyes, his throat was so tight he could barely speak. He had to get to her.

Back at the tent he gave the news to his friends.

'If you have to go then we will come with you. There is nothing for us here anyway,' said the Doctor, looking towards the Lawyer who nodded in agreement.

'Anyway, I have heard the women in England are very beautiful. I would like to invest in a complicated love life.'

The Doctor gave the Lawyer a disapproving glance. Nebay did not mind. He was glad they were coming. The only thing he had to work out was how to tell Theo, or whether he should tell him at all. It may distress him too much or he may simply not understand. He was not sure how Elise would cope either. She would be happy for him, but overly worried about the risk he was about to take. Maybe it would be best to say nothing at all. They relied on him, but so did his sister.

CHAPTER 43

There were cobwebs on the ceiling. Had he eaten spiders in the night? Theo mentally checked his body parts were present and functioning by wiggling each in turn and then shifted his attention to his mental faculties. What day was it? What had he done yesterday, or the day before for that matter? Other than a vague feeling of unease, similar to the unspecified anxiety that comes with a hangover, there was nothing. He should start with something easier. Where was he? At home.

There were noises in the apartment. Nebay or Elise? If he knew what day it was he would be able to work it out, possibly, but that information was not available to him. He did not like surprises. He got up and put his feet where his slippers should be, but they were gone. He hated it, how everything disappeared. He walked round to the other side of the bed. His slippers were there. He did not know how they had travelled, but they had definitely made the journey.

'Hello,' he called cautiously as he made his way to the toilet.

'Morning!'

It was Nebay. His voice was comforting, familiar. In the bathroom there was a funny old face looking at him. He did not like it, so he looked away. He went towards the kitchen, on the hall table there was a note with his name on it. Somebody called Sebastian had called and left a number. Theo did not feel like dealing with numbers.

'How did you sleep?'

'Good, I think. How do you rate it?'

'Sorry?'

'How do you know if it's good?'

'Well, do you feel rested?'

'I don't know. I feel… I feel…'

'Don't worry, take a seat. Here are your pills and a glass of water.'

Theo took the pills. They were small and bitter. He wanted to spit them up or out or whatever it was, but he did not want to upset Nebay.

'Thank you,' he said with feeling.

As the morning fell into the afternoon and the light became stronger, Theo forgot his earlier confusion. He just took a long time to wake up these days. He walked past the note again. He recognised the name, but he could not place it.

When Nebay left he lay a reassuring hand on Theo's shoulder.

'See you soon.'

And Theo thought, yes, see you tomorrow. He sat with a blanket over his knees, the radio played quietly in the background. His daughter was making noises in the kitchen. He looked at the picture of his wife on the mantelpiece. It was awkward living with a stranger and that is what Monique had turned out to be. One week after they returned from honeymoon, Theo was due to go to South America and give a series of lectures in Buenos Aires. The night before he had to leave they had had dinner together in their small apartment in Belleville.

'Why did you listen to your father when he asked you to marry me?'

'He never asked, he merely suggested that it would be helpful.'

'And why did you agree?'

'I owe them everything, Theo. My last relationship

ended badly. I got into some difficulty, financially, they paid my debt.'

'So, when you say you owe them you mean it literally. The contract between our father's businesses, that's what this was about?'

'Yes. Supply and demand. I needed a husband. You needed a wife. My father makes medical equipment, your father sells it. There's a lot of competition out there, but now we're family. It makes it much harder to say no.'

'But why marry me? Why do I have to be involved at all?'

'I guess my parents wanted me to make a more sensible decision this time, have stability, and your father had received another offer on the contract, undercutting my dad's firm.'

'This is not something I would have agreed to if I had been aware of the situation. You're not the only person affected by our agreement.' He resisted the word marriage. 'I made a big sacrifice thinking that I was going to make you happy. That's what husbands do. They put their wife's happiness first. I thought that's what you wanted.'

She came over to him and took his head in her hands. She kissed him.

'I'm sorry about what I said on our wedding day. This may not be the greatest love story ever told but that does not mean it cannot be good or be something we both enjoy. I stand by the decision I made, and I will try to make you happy.'

She unbuttoned her shirt and let it hang off her shoulders.

'I'm your wife, Theo, you can take me whenever you want. I'm yours, all of me.' She undid the belt of her skirt and let it fall to the floor. Half-naked, she looked young and vulnerable. Theo stood to kiss her, but he could do nothing more. He pulled her shirt around her and held her to him.

'What have we done?'

'We will be friends, in time.'

CHAPTER 44

It was 9.15am and Elise should have left for work over an hour ago. She watched the clock tick round to 9.30am. She had already rung the office to explain that she was ill. For the last three days it had been the same. There had been no sign of Nebay. She went to look for her father.

'Theo,' she said gently outside his bedroom door.

'Yes, yes, coming. I am coming. Is Nebay here yet?'

'No, he still hasn't come.'

Theo appeared at the door. His hair was all over the place and he looked like he had not slept.

'I think we should look for him, but I have no idea where to start,' said Elise. 'Has he ever told you where he lives?'

Theo sat down on a kitchen chair and placed his jacket over his knees. 'No.'

'He must have said something to you about his life here.'

'Not so much, not really. Hasn't he told you?'

Elise realised that there was still a lot she had not asked, and he seldom spoke about himself. She looked at her father and sighed.

'No, but we have known him for quite some time. We should know where he lives.'

'Why?'

'Because normally that's what happens.'

'Every man is entitled to his privacy.'

'Why are you being so difficult?'

'I'm not. I just don't know anything, and you seem to think that it is some failure on my part that we don't know where he lives.'

Elise pulled up a chair. 'That's not what I'm saying, Theo. I'm saying it's unusual.'

'Well, that's what it sounds like.'

'Okay, I'm sorry.'

'He mentioned a café in Belleville once, a place he went for food.'

'Good. Where in Belleville?'

'I don't know.'

'Okay, what was it called?'

'I don't know.'

Elise took a deep breath. 'Well, it's a start. Maybe if he went to this café regularly, then he lives in Belleville. That's more than we had.' She went to get her coat.

When she came back to the kitchen, Theo was still seated.

'What if it's no good?'

'We'll find him, Theo, we have to.'

'We did go to a bar once. People seemed to know him there.'

'Which bar was it?'

'Something about cats.'

'Cats?'

'They have dancing.'

'*La Feline*? He took you to an anarchist bar?' She laughed.

'They were very nice actually.'

'I'm sure they were. I just can't quite imagine it.'

The streets of Paris seemed quiet; everybody else was already in work. As she ducked into the open mouth of the metro she hoped that no one from the office would see her. If she had to make a lie up about a trip to the doctors they would want proof. She was already on a disciplinary.

'Elise, there's something I need to tell you,' Theo said quietly.

She waited while he formulated the words.

'I told him I wouldn't tell you. He disagreed. He said you had a right to know, but I was worried about your job.'

'You mean about his papers?'

'He told you?'

'Yes, and he was right, he had to tell me. I do have a right to know.'

'And you're not upset?'

'I meet people struggling to get visas every day at work. I give people bad news all the time. So if him helping us helps him, it's good. And also, I like him.'

A drunk had boarded the metro. In one hand he held his can of beer, in the other he gripped the rail, swaying slightly. He turned as if to a friend.

'Look at them all,' he said, taking in the carriage with a sweep of his arm. 'They're not even living. Prove to me you are alive, sing with me!' he commanded.

The carriage remained silent, each person making a conscious effort to look away from the man as he rambled through the first few bars of a song and held out a hat for spare change.

'You think this is life?' he asked. 'All this rushing around, all this work? You go home and stare at the TV, watch American films that rot your brain, barely have the energy to make love before it all begins again. That's not living. That's not life! Revolution! That is life! Resist. Resist. Resist,' he repeated, but instead of becoming louder he was losing volume with each word, falling in on himself. 'You have to pay attention,' he concluded, clearly upset now, lost in the darkness he saw in the world.

Theo got up shakily and handed the man a few euros.

'What are you doing?' Elise asked when he sat back down, but Theo did not respond.

The bar was closed when they reached it and he was not in the café, though the people that worked there knew his name.

Theo proposed a stake-out and before Elise had a chance to voice her opinion he headed to the café opposite. She watched the old man walk to an outside table protected from the wind by plastic walls and warmed by a heater. He looked so much happier all of a sudden. He had ordered them coffee before she had even sat down.

'I will have one of your cigarettes.'

'Will you?'

They sat down, huddled against the cold, and waited, but Nebay was nowhere to be seen. To pass the time, Elise asked her father about his childhood during the war and he told her about their long walk out of Paris, the hunger and the cold, about how the people they knew slowly disappeared, and about how his parents never ceased to fight against their present.

'It was a lot to live up to and I didn't. When my time came, I wanted only to survive.'

'You mean Algeria?'

'Yes, I was on the wrong side of the war.'

'Better than prison.'

'No, Elise, it was prison.'

She tried to imagine her father at war. Pictured him in his uniform, holding a gun, firing it.

'Did you kill anybody?'

He shook his head, but he did not say no.

CHAPTER 45

Nebay, the Doctor and the Lawyer took the bus to Calais the following evening. As they left Paris it felt good to be moving forward again, to have a destination, even though their chances of success were slim.

'If I make it, I can apply for my wife and children to come,' said the Doctor. 'It is almost too much to hope for, but I have to hope.'

'My sister has managed to prove her case. You can too, but you need a good lawyer.'

'Did somebody say my name?'

'Well, Mr Lawyer, it's true, you are exactly what we need,' said Nebay.

'Finally, recognition of my talent!'

'We will recognise your talent when you prove it,' said the Doctor.

'Well, you have never even managed to solve your own medical problem, so I would say the same to you.'

'Surprisingly, I cannot perform surgery on myself.'

'But you could at least try.'

'Come on, you two, professionals should not bicker on the bus.'

'Sorry, Professor, but you must admit that the thought of our lives being in the hands of the Lawyer is terrifying,' the Doctor was joking now.

'At least he offers a good rate,' replied Nebay.

'My favourite rate.'

'If you are suggesting my services are free, you can think again. I will keep a tab of every hour I spend, you can pay me whenever you are ready.'

'Of course! When I work in a big London hospital, you can have every penny. Here,' the Doctor handed the Lawyer a crumpled five euro note, 'a down payment.'

They disembarked at the port and made their way to the Calais Jungle, a spot that moved and moved again, but they had asked the new arrivals in Paris where people were currently staying. From one shanty town to another. Nebay wondered how many people like him lived in France under canvas. They set up the tent, going through motions long familiar to all of them. During the day they tried to get some rest. They would not sleep that night. Instead they would be at the port, sneaking through fences and under the noses of security guards. If they made it across they would not need the tent on the other side. Someone else could use it. If, more likely, they did not manage to cross, they would want the tent to sleep in again tomorrow.

Nebay wondered what would happen if things were the other way around. What if the UK ran out of its resources, what if the sea rose up and swallowed it, or a drought came and ate all the crops and dried out all the water? Would the starving British refugees make their way to the continent of Africa? And if they did, would they be welcomed, or would they be forced to make do along the borders in shanty towns with picket fences? If British refugees were treated in this manner he knew it would be an international outrage. When you had once owned the world you could not be forced to its margins.

When night fell they walked towards the port and slipped through a hole in the fence. As they watched the lorries for one that could carry them to another life they each remained silent, locked in their own thoughts. Crossing this stretch of sea meant something a little different to each of them but for all of them it was a strange form of homecoming. It was the idea of being able to settle somewhere, to learn the streets that would be walked to work, to bring back together those who had been lost to each other.

In the semi-darkness, the security lights did their best to illuminate the night. The group moved forward, crouched low. A lorry driver had left the canvas side of his truck slightly open while he went for a piss. He must have been doing a last-minute check to make sure there were no stowaways already on board. The Doctor was at the front and Nebay brought up the rear. They climbed in just as the driver was doing up his flies. Inside they found heaps of neatly stacked boxes. The Doctor and the Lawyer manoeuvred themselves around to the other side of the cargo. Nebay was about to follow when the driver returned. As the man began to draw the side panel shut he spotted Nebay.

'Get out of my fucking truck! I had two fines already this year. You buggers are bleeding me dry!'

Nebay held up his hands as if under arrest.

'Sorry, sir. I meant no harm.'

'You lot never do.'

Nebay began to step down. As his feet landed on the ground the driver punched him.

'That's to remind you not to try this again.'

Nebay breathed calmly and stayed where he had landed. He did not want to jeopardise his friends' chances.

'Any more of you bastards in there?' the driver asked, turning from Nebay back to the truck.

Silence answered him.

'If there are, and I come in there and find you, you'll get a lot worse than what he got.'

Again there was nothing.

'Any more in there?' he asked Nebay directly.

'No, sir, just me. I am on my own.'

'Well then, get lost.'

The driver went back to closing the door and mumbling to himself.

'Can't turn your back for one bloody minute. Can't even take a piss. Gonna miss the bloody boat now.'

He climbed back into the cab and sped off.

Nebay walked back to the camp alone. He hoped that the driver would not find his friends, that the sniffer dogs would not locate them, that the border guards would not search them out. When he reached their tent and lay alone in the stillness of the night without his friends to break the silence he suddenly realised how much he would miss them. Did he have the heart to carry on alone? He thought of Theo, the old man waking up and wondering where he was, Elise worrying, trying to track him down. He should have told them. He should have explained the situation, let them know it was not a lack of care for them but a great love of his sister that had chased him away. Knowing that his sister was free had filled him with the hope that they would soon be reunited, but when he thought it through now he realised how rash he had been. How could he expect to help his sister? He would arrive with nothing, less than nothing. He would arrive without even a name.

And if he returned to Paris? He would be stuck again. He would have Elise and Theo. It was something. It was more than nothing. But it was not enough. He would sleep and try again the following night. It was all he could do.

CHAPTER 46

Why had Nebay gone, why were people always leaving him? Every day Theo was presented with questions he found impossible to answer. He remembered the morning that Nebay had been running from the police. He could have been arrested. He could have left. He could have been hurt. The possibilities spiralled around him, making him dizzy with the thought of it all.

Being in Belleville calmed him. For two days they had sat in this café, talking, drinking coffee, eating lunch, drinking more coffee, and going home when it got dark. This was a place where Nebay was known. There were people here who could find him. Why had Theo never asked him where he lived? He remembered him saying that he lived with other people, that was all. Theo did not even know how many other people or what names they walked around with. Nebay did not talk about himself. There were thousands of things that Theo did not know about him. It was a terrifying distance. Was it possible that if he knew more, Nebay would seem even further from him?

He sat quietly with his daughter, their smoke drifting up into the cold air, mixing with their crystallised breath, forming a cloud around them. The strangers that passed them were just that, strangers. Theo realised that if Nebay had left and did not want to be found then he would never see him again. He was the sort of person, in the sort of situation, that leant itself to the terrible art of disappearance, just like Marianne.

'I lost her, you see,' he said to his daughter without expecting himself to.

'Who?'

'Marianne.'

'Who was she? How did you lose her?'

'She was my girlfriend in university, the person you reminded me of. She went to fight in Algeria, and I thought she was dead. For years I thought she was dead.' His face was getting wet again. 'I loved her.'

'Why did you think she was dead?'

'I went to where she was living, it had been bombed, there was nothing left. They said everyone died.' He looked at his daughter. 'I'm sorry, Elise, it left a hole in me and ten years later your mother walked into it. In the end we got married and after a few difficulties, a few upsets, we had you and you were the best thing, the only thing. I wouldn't change it, I couldn't.'

'Don't cry, Papa.' She reached out to hold his hand.

'But now all I want is to find her, and I can't, and maybe, even if I do, she will not want to see me.'

'When Nebay comes home we will help you find her.'

He squeezed her hand as tight as he could, but he could say no more. The water kept falling.

During the twenty years, he had believed her to be dead, he had seen her everywhere, in every woman, in every city, in every country. She had become a ghost who haunted him. In Cairo he had almost convinced himself that he had found her. Sweat drenched and wretched, he had seen a sole figure walking down the narrow street towards him, a woman with a boyish figure dressed in black, a shawl around her head half hiding her face. The light in the alley had been poor. He had watched as she slowly moved between the stalls, holding up colourful scarfs, bartering for spices, pausing in front of a book. He had sat transfixed as she drew closer to him, every bone in his body, every aching hung-over bone, had told him it was her. She was almost level with him, and he was just about to stand up and shout 'Marianne!' when he realised that of course it was not true. She was dead after all.

In that dusty backstreet, Theo had finally cried. The first tears had struggled to escape from his gritted eyes, but after the first had fallen there was no turning back and his whole body gave itself over to the act.

CHAPTER 47

It was getting dark on the third day when Elise finally saw Nebay's familiar form walking quickly up the street on the opposite side. He did not stop at the café but continued straight past it. She would have to run to catch him up.

'That's him!' Theo pointed in the direction of his retreating back.

'Yes, but he's walking so fast I think it's best if you stay here. Will you be okay?'

'I think I can manage.'

Elise was torn between reassuring her father and not losing track of Nebay. From the corner of her eye she saw him turn left towards Rue de la Mare. She thought of calling Mathieu or Celeste, one of them could have stayed with Theo, but Mathieu had someone else in his life now and Celeste had been at work all day. It would not be fair.

'I have to go.'

She stood up without further conversation. The waiter had been heading to the table. She could only hope that Theo would stay put, not forget why he was waiting and wander off. Thinking of this, she turned to the waiter quickly.

'If he gets up to leave remind him that he is waiting for his daughter and his friend.'

The waiter looked at her strangely and opened his mouth to speak, but she turned and started running down the street.

On rue de la Mare she saw Nebay as he turned onto rue des Pyrénées. She tried to shout but he could not hear her and continued onto avenue Simon Bolivar. Her breathing was becoming scratchy. She stopped to let the traffic pass as she crossed onto rue Rébeval. He would never hear her over the cars. He turned right and snaked up through the trees on boulevard de la Villette, but she had lost ground at the traffic lights. People stared at her as she continued, half running, clutching her side. She saw him make another left onto rue Vicq-d'Azir. He was heading towards the canal, still rushing, with his head bent to his chest. Again the traffic stopped her, the car headlamps cutting through the darkness like long, sharp knives. Finally, on rue des Écluses-Saint-Martin she gave up. She could run no longer. She shouted one last time, but to no avail. She lit a cigarette and continued to walk in the same direction, hoping only that he would stop or slow.

She found him on the bridge over the canal, standing on the parapet, staring down into the water. She ran the last few metres. He turned at the sound of her footsteps but did not look shocked to see her. It was as if he were almost expecting her or perhaps he was so lost in his own thoughts that in the outside world anything had become possible.

'Do not be stupid. I would never jump. I am not a coward,' he said when he saw the look on her face.

'Then what are you doing?'

'I am reminding myself of how easy it is to fall. How lucky I am to be here, to be alive, to have health.'

'In Paris we normally do that with a glass of wine, sitting in a chair in a restaurant. Come.'

'And that is why I love you Parisians. So elegant. Just like the Italians. But for me it is different. Sometimes I need to test myself.'

'Why?'

'To see what sort of man I am.'

'Where have you been for the last week?'

'I am sorry, but I had some things to do.'

'Why couldn't you tell us?'

'I did not know what to say.' He swayed slightly on the bridge. 'I wanted to see my sister.'

'You never told me about her.'

'I don't suppose I did.'

'Where is she now?'

'She is in the UK, and finally, she is free.'

'You tried to cross?'

'Yes. I did not make it. I tried for three nights. Elise, what can I do? Even my best friends have gone.' He turned to her, suddenly looking a lot younger than she had imagined him to be.

'I don't know, but we will work something out. Come down. Theo is waiting for us. We will fix this together.'

He looked down into the water once more before jumping easily onto the pavement and landing firmly on both feet. He put a hand on her shoulder and looked her in the eye.

'Do not worry, Elise, I meant what I said. I would never do this thing. I have too much left to live for.'

Elise embraced him tightly. 'Yes, you do.'

CHAPTER 48

Standing on the wall, his feet securely planted while the water below beckoned, asking him to offer his sacrifice, to finally give up, he had thought of Emmanuel. Or maybe, Emmanuel had thought of him, from that other place, the one that Nebay sensed at the edge of this life. He had been given the image of an afternoon they had spent together, a long lazy fall into night, they had spent their time in the sheltering shade of a giant sycamore tree, talking, reading, laughing, making love. The simplicity of it all had been overwhelming, the beauty of doing nothing with the one you loved, of time quietly passing around the eternal moment which you shared. Even now, with the evening traffic rushing past him, and the chill breeze coming off the canal, he felt held by this memory, cocooned by it. Rather than feeling his loss, he had an overwhelming sense of all that was still possible.

In Calais he had tried, and he had failed, and now here he was, back in Paris. When he had turned and seen Elise standing there he had not even been surprised. She had become a new sort of family to him. It was as likely that he would turn and find her or Theo as it was that he would find his own shadow.

'How is Theo?' he had asked as soon as they were walking.

'He has missed you. You are very important to him, you know.'

'I have realised that he is important to me also. You both are.'

Elise gave him one of her funny little smiles.

'Have you talked to Mathieu yet?'

'He is still with someone else.'

'You should tell him how you feel.'

'Have you come all the way back here to counsel me on my love life?'

Nebay laughed, 'No, but I seem to be doing it anyway.'

'Theo told me about Marianne, did you already know?'

'Yes, I have been helping him look for her.'

'He shares a lot with you.'

'And not with you?'

'Not really, but we have been talking these last few days.'

'You two were not very close when he got ill, were you?'

'We had very slowly lost the ability to talk. I was tired of being angry with him, but so tired I couldn't forgive him either.'

'Have you forgiven him now?'

Elise looked up at him, 'I suppose I realised there was nothing to forgive, or at least, that I have finally decided to let it go.'

Up ahead, Nebay saw Theo, frail in his large coat, sitting in a café. He slowly stood as he saw Nebay approach. His glasses sat awkwardly on his face, as if designed for a larger man, and his hands shook as he adjusted them. His scarf opened during this process to reveal his scrawny neck, barely holding up the old man's head. There was hardly anything left of him. When they embraced, Nebay could feel his birdlike bones.

He sat down with them and they kept the conversation as light as possible. In the back of his mind he thought of the Doctor and the Lawyer and hoped that they had crossed safely, that while he sat here at a café in Paris they were spending their first days in the UK, moving towards their futures.

CHAPTER 49

There he was, Nebay, sitting right in front of him. Theo held out his hands to him over the table and grasped his fingers tight when they were offered, feeling their strength.

'You scared me.'

'I am sorry, Theo, I had things to do.'

'What things?'

'I wanted to visit my sister, but it was not possible.'

'But she is so close.'

'I know.'

They ate a meal together and for a moment Theo fancied they looked almost like one of those families he had seen through restaurant windows, whiling away their lives together, giving and receiving comfort. He smiled.

They took the metro home. Nebay came with them and Elise made him a bed on the sofa. That night as Theo fell asleep he felt content, but in the middle of the night he woke. He had forgotten something important. He went into the hall in his pyjamas and looked at the piece of notepaper on the table. Sebastian, of course. He returned to his room, taking the note with him. It was still in his hand as he fell back to sleep.

He had been running late for a class he was teaching; Monique had kept him at the breakfast table talking about moving into his parents' old apartment now they had both passed on. He had not known what to say. It felt like it would be moving backwards rather than forwards. It was old and stuffy. 'But it is cheap,' she had countered, which had surprised him. She did not usually worry about these things. 'And there is more room.' Another thing he could not deny, he just did not understand why it mattered. They were not short of money or space.

When he had finally arrived at work he had taken the small flight of steps at the front of the university building two at a time, nearly tripping over the last one. He paused for breath before entering the large door, smoothed his hair down, and straightened his shirt and tie. In the entrance hall was a large poster advertising this month's speakers with photos. The third one down was Marianne. He stopped. Something was trying to escape from his chest. The third one down was Marianne. He moved closer to the poster, his hand outstretched, and touched it. Her name was there under her picture. It was her.

He realised he was kneeling on the floor in front of the display. A security guard was walking over to him. He stood up, walked to his office, his hands were shaking, his whole body was. He cancelled his class, took some deep breaths, and rang administration for Marianne's contact details.

He woke up with tears in his eyes, surrounded by darkness. He longed for light. He manoeuvred himself out of bed and went to the kitchen, turning on all the lights, walking in circles around the island in the centre of room. His frenetic movements knocked a cup off the side, and it crashed to the floor. He bent to pick it up and cut himself, his blood fell freely to the floor. Nebay came in, awoken by the sound, and bundled him to the kitchen table, sat him down on one of the old wooden chairs that had been new wooden chairs when Monique bought them.

'Hold out your hand,' Nebay said to him, and he did as he was told, the tears still falling, the pain in his hand far away.

Nebay dabbed at him with something that stung and wrapped up his hand. The bleeding stopped. He came back to himself.

'She's alive,' he whispered to Nebay who took him in his arms and held him until the tears had finished.

CHAPTER 50

The metro sped through the abandoned Croix-Rouge station. In a flash, Elise saw the empty seats and curved walls. She imagined it crowded with people, populated with ghosts. It had closed in 1939 at the start of the Second World War, three years after Theo was born. Bold colours now stretched across every surface as if it had only ever been an oddly shaped canvas, a blanked-out page from a history book. Maybe if she had pursued her career as an artist she too would have been down here in the dark scratching artwork into the dirt and dust, clawing at collective memory with her paintbrush or spray can, covering everything until nothing was visible anymore, creating a new truth.

She bit her ragged nails. The thought of facing Simon made her feel cold. What if he found out about Nebay? She had managed to get to work every day through the power of not thinking, not questioning. She had treated it as a task that had to be completed, had made it clear to herself that there were no other choices. This was the only way. Work, and look after Theo, and work. But how long could she keep this up for? She had tried for other jobs but with an arts degree and a long history of waitressing, the rejections had piled up. She wished they still came as physical letters so she could have used her standard approach, adopted in the months after she'd finished university, of making them into paper aeroplanes and throwing them out of the living room window, watching them as they spiralled down onto the street below and ducking out of view if any of them happened to land on a passing pedestrian.

At Gabriel Péri, she got out. The bodies around her dragged her forward against her will. She felt like shouting 'Wait!' but what would they do? Stop? And then what? She had to trust her legs to carry her. That was all she could do. As she mounted the final steps she took out a cigarette and at the top she paused to light it. This had somehow become a habit again, a ritual, the last cigarette before the office, a few more moments to herself. The rest of the way she walked swiftly, her head to the floor, her mind focusing on the scuff of her shoes along the pavement.

'Good afternoon,' said Simon, looking at his watch.

She regarded him for a moment – his weaselly eyes, his parched and dappled skin and half untucked blue shirt – and said nothing in reply. There was no reason to be scared of him. He knew nothing about her life outside of work. True, she was on a disciplinary, but all she had to do was keep her head low and do her job.

For the rest of the morning she went through visa applications on the computer screen. She checked that the information given was correct and matched the documents provided. She checked the spellings of names, the reasons for travel, the lengths of intended stay. She stared at photos and wondered about the lives of these people. In theory they were different to her only in that they required a visa whereas she did not, but often they looked different to her as well. Being born in Europe was a kind of magic, it gave you special powers of freedom and movement, and all you had to do was survive birth. There was another alert notice about the new fake passports. She paused to read it again. Where did you get one?

During her lunch break she chain smoked cigarettes with an instant coffee from their small staff kitchen. Her hand was cold as she held the cigarette to her mouth. Every now and then she swapped hands so that the cold one could hold the coffee.

'I thought you didn't smoke,' Simon said when she came back in, looking at his watch again.

'I don't, I'm just having a relapse.'

'Are you worrying about something?' His voice suggested kindness, but this seemed unlikely.

'No, not really. Obviously I'm worried about my father, but other than that everything is fine really, just fine.'

Simon shook his head slightly. 'If there is anything you need to talk about just let me know.'

Elise went back to her computer, turned the screen on and printed the paperwork she needed for this afternoon's interview. Her hands were shaking, and she placed them on her knees under the desk, hoping that no one noticed. Nobody at work knew about Nebay. There was no reason to worry. And yet.

Simon followed her into the interview room, picked up a chair from the table and took it to the back corner, behind the interviewee. She was under supervision.

'Do you know why you're here?' she asked the man opposite her, Hayyan Qureshi.

'No.'

'Are you sure?'

'Yes.'

'They do not believe these papers belong to you,' she said, and Simon gave her a look. 'We do not believe these papers belong to you.'

'They are mine, they have my photo, have you looked at my photo?'

'Of course.'

'Well, doesn't it look like me?'

'Yes, but just because it looks like you, does not mean it is you.'

'I don't understand.'

'Did you buy the papers?'

'How would I have bought papers? I have no money.'

Simon gave her another look. Elise swallowed and continued.

'What is your date of birth?'

'The 23rd of February 1995.'

'Where were you born?'

'Aleppo in Syria.'

'Which district?'

'Karm al Jabal.'

'When did you leave Syria?'

'March 2012.'

'Why?'

'I had been a part of the demonstrations, many people I knew, my brother and my father, were killed. It was not safe for me.' His hands had started shaking too.

Elise stopped herself from reaching over the desk to take his hand in hers, to offer comfort. She looked up at Simon, he shook his head.

'Why did you take part in the demonstrations when you knew it could put you in danger?'

'We wanted democracy. We wanted our rights.'

'When did you receive asylum in France?'

'July 2012.'

'Why, when you have asylum here, do you want to go to the UK?'

'My uncle is there. I have not seen him since I was a child. He has invited me.'

'Where is your uncle from?'

'He is a British citizen.'

'But where was he from before that?'

'Syria.'

'How long do you intend to stay in the UK?'

'Two weeks.'

'Where will you stay?'

'With my uncle, in London.'

Elise looked once again towards Simon, but it was no use, his expression was clear. This man was not going to the UK.

'I'm sorry, but we cannot grant you a visa at this time.'

'Why?'

'I have to go,' Elise stood quickly, nearly knocking over her chair as she did so.

'You have to give me a reason why.'

She closed the door behind her and went to her desk.

'Not so hard after all, is it?' said Simon cheerfully as he walked past her.

Elise did not look up, just shook her head, and pretended to be intent on typing up her notes. She heard Simon laugh as he walked back into his office.

By the time she left work she was so on edge she could not bring herself to sit down in the metro even though it was relatively empty for the time of night. She felt almost as if she was on the run, as if she would turn around and see Simon walking up the carriage towards her shaking his head. She leant up against the pole and closed her eyes and tried to think of nothing. She listed colours: cerise, burgundy, magenta, but she could not escape from red.

An image of Monique came to her. She tried to concentrate. Sometimes she worried that she would forget what her mother looked like. Every day she checked the photo on the mantelpiece to make sure the picture she carried with her to work that morning was still accurate.

They had gone for a picnic, just the two of them, and had sat on a bench in the Jardin du Luxembourg eating bread and cheese. The sun was out, but it was still quite cold, and Monique had put a shawl over Elise's knees to keep her warm. Under the chestnut trees near the statue of Sainte Bathilde, Monique told her the story of the Queen of the Franks once again.

'Where was she from?' asked Elise.

'She was Anglo-Saxon, which means she was English.'

'And what happened to her?'

'On a wild, wild night she was captured by pirates and sold as a slave in Gaul.'

'Was she scared?'

'Of course not, never.'

Elise would always pause at this moment to imagine life as a pirate.

'What was the ship like?'

'It was massive and old and had a pirate flag. It creaked in the night while Bathilde was trying to sleep.'

'Did she have to sleep in a hammock?'

'She had to sleep on the floor with the rats.'

'I wouldn't want to sleep on the floor with the rats.'

'Well, you will never have to. Unless, of course, I become a little short of money. Maybe if I wanted to buy those expensive shoes we saw... maybe then I might sell you.'

'No! Mama, you can't sell me. I'll be very good. I'll get a job. I'll buy you the shoes.'

'You are eight years old, Elise, a bit young for a job, but the perfect age for a pirate.'

'Fine then, I'll become a pirate and I'll go and find Papa.'

After her death, Elise had found a love note stuck into one of Monique's novels. It was not from Theo. At the funeral a strange man she had never seen had come and stood at the back. As she had walked past him he had whispered to her.

'I am sorry. I would never have left her if I knew that this was how she would react.'

She had stared up at him with cold, dry eyes. This man was telling her that it was his fault that her mother had killed herself. He was saying that it was nothing to do with her or Theo. She had not believed him. She had chosen to blame her father instead, and finally she had forgiven them all, even the deluded stranger. Now all she feared was the genetic makeup she shared with the woman who had given birth to her, the cells which held both her creativity and her pain, but she would no longer let it hold her back.

When she finally reached the Odéon she was exhausted, but not yet ready to return home. She wanted some time to think. Theo was getting worse. Nebay needed to get to the UK. In her mind these problems were inextricably linked. Theo would not survive losing Nebay, she was sure of it, but Nebay could not abandon his sister either. He needed a way to travel safely. Could she help Nebay and keep her job? What she intended would irrevocably compromise her position.

She rang Celeste, 'I need to borrow some money.'

The following day, on the way to work, she stopped by the group of migrants she often saw at the café and started asking questions. She was going to help Nebay to see his sister.

CHAPTER 51

Nebay had woken with the rough bristle of an old carpet cushion burning into his face, his head a little foggy after his disturbed night's sleep. He moved onto his back and studied the cobwebs at the corners of the ceiling that had made their way down to the top of the gilt frames. On the wall opposite him, in between the two windows, was a black-and-white family portrait: a man and a woman with a baby in her arms. They were very young. The man had Theo's wiry, untameable hair and the woman his eyes. Theo had been born in history. Nebay reached for his notebook and wrote down the phrase, 'born in history'.

The apartment was quiet. Elise had gone to work without waking him. Theo must not yet have woken up or he would have called out a morning greeting. He pulled on his trousers and went to make coffee. As he waited for the water to boil, leaning against the counter next to the gas stove, he wondered if Theo had actually managed to track down Marianne, if that's what he was trying to say last night. It may be one of the few things that would bring him back to himself, for a while at least. Theo was running out of time. As the thought surfaced, Nebay choked it back down again. He was not ready to lose anyone else.

With the Doctor and the Lawyer gone, Nebay had no one to find a room with and he could afford nothing on his own, having given all his savings and pay to Asmeret. He had stayed on the sofa before, justifying it to himself because Theo was so ill, but the truth was that Theo was getting a little brighter again. Nebay knew that if he asked he would be able to stay for as long as he wanted, indefinitely even, but it was the idea of doing it that stumped him. Requesting help was not something he felt comfortable with. He admitted that this was partly through pride, but it was more than that. Relying on others could get you into trouble and in this particular situation it could get Elise and Theo into trouble too. His bond to these people did not stop him from being an illegal immigrant. The police would not care who loved who and how much. They would want to see papers and when no papers could be shown they would all be marched down to the station, Theo included. Nebay would not let that happen.

When Elise got back from work he excused himself and left. He had found an empty building not that far from the apartment and that night he made his way around the back carrying a screwdriver in his pocket. It was just strong enough to prise off the thin sheet of board from the back window. It was not locked and slid up with only a little effort. It looked like an old courthouse and it was not long before Nebay found the room with the judge's chair and public gallery. The leather of the seats was old and torn. Dust and leaves lay in drifts along the walls and up against the tables. How long was it since the building had last been used? Had the hammer gone down on people's lives? Were they taken from this room to the place of their execution?

Looking around, he imagined what it would feel like to know that these walls were the last you would see. The cornices had flowers engraved in the corners. That, at least, was something. If life was a series of rooms then the one Theo was in would look very much like this one. The last one.

Nebay wandered further, looking for somewhere to lay down his sleeping bag. He was careful to keep the torchlight away from the windows. Even though they were boarded, a stray beam and a passing policeman could lose him his night of rest. Off the main corridor he found an empty store cupboard with no windows. He made his bed quickly, undressed, and lay down in darkness. Within minutes he was asleep. He would have to leave again before it was light.

As day grumbled through the streets, Nebay crawled out of the window. A police officer holding a cup of coffee in one hand and a croissant in the other spotted him and made to run after him, but Nebay was fast and the young policeman was hungry.

CHAPTER 52

It was Friday, he had checked the calendar. He was ready to make the call. He had procrastinated for too long. He needed to focus, to hold it in his head. He needed his head to work. Nebay walked in looking agitated.

'Has something happened?' he asked.

'No. I'm just a little tired, it is always the same with a new place, you do not sleep.'

'Is the room you rented okay?'

'It is fine, it will just take some getting used to. How do you feel about going out to breakfast? I am starving.'

Theo held the note in one hand and the receiver in the other.

'I was just about to make a call…' his nerve was leaving him, 'but I can do it afterwards.'

'Do it now if you want. There is no rush.'

'No, no. I think it's better if I leave it till later.'

They left the apartment and strolled through a rare moment of late Autumn sun; it held a promise of better days to come. He wished he had made the call. He may never get up the courage again.

'So, who were you going to call?'

Theo looked down.

'Sorry, none of my business. You do not have to tell me.'

'No, I want to. I think I have found her, Marianne. Or, at

least, a number for her. I was calling the friend who will give it to me.'

Nebay stopped and turned to him.

'Why did you not tell me? We should call straight away.'

'I don't know. Maybe she won't want to talk to me.'

'And we might all die tomorrow. Come on, Theo, no more excuses.' Nebay handed him his mobile phone.

'I left the number at home.'

'Okay, well, we will do it as soon as we are back.' Nebay smiled and rested his hand on Theo's shoulder. 'We all deserve our moments of happiness, even you, old man.'

Back at the apartment he dialled the number.

'Sebastian?'

'Theo, you took your time getting back to me.'

'Sorry, I had a few bad days.'

'Don't worry, look, I talked to Marianne, she said I could give you her number.'

Theo breathed freely for the first time in days, or weeks or maybe even years.

'Thank you, Sebastian, thank you so much.'

'Don't worry, old friend, let's go for a drink sometime, see how many waitresses we can chat up.'

'Can't wait,' Theo replied, knowing they would never do it.

He wrote down the number with a shaking hand. Now he had it he did not know what to do with it. He stood in the hallway wondering what she would make of this old person he had become. When he finally called the number there was no answer and no voicemail option. In a strange way he was relieved.

The last time he had seen her she had worn a scarf wrapped around her hair. He had seen the scar it was supposed to hide or detract from and wanted to reach out and touch it, to kiss it, to wipe out all the pain that this one physical sign suggested. Instead he kissed her lightly on both cheeks and sat down on his hands to prevent them from moving without his say so. They were as they had been when she left that morning, in that time long past, and they had yet to speak a word. He held her stare.

'Theo,' she said his name and he wondered why anybody else bothered to say it all. It was only truly his when it came from her lips. 'It's good to see you. I am sorry it has been so long.'

Everything he had wanted to say in the years between her leaving and now piled up inside him so that no words could escape, they had blocked the entrance in their rush to be free. She looked older, wiser, even more beautiful. The scar, that on some would be a disfigurement, only accentuated her features so that she became almost regal. He could not take his eyes from her. He could not waste one second.

'Yes, it has been a long time. I want you to know that I came to find you in Algiers, but they told me that everyone in that house had died. I should have stayed and kept on looking.'

'For a dead woman? It is fair to say that everybody in that house did die.'

'Where have you been all this time? Why didn't you come and find me?'

'I didn't think you'd want me to. I was moving a lot at the time, giving talks, travelling. I spent some time with workers co-ops in South America. I passed through Paris a few times, but I had no way to contact you. Eventually, I moved back to Algiers.'

'I was in South America as well,' he said.

'Argentina.'

'Ecuador.'

'I wish we had met,' she said quietly.

'I wish it too.'

They paused. He put his hand on the table and she took it silently. The feel of her skin was everything he had ever wanted in life. He rubbed her fingers between his. They were small, bony and warm. Without realising he was doing it, he brought them to his mouth and kissed them. He held them there until he remembered Monique. He placed her hand back on the table and forced his own onto his lap. He could not trust them.

'I'm married,' he said with a weak smile.

'I'm supposed to say I'm happy for you.'

'Yes, and are you?'

'I am happy you are well. Who is she?'

'Her name's Monique, my mother introduced us. She's the daughter of a friend of my father's, a business associate.'

'I see. I don't suppose it's my place to tell you off about living a middle-class Parisian life anymore.'

'I don't suppose it is.'

'Can you take a walk with me even though you're a married man?'

'I don't think there's a law against it.'

He put his arm around her as they walked towards the river and leant his head into her hair. She smelled the same. He kissed the top of her head and closed his eyes. For a second he allowed himself to believe that everything was different. They stopped for a glass of wine. It was approaching seven o'clock. He would have to leave her soon.

'Do you love her?' Marianne asked, her voice strained.

'I have tried.'

She stood with him and they kissed, their lips lingering, their hands clasped.

'Leave her, come with me like you meant to.'

Theo looked into her eyes. He wanted to say 'Yes, of course, I need you.' But he had spent so long recovering, had promised himself he would be a new man, someone who took responsibility, stuck to his decisions, did not hurt people unnecessarily. And yet.

She pulled him closer. The warmth of her body seeped into him. Her breath on his cheek sent an ache through his whole being. They kissed again.

'Do you remember when you asked me to marry you, just before I left?'

'Of course.'

'I almost said yes.'

'Would you say yes if I asked you now?'

'I believe I would.'

With her in his arms he felt whole.

'We have the chance to be happy, Theo. Can you honestly say you have ever felt that with anyone else?'

'No, of course not. You were always the only one for me.'

He looked into her eyes, saw the light there, the one he thought had been extinguished from the world.

'I'll talk to her, explain. Will you wait for me?'

'That depends on how long you take.'

CHAPTER 53

It was evening. Theo was taking a bath. Nebay had stayed late to make dinner. Elise had not argued. She was tired and she needed to talk to him. It was just a question of approach. She did not know if he would accept her help.

Theo called out from the bathroom.

'Don't worry. I'll go.'

Nebay went before she even had a chance to stand up. He was gone for so long that she decided to follow him. The bathroom door was ajar. She poked her head around the corner. Her father was still in the bath and Nebay was helping to sponge his back. They could have been father and son. She left without saying anything. Theo would hate to know she had seen him in such a vulnerable position.

When Nebay came out she offered to make him a drink.

'There's something I need to talk to you about.'

'Okay. It sounds serious.'

'It is.'

Nebay pulled up a chair to the table.

'I want to help with your papers. I saw what you did for Theo just now. There is no one else in the world that he would allow to care for him that way.'

'I have already been rejected in both England and France.'

'Still, I think we should try. We can add character witnesses, say you've been looking after Theo, contributing…'

'You should not put your name to this. You cannot admit to employing an illegal immigrant.'

'I've made up my mind. We're going to do this one way or another.'

Theo came into the room.

'What are you two talking about?'

'Nothing, Theo, we're just chatting.'

Elise gave Nebay a look and he gave a small nod to show that he understood. There was no need for Theo to know. After dinner, Theo went to bed early, leaving Elise and Nebay at the table.

'If we're going to do an appeal you're going to have to tell me more about why you left Eritrea.'

'I really think you should just leave it.'

'Why? What sort of life can you have living like this?'

'Because I have already given them enough, they want you to relive every trauma from your life, every detail. I cannot, Elise, I cannot do it. They cut you right up through the middle, expose you, and then they say no.'

'But your sister has managed it.'

'My sister has always been braver than me.'

'There is another way.'

'Go on.'

'Forged documents.'

'They cost though, too much. I have nothing.'

'I'm pretty sure we owe you and I've been making enquiries. I can get a good deal.'

'It is risky.'

'It's risky whatever we do.'

CHAPTER 54

He was exhausted and the thought of his dusty little cupboard did not comfort him. As he rounded the corner onto the street of the old courthouse, two officers approached him. He could tell by the way they moved towards him that they were going to arrest him. He thought of running, but it was no good. There were two more officers behind him. They pushed him up against the cold stone of a wall and took hold of his hands, burying them into the base of his spine while they cable-tied his wrists together.

'May I ask why I am being arrested?'

'What reason would you like? Evading arrest? Breaking and entering? Squatting? Shall I go on? I could probably add working illegally.'

'I think you must have me confused with someone else…'

That morning he thought he had got away with it. He was sure that the officer had not seen his face clearly enough. Was he being picked up just because he resembled himself, as it were? Did they have any proof? Even working illegally would be hard to pin on him. His employers would not testify and admit they had been employing illegal immigrants. The friends he was working with had left. All he had to do was plead ignorance and stay quiet. They would hold him for a few days because he was undocumented, but then they would throw him back onto the street. It would take a few days, but he would be free again soon enough. His only concern was Theo and Elise. He would have to let them know.

In the back of the police van he thought of the conversations he used to have with his sister when they were younger. They thought of Europe as a place full of freedom. They had left Eritrea to avoid precisely this kind of treatment. How stupid they had been. He imagined his mother's face if she knew that two of her children had been held by European authorities, but then she was not the sort of person who was easily shocked. She had always warned them that you could trust very few people, and even fewer policemen and politicians. During the revolution she had campaigned for petitions to be signed so that they could be sent to all the countries of the United Nations. All they had asked was that a law created by the UN be upheld; that Eritrea be allowed independence. But the petitions were met with silence and the Eritrean people continued to die.

The grey building that swallowed him up seemed apt for its purpose. He hung his head like he was supposed to and gave his name at the desk. He played the game. A game he felt he had been born for, just as Emmanuel had been. There were high stakes and no winners.

CHAPTER 55

Theo called the number every hour, but there was no answer. He woke up and started again. Was it possible that she had given him a false number like the girls used to do in university when they were not interested in you? No, they were not children anymore, she must just be out. Where was she? It was not a Paris number. He resorted to the phone book once again and looked up the area code. She lived in Calais. He imagined her living by the sea, having a small garden, sharing it with her, picking flowers and arranging seashells while she did the crossword or made kindling. She was always very handy with an axe.

He felt like his heart was trying to escape from his chest, his blood pumping in his ears. Elise had booked him a doctor's appointment because he seemed so jumpy. She thought they had put him on too high a dose of one of his medications, but he knew this was not it. He was coming alive again. The hope of seeing Marianne had rejuvenated him. He was going to have a second chance, and when he was feeling kind towards himself, he even felt that he deserved it. He just needed a little more time; needed to stop the slip-sliding of his brain and stay focused.

On the third day of his attempt the phone was answered.

'Hello?' he said cautiously into the receiver.

'Yes?' It was not Marianne.

'I'm calling to speak to Marianne Anouar.'

'I'm afraid she is not here at present. Who shall I say called?'

'It's Theo Demarais. When will she be back?'

'She's in hospital for an operation, it will be a few days until she can return home.'

'Is it serious?'

'I'm sorry, but I think it's best you talk to her about it.'

There was something familiar about the woman's voice. A daughter?

'If it's serious I would like to be there.'

'Like I said, she'll be home in a few days. Call back then.'

The phone was put down. He considered what she had said. He could not wait three days just to talk to her. It was impossible. He ran down the stairs, or at least he tried to, it was more of a hobble, and out into the street. A few taxis passed him. He was only wearing his overcoat and pyjamas. Eventually, someone stopped. When Theo breathlessly shouted 'Calais,' the driver thought he had misheard him.

'Where?'

'Calais!'

The taxi driver looked him over again, clearly wondering if this old fool had enough cash to meet his demands. Theo pulled out his wallet and waved it at the man.

'I can pay, damn you, just drive!'

At that, the taxi driver, now pleased with his long fare, pulled back out into the street and started heading out of town. For a moment Theo sat back and revelled in what was about to happen, but then he looked down at his apparel, caught sight of himself, unshaven and unkempt in the rear-view mirror. There were globs of something in the corners of his eyes.

'Stop!' It was no good, he could not do it. He could not turn up looking like a mess. He needed to buy flowers. He needed a suit. 'Turn around.'

The taxi driver scowled.

CHAPTER 56

Elise woke up to a voicemail message. It was Nebay's voice, but it was quiet and sounded far away.

'I have been detained,' he said. 'They are holding me at the police station on Rue de Nantes.'

Surely this could not be right. She had said goodnight to him yesterday evening on this very spot. She listened to it again.

'Nebay? Is that you?' called her father.

'No, Papa, it's me. I don't think Nebay will be able to get to us today.'

'Why?' Theo appeared at his bedroom door. He looked disappointed.

Should she tell him?

'He's not very well. I think it's a cold.'

'He should have come here. I could have looked after him.'

'He didn't want to be any bother.'

'I see, I see. He's a good man.'

'Yes, he is.'

Elise went into her father's room to help him dress.

Theo rummaged in his wardrobe.

'Why are you standing there?'

'I am waiting to help you. Do you want me to pick something out for you?'

'No, I will do it myself. Nebay usually helps me, but he's not here.'

'I know, Papa, it was me who told you.'

Theo ignored her and continued worrying the wardrobe.

'I don't know what to wear,' he said finally.

Elise took a deep breath. 'Do you want me to help you?'

Theo turned to her. 'Okay.'

She picked out underwear, a shirt, trousers and a jumper. Her father looked at them sulkily.

'I suppose they will do.'

'Do you need help to put them on?'

'No.'

'Are you sure?'

'Yes.'

Elise left him to call the office. Simon sounded unimpressed.

'Another family emergency?'

'You could say that. I need to look after my father, our carer is sick.'

'Well, you needn't bother coming back. You've won. They're shutting us down.'

'What do you mean?'

'We're not efficient enough. All those positive interview results you hand out, they add up. By not doing your job, you've helped to do us all out of one. The Home Office are taking over. Your severance will be in the post.'

He hung up, but Elise was still holding the phone. She allowed herself a moment to let it sink in. She was free of them, and the money would help to tide her and Theo over. It was one good thing. Her father came into the hall with his shirt buttoned wrongly and wearing only one sock.

'Is Nebay here yet?'

'No, Papa, he cannot come.'

Theo walked through the living room. She found him standing by the mantelpiece.

'Who is this woman?'

Elise went over to him. It was a strange question to ask. There were not many photos up there and a few were of elderly relatives even she could not name, but when she saw which photo he held, she recognised it instantly.

'Theo, that's your wife, Monique, my mother.'

'My wife?'

She double-checked that her father had taken his medication and rang the doctor, but they had little to suggest other than hospitalisation. Hallucinations, delusions, fits of rage. Anything was possible now.

She tried the police station, hoping to track down Nebay. The phone rang for a long time and the officer that picked it up sounded grumpy.

'I believe you are holding someone by the name of Nebay?'

'Second name?'

She could not believe that she did not know it.

'He is from Eritrea.'

'I'll need a second name, madam.'

'He's a family friend, please, do you have someone by that name?'

'We only deal with full names and I'd be careful to whom you refer to as a family friend. Goodbye, miss.'

Stupid. She would have to ask Theo, but it seemed impossible that he would know. He was sleeping in his chair in the sitting room. His head was bent forward. His chin rested on his chest. She could not get used to him being so old.

'Papa?' she said gently, laying her hand on his arm. 'Can I ask you a question?'

Theo woke with a start. His eyes were clearer.

'How can I help?'

'Do you know Nebay's second name?'

He did not miss a beat. 'Woldu, it is his father's name.'

Elise looked at him, shocked. 'Thank you.'

She rang the police station again. Luckily, a different officer answered. It was a woman.

'Are you holding a man by the name of Nebay Woldu?'

'May I ask who is calling?'

'His legal representative,' she lied.

'Yes, he's here.'

'I'll be there shortly.'

She took out a dark grey skirt suit and black high heels. She piled her hair high on her head and chose a pair of pearl earrings that had belonged to her mother. From her father's office she borrowed his briefcase. She rang Celeste. She was working, but promised to come over when Elise next needed help and with a little more notice. She rang Laila, but she did not pick up. The only other option was Mathieu, who she had not spoken to since he told her about his new partner. Her hand hovered over the phone.

'What are you doing out there?' asked her father.

'Nothing!' she replied, dialling the number.

He answered on the third ring.

'Everything okay?' he asked, guessing correctly that she would only have called him in an emergency.

She explained the situation and he promised he would be there as soon as he could. Theo came out into the hall.

'Who were you talking to and where are you going with that?' he asked when he saw her with his briefcase.

'Interview.'

Theo paused to consider this. 'Okay.'

'And you'll be pleased to know that Mathieu is coming to spend some time with you while I'm out.'

'Mathieu?'

'Yes,' she replied, too distracted by her preparations to question his tone.

She slipped her work ID badge into the briefcase with a few bits of blank paper. She was ready. In the kitchen she poured herself a coffee and waited impatiently for Mathieu.

CHAPTER 57

The large cell smelled of stale clothes and male sweat. He tried to avoid conversation with his fellow inmates, but it was impossible. For a start, he had cigarettes, and people will do anything for a smoke inside. There was a young Ethiopian guy in there with him. He was tall, elegant and quietly spoken. His name was Thomas.

'How long have you been in France?' he asked Nebay in the emptiness of the afternoon.

'A year this time, and you?'

'Six months. I was in Calais, but I had to leave. I had some trouble there.'

Nebay knew better than to ask what this trouble had been.

'Where will you go now?'

'I don't know. Maybe back to Libya to find some work. I drive trucks. Someone always needs a truck driver.'

'You do not seem like your average truck driver.'

'Maybe I'm not, but it is a job that pays. In another life I would have been something else, a musician maybe, I play the flute, but in this life I am just an unemployed truck driver.' He laughed and a smile remained on his lips.

'It seems that you are more than that to me.'

'Well then, you see more than most people.' Thomas held his gaze a little longer than necessary.

Nebay wondered what it would feel like to hold this man

in his arms. It had been so long since he had held and been held. But the thought of Emmanuel stopped him in his tracks.

'It has been nice talking to you,' he said and turned away from him.

Thomas placed his hand on his waist as he did so.

'You can't live with ghosts forever. I know that look. He cannot see you now.'

'It doesn't matter what he can see. It matters that I left him.'

'Everyone here left someone, many people, their whole lives. They did it so that they could go on living.'

'I am living.'

'No, my friend, you are not.'

'Well, I am alive.'

'And that is a gift you should do something with.'

'Even though it was bought with the lives of people I loved?'

'For this reason alone, you owe them that.'

Nebay looked long and hard into this man's eyes. How could Thomas see so much in so short a time? Was it that obvious? Did he wear his pain like a scar on his face? He realised he had taken Thomas's hand. A guard walked by and he dropped it.

'Think about what I have said,' Thomas added and went to talk to a group of men huddled in the corner around a pack of cards.

Nebay sat on the floor against the back wall, his knees up to his chest, his arms around them. What did he owe the dead? Before Emmanuel had died, there had been rumours in the barracks about their relationship, an offence in Eritrea. The other guys had started making remarks. Nebay had asked Emmanuel to ignore them, but he had found it difficult, wanted to stand up to them. Their comments quickly became threats. They started following Emmanuel and shouting abuse at him. Their officers did nothing, sometimes they joined in. Nebay wanted them both to leave, but Emmanuel said they needed to prepare first.

One night, a few guys from the battalion had found them

together in a storeroom. They had only been talking, planning their escape, you cannot just leave the army in Eritrea after all. You have to do your National Service. They had been overheard. The men threatened to beat them right then, until they had been called off to attend to some border skirmish. That was the night that they should have left.

A week or so later, the same group followed Emmanuel to the toilet during the night. They said that if he liked men so much then he could do them all a favour. When he refused what they asked of him they started to kick him. He tried to defend himself, so they pushed him to the floor and hit him harder. They may not have meant to kill him, but that was what happened.

Nebay never saw him again.

A friend had come to his bunk very early in the morning and had explained in a hushed voice what had happened. He had told him to go before the same thing happened to him. Nebay had had one choice, he had run.

The shame of it killed him, the injustice, the helplessness. Why had he not woken in the night? Why had he not sacrificed his life to avenge Emmanuel's murder? Thomas was right, he had wanted to live.

CHAPTER 58

Theo felt abandoned. His daughter had left him. Nebay had left him. Marianne seemed further and further away. How would he ever get to her? How was he supposed to organise himself when everyone was rushing off all the time, before he even had a chance to get his thoughts in order, before he had a chance to speak. If Nebay was here, he could have told him about the phone call. Nebay would have given him time to come up with the sentence. He liked Mathieu, but he was not who was needed. It was Nebay he needed.

'It's not good enough,' he said out loud without meaning to.

'Sorry?'

Mathieu was peering at him as if trying to extract knowledge.

'I said nothing. Where is Nebay?'

'He can't come right now, something has happened.'

'What has happened?'

'Nothing, Theo, nothing has happened. Forget I said anything.'

How could something and nothing have happened? Mathieu was silent. He was offering no more information. Why would nobody answer his questions?

'I will not be treated like this! You will tell me what is going on!'

Mathieu jumped up as if he thought Theo was going to hit him.

'Tell me!' Anger boiled within him. It needed an escape route. Everything was going wrong.

'Nebay has been detained. The police picked him up. That's all I know.'

Theo stood and as he did so the books that had been piled on the arm of his chair collapsed. The sound of them thumping to the floor seemed to confirm to him that his anger was well-founded.

'Look at this! Mess everywhere!'

'Theo, you need to calm down. You could hurt yourself.'

'I am not a child!'

'I know. That's not what I'm saying. It's just…'

It was too much. His own anger hurt him. He had already hurt himself. Picking up a silver-framed picture from the centre of the mantelpiece, he raised it as if he were about to smash it on the floor.

'Theo, no. That's a picture of Monique. It's Elise's favourite.'

'That is not my wife!'

Why did nobody understand? Mathieu was near him now. He took Theo's hand gently and they lowered the picture together.

'Please sit down. I can get you something to drink.'

What was happening? Who was this person? Tears burnt his eyes.

'I am sorry.' His body crumpled. He could feel it all sliding away from him. The floor felt safer. The lower down you got the more solid it became. He closed his eyes. Where was his daughter? Where had everything gone?

The night he had returned to Monique after meeting Marianne, he had been ready to leave her, ready to start anew, and Monique had greeted him with a pregnancy test. Before he had had a chance to question it, she had told him all he needed to know.

'It's yours. And this time it's going to work out, I can feel it.'

For the rest of the night he had sat alone and upright at the kitchen table as the clock ticked round till morning. One hand rested on the cold Formica, the other on his knee. He had not moved a muscle, as if by staying still he could stop time. If he breathed slowly enough maybe he could even reverse it. He was empty.

In the morning, Monique brought him coffee. She placed it down carefully as if she did not want to disturb him. She moved away from him, turning to rest against the sink, one arm bent over her stomach, the other one propping up her chin.

'I guess you'll just have to tell her no,' she said with no hint of reproach.

He looked up into his wife's eyes and nodded. After the decade they had spent together, she knew him after all.

He had not seen Marianne again. He knew he would not be able to leave her twice. She sent him letters, but he could not bring himself to respond to them. He did not have the words. In the end, she stopped.

CHAPTER 59

The police station was busy, and Elise waited in line. When she reached the counter the officer eyed her outfit.

'Legal visit?'

'Yes.'

'And who are you here to see?'

'Nebay Woldu.'

The officer's voice was familiar. Was this the man she had spoken to on the phone? Would he catch her out?

'ID.'

She handed him her work ID.

'You lot don't normally visit people in here.'

'It's an ongoing case.'

'I see.' The officer paused as he looked from the photo ID to Elise's face. 'Okay. An officer will show you through.'

The plastic-topped table and mismatched chairs reminded Elise of her office. It made her feel uneasy. The officer who had walked her down remained outside the door. Nebay walked in looking drawn. His eyes were set deep in his head and he looked tired. He sat down heavily and smiled wearily at her.

They greeted each other silently, there were too many words to say.

'How is Theo?'

Elise looked down at the criss-cross of cracks in the tabletop.

'Not so well. Have they said how long they will hold you?'

'I do not know. My case has gone to the judge. They will probably just let me out again in a few days, but I don't know when.'

'How did they find you?'

'They were waiting for me at the place where I was living.'

'Did they hurt you?'

'No more than they hurt anybody else in here.'

'I should have asked you to come and stay with us.'

'You did, it was my choice to move out.'

'Where were you staying?'

'A squat.'

'I thought you'd rented a room?'

'I couldn't afford to.'

'You should have said something! What can I do to help?'

'Nothing for now. Let's see what the judge says. I will try to call.'

'What's it like here?'

'Not good. Too busy, too many people,' he shook his head.

'Hopefully it won't be for long.'

Elise felt small and inadequate. Had she thought that she could save him? A policeman knocked on the door.

'I think I have to go.'

'Thank you for coming.' Nebay sounded formal.

Elise stretched out her hand as she stood and Nebay shook it. To anyone looking in, it would have looked like the end of a normal interview.

Mathieu looked tired when she returned to the apartment even though she had only been gone for a few hours.

'Are you okay?' she asked.

'Yes, I'm fine. I just didn't realise how ill Theo had become. I'm sorry, Elise. You must be exhausted.'

'We get by.'

'How was Nebay?'

'I don't know, he sounded defeated. I've never seen him like that before.'

'You know you can still ask me for help whenever you need me, we're friends, you and I.'

'I know it now.'

He left and she slumped into the hall chair. She wished that she had talked to Mathieu for longer, she had so much to say, but Theo had been calling her name, he still was. She just needed a minute.

That night she could not sleep. Her thoughts were thick like oil paint. They coagulated into brown, then black. She was twelve. Theo was away, touring a lecture on the use of cartography as a weapon in the Second World War. He had taken some extra work with the cartographic society in Peru. He had been gone for months. She had arrived home from school a little early. It was a hot Friday in summer and the city had emptied out as if someone had tipped it upside down and shaken it. As she entered the apartment she had called out to her mother but had received no reply and had assumed that she was at the shop or was having one of her afternoon naps, she was sleeping a lot. Elise checked her bedroom, but the unmade bed was empty.

She had gone into the kitchen, made herself a sandwich, poured a glass of orange juice and taken both to the living room to watch TV. After half an hour her programme had finished, she had eaten her sandwich, drunk her orange juice, and her mother had still not returned. She needed a pee and went to use the bathroom, but the door was jammed. It was an old apartment so this happened regularly, the wood expanding and contracting with the change of seasons, sometimes even the steam from the shower would do it. She sat down once again in front of the television but could only half concentrate on the new programme because of her full bladder. She rocked a little on the edge of the chair to take her mind off it. Another half an hour passed. She tried the door again, but it would not budge so she went downstairs to ask Mr Beauclerc, a friend of her parents, if she could use his bathroom.

He came to the door and let her in without any fuss. She walked down the corridor to the toilet. On the way out she paused at the budgie cage and held her finger up to the bird. It looked at her with its head to one side.

'If your mama's not home soon you can always come back down here and watch TV with my grandson,' he said, motioning to the boy she could see through the open door at the end of the corridor. He was so fixated by the television that he did not appear to have heard them.

'Thanks.'

Elise went back upstairs and sat on the window seat to stare at the passers-by below and watch for her mother. She went to the kitchen, found a stale croissant left over from breakfast, and ate it in silence back at the window seat, making crumbs. The clock on the mantelpiece sounded louder than usual. Elise began to feel as if she was in some kind of trance, completely separated from the little people scrabbling around on the pavement. She pinched herself to check that she existed. At some point she tried the toilet door again, but it was still jammed. She returned once again to her perch. Outside, the clouds had cracked open and fat rain fell from an angry sky onto the sun-warmed pavement. Elise was sure she saw steam. The city was boiling. Darkness fell with the rain and still her mother did not return. The street lights turned on one by one. The people disappeared. The rain stopped and left everything quietly gleaming.

It was late. Elise went to find Mr Beauclerc who this time came to the door in his pyjamas, wearing his reading glasses and a heavy cardigan that still smelled faintly of sheep. He looked at Elise with concern and it was only then that she really started to worry. Mr Beauclerc called around a few shared friends but got only tired voices and no news.

'How about we go upstairs and search for clues,' he said

in that overly cheerful tone that adults use with children when they're trying to convince them that all is well.

Elise asked to borrow his toilet again before they left.

'Still won't open, eh? We'll see if we can fix that while we're up there.' His tone was distracted, and he hurried Elise out into the corridor once again.

They climbed the stairs together, Elise on the outside tracing the flowers on the banister absent-mindedly as they went, her small hand dawdling over the points of sunflower petals and the long leaves of lilies.

The first thing Mr Beauclerc did as he entered was to try the bathroom door, gently at first and then with the full force of his shoulder behind it. He failed twice, the blows rattling the large mirror above the table on the wall opposite. With the third blow from his shoulder the door opened, and there she was, her beautiful mother, her eyes closed as if sleeping, her body hanging loose and long.

The police arrived, the paramedics, the men with the trolley. They stole her mother away from her. She ran after them as they took her mother down the steps, her face covered, her body bagged. Celeste's parents came to collect her, and that night the two girls had shared a bed, but Elise didn't sleep. She didn't even cry. None of it would be real until her father came home, but he took so long, too long, and her grief kept burying itself deeper, until it became something else.

Elise awoke in the middle of the night to Theo calling her name. For a moment she lay without moving in the darkness, her mother's face, her blue lips and red cheeks on white skin still with her. But then he called for her again, fear in his voice, and she pulled on her dressing gown and went to him.

'Who is that woman?' he asked her.

He was pointing to the corner of the room.

'There is no one there, Theo.'

'She keeps staring at me.'

'Papa, come on, look at me. There is no one else in the room.'

'She's angry, I've done something wrong.'

Elise took her father in her arms and held him close. They would get through the night together.

CHAPTER 60

Nebay rubbed his fingers over a message scraped into the wall. It read *Long live the revolution*. The letters were etched deep. He wondered about the person who had written it. Whose revolution it referred to. All? Or one specifically?

His sister had spent time in a cell like this, filled to the brim with people who could not conform. He would have ended up in the same place if he had not left, if he had survived long enough to be transported there. Emmanuel would not have wanted that. He would not have wanted blood spilled after his blood. He had believed that they should stand up for themselves, fight for their right to exist, but only ever to the extent that they could go on living, that it would bring them something good, change something for the better, and in the army there was no way to do this. People wanted to survive, and survival meant compliance, and compliance meant killing a little of yourself, and that, well that led to the sort of behaviour which had ended Emmanuel's life. That was how he saw it. Damage following damage, pain on the back of pain.

Thomas came and sat opposite him.

'Have you thought about what I said?'

'I am thinking about it even now.'

'And what did you conclude?'

'That I have had enough of this half-life, that it is not what he would have wanted for me.'

'What was his name?'

Nebay paused, to speak his name seemed too much, but Thomas reached out to him, placed his hand on Nebay's.

'You must name him so that he can live again in the world, so that people know that he existed. It is important to honour the ones we lose.'

'Emmanuel, his name was Emmanuel Eyasu.' Nebay could not prevent his voice from breaking, snapping like a bone through skin.

'It's okay, you have begun,' said Thomas as he drew him into an embrace. Nebay allowed himself to be held. For a moment, the first that he could remember since before Emmanuel's death, he felt safe.

CHAPTER 61

The snow covered everything, masking the streets and the pavements, obscuring the signs and the landmarks. Theo watched the scene from the living room window. He had been sitting there for so long that he witnessed the frost arch its way across a pane of glass. He could hear someone in the kitchen and briefly wondered who it could be. There was the suggestion in his mind that it was his mother, but that seemed wrong. He was in the wrong time, had slipped into the past, he tried to claw his way out. It must be someone else, a friend perhaps.

'Nebay?' But even as he spoke the word it seemed unfamiliar to him. What did it mean? He had said it like a name.

There was no answer.

In his hand he held a crumpled map. He looked down at it, unaware of picking it up. Stretched across its south-westerly corner he read the words 'Mountains of Kong' and smiled to himself without truly understanding why. A woman entered and he thought to share his discovery with her.

'Look here,' he beckoned and pointed to the peaks, 'such a funny name.'

'I know, Papa, you have shown me many times. It's one of your stories.'

'My stories?'

'Yes, an Englishman placed the mountains on the map based on the story of an explorer and a Frenchman proved him wrong nearly a hundred years later. You always say that this is why maps are so important, because once it's on the map it's in the world, even if it doesn't exist.'

'I said that? All I can think is that it sounds like a good reason not to trust the English.'

'Yes, Papa, you say that too.'

The woman went away again, back to the kitchen. He could not help but think she looked tired and a touch annoyed. What had he done wrong? He was merely sharing an amusing observation. He looked out of the window again at the snow-covered street and back at the paper in his hand. What was it again? Why was he holding it?

On the mantelpiece there was a photo in a silver frame. It showed a woman who looked a little like the woman in the kitchen. Her hair and make-up suggested glamour. She did not look like his type and yet he felt as if he knew her well. He wondered how he could have come to know someone so different to him. He had always thought he would end up with an earthy type, someone who could survive in the wilderness, someone like Marianne in her dungarees with the flared trouser legs and brass buttons. Marianne, again it was a word he had thought of as a name. Was it?

'Who is that woman?' he asked of his friend when she came back into the living room. The question sounded familiar to him.

'She was your wife, Theo.'

Theo thought he caught some accusation in the young woman's words.

'Ah, yes,' he replied to mask his confusion, 'of course. She was very beautiful.'

'Yes, Papa, she was.'

Theo breathed deeply, feeling that he had somehow won that round. He had said the right thing and the tension in the room defused a little. Sipping his coffee, he felt himself relax.

'It's very... um... outside. It's very...'

'Snowy?'

'The white stuff?'

'Yes, the white stuff is snow. It's winter.'

'Of course, of course it is. And what was her name?'

'Whose name?'

'The woman, the wife in the photo?'

'Her name, Theo, my mother's name, was Monique.'

The young woman left again, and he heard things clatter in the kitchen and possibly the sound of something breaking. He had done it again. He had done the wrong thing. He looked at the picture. Stared at it hard. He remembered that woman from somewhere. He concentrated. She had been in the bath; all of her clothes on and her make-up everywhere. He had picked her up and dried her and put her to bed. An attempt, the doctors had called it an attempt. An attempt at what?

Theo stood and walked towards his office. He felt suddenly tearful. Everything seemed to be leaving him. He sat down in his chair and stroked the arms. The warmth of the wood comforted him. This is where he had worked. Maps were pinned haphazardly to the wall, photocopies, covering up other, original maps in frames. His desk was stacked with paperwork and handwritten notes. It was overwhelming and he wanted to push it all off, tear down the maps and start again. Could this really be his life? This mess of paper, this apartment, these memories and holes where memories should be?

He opened the desk drawers, thinking that maybe he could put the mess in them, or that their contents might reveal something. There was a half-empty bottle of brownish liquid in the first one. He brought it out and took a drink straight from the bottle. The taste was sharp and familiar. He took another swig and replaced it exactly as he had found it as if it belonged to someone else, as if he was stealing. The next drawer was full of paperwork – there was no room for any more – and the one after that contained a small leather photo album. He picked it up. The leather was smooth and well worn. Inside was a photo of a young man that looked like him, with a girl in dungarees. They were smiling and holding each other around the hips. It looked as if they were perched on the top of a mountain and on either side of them everything fell away into the mist. This was it. This was her. This was what the word 'Marianne' meant. It meant love.

CHAPTER 62

It was cold in the apartment, but Elise was too worried about money to put the heating on higher. She put on an extra jumper instead and sat Theo near the fire. He had started to have difficulty swallowing so she had made soup for lunch. She brought it through and placed it on the table next to her father.

'There you are, Theo, eat your lunch.'

He looked at her vacantly. She held the spoon up to his mouth and he swallowed it reluctantly. She offered him the spoon to hold.

'Come on,' she said gently. 'You can do it.'

He did not move his hand to take the spoon. It was as if he had given up. She leant to get the small stool from beside the fire so that she could sit more comfortably. Theo picked up the spoon from the table and threw it across the room. Elise went to pick it up.

'I know, Papa. I know you are not a child, but you need to eat and if you won't do it then I need to help you.'

He shook his head as if to say there was no point.

'There is, Theo, there always is.'

At her feet there was a notebook. It seemed to her as if he was swimming through time, occasionally bumping up against the rock of memory. With no forewarning he would launch into a jumbled story from his life. Of course she had no way of telling fact from fiction unless it was an episode she was already familiar with, but this was all she had left. Truth had become irrelevant.

'Godin lost his wife in Peru.'

'Are you saying that because of Monique?'

'I don't know what you mean.'

'Because Monique died while you were in Peru?'

Theo looked at her uncomprehendingly. She gave up.

'They were separated for twenty years. She trekked through the rainforest to find him. Everyone else died. Only she survived. Now *that* is love.'

She had not heard this story before.

'Who was Godin?'

'I don't know.'

Elise put down the notebook and picked up the spoon. Celeste and Laila would be here soon. She just had to hold it together a little bit longer.

'Come on, Papa, try your soup.'

'I don't have any children.'

'Okay, Theo, but do you want some soup?'

There was no response. She gave up and took the bowl back to the kitchen. As soon as she left the room, Theo began calling out. She was about to answer when she realised that it was not her that he wanted after all.

'Marianne? Marianne!'

She did not know what to do. If she went next door would he believe that she was this lost love of his? This ghost that haunted him? She had no choice.

'I'm so sorry, Marianne. I shouldn't have done it. I should've been better.'

He was crying. Nothing made sense anymore. This could not go on.

She was standing in the hallway, trying to work out what to do. By the phone there was a number written down in Theo's spidery handwriting. Next to the number was a name. Elise hesitated. In her reflection in the mirror above the side table she saw her mother's eyes looking back at her, but it was too late to think of all of that now. He was slipping away. She needed to do something to bring him back. She tapped in the number. An old woman answered.

'Hello...' Elise was at a loss for what to say. She should have thought this through. 'I am Elise Demarais. My father is Theo Demarais. I believe you know him or knew him.'

'Yes, I did.'

Elise realised that Marianne probably thought that she was calling to inform her of her father's death. That is what happened at their age. She had seen her father go through it. You were reminded of an old friendship only to be told that it was now irrevocably ended.

'Well, he's been rather ill. He wants to see you.'

'Why?'

This woman was not an easy person to talk to.

'I think, maybe, to apologise for something. I'm not sure. Like I said, he's been very ill. He keeps calling your name.'

Marianne sighed, as if relenting.

'How is your mother taking it?'

'My mother is dead. She passed away twenty years ago.'

'And he left it this long to get in touch?'

'Erm...' Elise felt as if she was suddenly caught in the middle of somebody else's argument.

'What a stupid man. Your father has always been a very stupid man.'

'Oh.'

'Of course I will see him, but I'm recovering from an operation myself. He'll have to come to me.'

She gave Elise her address and hung up. There was a knock at the door. Finally, Celeste and Laila were here. They arrived loaded with provisions, dumped them on the kitchen floor and hugged Elise between them.

'Thank you so much for coming. I'll try not to be too long.'

She went to take the money from her father's safe in his

office. There was something she had to do before Nebay came home and talked her out of it.

Mathieu met her at the metro.

'How are you?' he asked.

'Better for seeing you. Thanks for coming.'

'No problem, but now can you at least tell me what we are doing?'

'We're taking matters into our own hands,' she said as she showed him Nebay's passport photos and proceeded in a whisper to explain her plan. Mathieu was worried about her safety.

'That's why you're here, for back-up.'

They sat in the empty carriage in silence as the stations passed by them like miniature theatre scenes.

When they finally arrived, the street they walked down was dark and narrow. Mathieu walked by her side but looked nervous and she instinctively moved a little closer to him. She had memorised the address, not wanting to carry it around with her just in case she was stopped along the way. She could not be too careful. Stopping outside number 23, she knocked five times and waited.

A large man greeted her warmly. They stepped inside and found an office like any other. After handing over the photos, they sat in the waiting area side by side.

'This is not what I expected to be doing with my evening,' said Mathieu. 'You are even braver than I thought.'

'It's bravery born of necessity; it doesn't count. I'm still completely terrified, I just hide it well.'

A few moments later, Elise was handed an envelope. She checked the contents. The tiny red book inside contained the possibility of a new life. Her hands shook as she opened it. Nebay's face stared out at her, a Frenchman.

She waited on the platform with Mathieu so that he could catch the last metro home. With Nebay's passport securely in her bag she felt suddenly stronger. They had achieved something that a few months ago she would never have thought possible.

'Mathieu, I've been thinking.'

'Yes?'

'I miss you.' She paused. 'I know you're seeing someone else, but there's something I have to say.' She looked him in the eye. 'I love you. You don't have to say anything in reply. I just had to tell you.'

A mix of emotions sped across his face, which she could not decipher.

'Can I ask what made you change your mind?'

She hesitated before replying, contemplating her words.

'I realised that the promise I made myself was the wrong promise to make. I thought I had to be on my own to keep myself safe, but I don't, not if the person I am with is you.' She took a breath, and fought against her desire to run, to leave before the inevitable rejection. She would understand completely if he said nothing at all, or asked for more time, or stated that he was in love with the woman he had met.

He kissed her.

'What about…'

'I ended it a couple of days ago. I didn't love her. It turned out I couldn't.'

'And me?'

'Well, I think that might have been the problem.'

He kissed her again as the metro pulled up and waved through the window as it sped off into the darkness. Despite everything, she walked home with a smile on her face. When she got back to the apartment, Celeste and Laila were in the kitchen.

'Have you finished your clandestine activities for the evening?' asked Celeste.

'I have.'

'And are you finally going to tell us what it was about?' asked Laila.

'No.'

'Okay, then will you at least tell us why you look so bloody happy all of a sudden?'

'I might, Celeste, I'll think about it.'

'It's Mathieu, it's written all over her face. Look, she can't stop herself.'

'You got me. I admit it. How was Theo while I was out?'

'Luckily for all of us, he slept all evening,' said Celeste.

'Will you help me get him to bed?'

The three women supported Theo to his room, Celeste and Elise under one arm each and Laila opening doors and removing obstacles.

'Mama?' he asked quietly, as they laid him down to rest.

CHAPTER 63

The following day, Thomas left him alone, gave him time to heal. Occasionally he would catch Nebay's eye across the cell, but that was all. If the other men noticed they said nothing or simply did not care, but it still made Nebay nervous. He began to feel protective towards him. He had seen what could happen when a man expressed his feelings in this way.

In the night, Nebay woke, stiff from the concrete floor, to find Thomas next to him.

'Hello,' he whispered.

'Hi.' Thomas placed an arm across his chest and rested his head in the crook of his shoulder.

Nebay held the pose stiffly, fearing that the other men would wake and see them, but when he peered around the room he could see that many used their neighbour for a pillow or for extra warmth. He began to relax. He felt Thomas's breath take on the even pattern of sleep. He could feel his hair against his neck and chin. He wrapped his arm around Thomas's waist. He had forgotten how wonderful this felt.

When he woke in the morning, Thomas had moved and was sipping the light brown liquid they called coffee from a plastic cup.

'I have one for you,' he said and held it out.

'Thank you,' Nebay said and smiled back.

The coffee warmed him from within. He had not felt this good for months.

'So, where do you live now?' Thomas asked him.

Nebay thought about it for a moment. 'I have no idea.' He could not stay on Theo's sofa forever. 'What about you?'

'With some friends. One bedroom, many beds.'

'Oh, yes, I am familiar with this arrangement.' He thought of the Doctor and the Lawyer. He missed them.

'It reminds me of the army.'

'Sorry?'

'All the beds together, there's almost something comforting about it, familiar.'

'I guess there is, I had not thought of it like that.'

'So, we both did our National Service.'

'On opposite sides of the border.'

'Thank God we didn't shoot each other.'

'Do not thank God. Thank something more reliable.'

'Like fate?'

Nebay thought of Emmanuel. 'No, not fate.'

'Then what or who?'

'Thank chance. It is all we have.'

'Is it?'

Nebay laughed quietly. 'Maybe not. Not if we are lucky.'

The custody sergeant came to the cell door.

'Nebay Woldu?'

'Yes?'

'You are being released.'

He stood to leave. He had never thought he would feel sad to be leaving a police cell.

'Call me when you get out.'

'I will.'

They stood for a moment, their hands on each other's shoulders. It felt like all they could do.

'Break it up, ladies. I've got work to do.'

Nebay moved away swiftly and turned to face the policeman.

'Relax, Nebay, I will see you soon,' said Thomas to his back.

He knew that Thomas was right, but he hated it. He could not even turn back to look at him.

Outside on the street, the same street he had stood on only two days ago, he was amazed that nothing had changed; the same grey stone, the same trees, the same people walking along. A few snowflakes were falling, that was all.

Before calling Elise and Theo, he needed to walk, to feel the air on his skin, to live in freedom for a moment before responsibility took over once again. His step suddenly felt a little lighter. He smiled at the strangers who passed him, hugged into their winter coats, scarfs up to their ears. He kept on walking until he found an internet café. He wanted to know if his friends had succeeded in their journey. There was a message from the Doctor.

Dear Mr Professor!
We miss you! But are safe and well in the UK, at least as well as we can be in these delightful detention facilities they offer. The Lawyer is working on both of our cases, he says he will offer you a very good rate when you arrive. We saw a picture of your sister in the newspaper. She is famous! The Lawyer said that he would even be prepared to consider marriage to an Eritrean woman, but don't worry, I've convinced him otherwise.
We wait to hear from you and hope that you are okay with your old man mapmaker.
With love,
Ateef and Sylvestre

The wonder of it. That they could remain so positive exiled behind tall walls and security fences. Their words made him miss them all the more.

CHAPTER 64

Theo had woken in the night to a strange sound. He had found his mother, Alice, in the kitchen, prising up the floorboards with a chisel his father used for woodwork. He could see it all as if it were yesterday, no, not even yesterday, as if it were happening now.

She had moved the kitchen sideboard, it sat at an awkward angle butted up against the table. Into the hole she had made she was pouring their memories. Photos in silver frames, his grandmother's candlesticks, a dish his parents never used because it was a wedding gift, his grandfather's pocket watch which would one day be his, but not until he could look after it.

'What are you doing?' he asked in his tired four-year-old voice, but she did not reply.

Instead she came over to him, lifted him neatly from the floor, carried him to his bedroom, and took out the satchel which they had saved for him to use for school when the time came. It had been his father's before him.

'Get dressed,' she said as she placed his pyjamas and a change of clothes in the satchel. She handed it to him. He picked up his ragged teddy bear and followed her out of the room.

His father, Antoine, came through the front door carrying his medical bag.

'Everyone's nearly out,' he said to Alice while manoeuvring Theo's sleep-slackened body into his coat and hat, 'it's time.'

His mother was carrying two suitcases and his father took one from her.

'You look after the boy,' his father said.

Outside, light was slowly creeping into the early summer sky. Paris was silent, as if everyone had decided altogether not to speak. The families he saw, scurrying towards the metro station like them, walked quickly, but said nothing. Theo fell asleep on the train only to be woken roughly when they reached the last stop.

'Come on, my boy, no time to lose,' his father said, carrying him out of the carriage. Theo tried to wake himself, but it was no good. He fell back to sleep on the rough wool of his father's coat, to the rhythm of his hurried footsteps.

When he came round it was to the roar of something flying overhead, a shockwave that made his father fall backwards, a sudden scream that seemed to come from the earth itself. He was still held in his father's embrace, but now they were sprawled upon the ground. His mother lay next to them. Something had painted the world red. The air was heavy with smoke, it burnt his eyes and made him cough. He struggled to sit up. For as far as he could see there were people, more people than he had known existed in the world, and beyond them an endless expanse of unfamiliar country, long flat fields under a pale blue sky. In the far distance was a plane, growing bigger by the second.

'Papa!' he shouted over and over until his father's eyes opened.

When Theo woke for real, he was crying for his dead parents as he had not done in years, as he had not even done in the moments of their deaths. And the fear from this memory lingered in the present. The immobilising fear of that day in 1940 when they had been forced to leave their home as the Germans moved into their city. How little he had understood of the reasons and the bodies and the blood. How little he understood even now, less and less with each passing day.

CHAPTER 65

'I have been released. I'm on my way to you.'

Elise sank down to the floor next to the telephone. Finally. Nebay was coming home. She went to wake Theo. It was past midday and he was still not out of bed.

'Nebay will be back soon,' she whispered to him.

'Nebay?'

'Yes.' Elise hoped his return would help Theo, bring him back to the present for a moment, and then there was Marianne. Surely when he saw her, he would remember.

She rang Mathieu to tell him.

'I'll come over.'

Nebay arrived first.

'How are you?'

'Better now I'm out of that place.' Nebay was looking at the world map on the kitchen wall. He seemed transfixed by it, and though he looked tired there was also something different about him. He had lost his air of defeat. He almost looked happy. 'This is one of the routes that I took,' he said, and he drew a line with his finger.

'Eritrea, Sudan, Libya, Italy, France, Britain. Repeat.'

'What was it like?'

'I lost two friends on the boat from Libya to Italy. Dawit Bekele and his wife, Mazza. They drowned. I lost another on the way to the UK, Ife Hassan. She was run over by a truck at the ferry port. I got all the way to London. A friend has told me I should name the ones I have lost, to give them a place in the world once again. So I will name them for you. There were others, whose names are lost, maybe one day I will find them.'

He continued to look at the map on the wall. Elise stared with him. The lines shifted in front of her tired eyes. Finally, he turned to her.

'But the first person I lost was Emmanuel. He was the reason I left.'

Elise nodded, aware that he had shared something deeply personal.

'Get some rest, you look exhausted.'

Mathieu arrived and held her tightly.

'What's next?'

'Tomorrow we will go to see Marianne.'

'Have you given Nebay his passport?'

'No, I know it sounds strange, but I didn't know how. I'll leave it out for him, for when he wakes up.'

When Mathieu had left and while Theo and Nebay continued to sleep, Elise went once more into her father's office. The room was an atlas of his life. There was a map of every country he had ever visited. Notebooks from his travels were piled on the shelves. Volumes he had written or contributed to were everywhere. Sitting on his chair, she looked around. There was a framed portrait of Monique above the filing cabinet. Through the window of the office she could see into the apartment opposite, a young woman was making coffee in her chemise. There were pink geraniums in the window box. Her mother's favourite. On the back of the door was a hook where he had always hung his jacket after work.

As a child she had often burst into Theo's office trying to catch him up to something exciting but usually she found him sitting, staring out of the window or else preoccupied with a well-chewed pencil and a crossword puzzle. He had always used pencils for crosswords so that he could change the answers later. He often got them wrong the first time around. She would sit upon his knee and they would work on them together.

She leant upon his desk, her elbows digging into the debris of what little was left of him, and allowed herself to cry.

CHAPTER 66

In the morning he woke groggily. His eyes felt gummed up as if someone had poured glue into them in the night. His throat was dry. He reached for the glass of water he had left on the table and his hand found something else instead. It felt like a small book. He turned his head. It was a dark red colour. He picked it up. It was a passport. He opened it up. His face was in there staring right back at him. There had to be some sort of mistake. Elise. What had she done?

He sat up and rubbed his eyes. He looked at the passport again, turned it over in his hands. It had a certain weight to it even though it was so small. He opened it again. It was all there; the watermark, the hologram, the picture of his face. How had Elise got that? And then he remembered, getting photos taken in the station one day. Something Theo had wanted, or at least that was what she had said. He could not stop staring at it.

He could go and find his sister. He could leave anytime. He could take a bus, or a plane, or a train. He could travel. He could travel home if he wanted. He was French. Would his name come up? Maybe. Yes. But as a Frenchman would they dare to touch him? Maybe. No.

But Elise, she had risked so much to get this for him. How much had it cost? She would say he owed her nothing. He could hear her say it already.

Was it real?

It looked genuine.

One hundred per cent genuine.

Would it work?

He looked at the picture of his face one more time. It was him, for sure. He did not know what to do so he lit a cigarette before he had even made the coffee. Suddenly, everything was possible.

When he walked into the kitchen, Elise was already there. He placed his passport on the kitchen table.

'You are an extraordinary woman, Elise Demarais.'

'And it's taken you this long to realise?'

He laughed. How could he not? When the world was so unpredictable.

CHAPTER 67

The face that hovered in front of him made him smile. The man was home. Nebay. The knowledge of this recognition lifted him. He was not entirely gone.

'Your face is hanging down.'

'I'm just a little tired.'

'You weren't here before. They stole you.'

'They did, but I am back now.'

Theo took Nebay's hand. 'Good. Now you will stay.'

The woman came in. It was his daughter. He knew it when she stood next to Nebay. Maybe they were brother and sister. She said words and he smiled because he remembered when she had none, when she was a small, fat, screaming thing.

'Elise said that we're going to visit Marianne today,' said Nebay.

'Marianne?'

'Don't worry, I'm sure it will all come back to you as soon as you see her.'

Marianne? He had thought she was dead. No, no, that was wrong. It had been a mistake. Some people did dying for real, others did not. The bath woman, the woman from the photo, she had done it for real.

'Don't cry,' he said to his daughter as she walked into the room holding a round thing full of something. She looked just like the woman from the story in his head, but she was just a child, his child, but then how could she be, when he was only a child himself?

It was early when they woke to the banging on the door. Theo got up cautiously, going only as far as the door of his bedroom, his head at the height of the door handle, and peered out through the crack. There were policemen talking loudly about Jewish people, asking his parents if they had seen their next-door neighbours recently, asking them how they felt about Jewish people in general, asking if they had any Jewish relatives themselves, reminding them how illegal everything was. They wanted to come in, but his parents stood strong by the front door, blocking their entrance.

'How dare you come here at this time in the morning and disturb my family's sleep over some Jews, this is unacceptable.'

In the end the officers apologised and left. Theo went back to bed but left the door open. He could hear his mother crying. Their French citizenship, he heard her say, would mean nothing if they discovered the Jewish blood that ran in his and his mother's veins. How would they find out what was in their veins? He looked at his small wrist, little blue lines running under his skin, and wondered.

CHAPTER 68

The block of flats towered above her. Elise took a deep breath and walked forward, hoping that Nebay would be okay waiting with Theo in the car. In the window nearest to her was a sticker for a charity called Salam with collection times for free food. Was this what her father's ex-girlfriend did?

'Hello,' said the old woman as she opened the door.

Marianne had a scar that ran down the right side of her face, disfiguring her right eye, squashing the lids together. Moisture collected in its corner, congealing into a crust. Her other eye was bright and alert.

'Hi, my name is Elise Demarais. We spoke on the phone.'

'So, you are his daughter.'

'Yes.'

'Come in.'

Marianne led Elise down the long corridor to a small kitchen at the back that looked out onto a verdant garden. She went to put the kettle on. Elise sat at the kitchen table.

'I saw your mother once. She was very beautiful.'

Elise was confused. 'You saw her?'

'With my good eye,' she added by way of explanation.

'No. What I meant was when?'

'A long time ago. In the sixties. He left me, I wanted to know who he had left me for.'

'Oh.'

'Like I said, it was a long time ago, and I had already abandoned him once. What could I expect?'

'He said he thought you were dead.'

'Yes, for twenty years.'

'But why didn't you contact him and tell him you were alive?'

'I had no idea he'd come to look for me and found my old house, the army had destroyed it. I thought he'd given up on me, on us.'

'So, how did you get back in contact?'

'He saw I was giving a conference at the Sorbonne. Poor man, it must have nearly killed him.'

'But he was already with my mother.'

'Yes.'

'Had I been born yet?'

'No. How old are you?'

'Thirty-two.'

Marianne was quiet for a moment while she worked something out. 'Well, that explains something.'

'What?'

'Nothing, dear. Now, where is this old man anyway?'

'He was sleeping, I left him in the car with a friend.'

The doorbell rang and Marianne went to answer it. Nebay came in breathing hard.

'He's gone.'

'What? How?'

Nebay looked towards Marianne.

'He went to relieve himself. I gave him a second of privacy and he left. I've looked down the street both ways. I don't understand it.'

'I should come,' Marianne said.

'No, don't worry, you stay here. We'll search for him. He can't have gone far.'

They stepped out into the cold and the sea breeze slapped them in the face. Already the day was turning darker, a storm was coming in on the waves. They had left late trying to get Theo into the car.

'I shouldn't have left you alone. You're exhausted. I'm sorry.'

'Don't worry, we'll split up, it'll be quicker. Take the car. I'll walk.'

CHAPTER 69

Nebay made his way along the deserted port roads, the grey of the concrete merging with the grey of the sky and, far off, the sea. He thought of the last time he had been here, only a short time ago, yet so much had changed. He hoped that Theo was not far away, being here made him feel uneasy. He called out his name, but it was snatched up by the wind and the seagulls, tossed and turned on the waves, it was useless. He carried on walking, looking to either side of the road, the scrubland and abandoned buildings that spoke of life and industry now spent.

'Theo!' he called again, and again his voice disappeared as soon as it had left him.

Where could he be? He reached the fence, there was a man-shaped hole made by eager bodies searching for hope. He climbed through. At the far end of the empty compound, an area big enough to park a hundred trucks, he saw a figure walking slowly away from him. He started running, but as he did he noticed two security guards running through the main entrance gate to his left. As he started to run faster so did they. It had become a race. He would win it.

He cried out 'Theo' at the top of his lungs, but realised that this lost old man may not even be able to recognise his own name. It was all too late.

CHAPTER 70

They had been in a thing, a car. He preferred the other thing, the big one you could walk around in, but he had not been allowed to go on it. Theo got to the bush, relieved himself and looked around. He could see the sea. He remembered the garden that he would tend with Marianne. If he started walking he knew that he could find it. The roads were no good. He went straight through the bush into a flat place and headed towards the sea. A big boat thing honked its horn. He jumped a little but carried on. He could not be stopped now.

At a tall metal fence he stopped, this was all wrong, she did not live here. He sat down to think about it. What was he doing? Who was he looking for? He stumbled through the hole in the fence. It was getting dark. Marianne was not here, but he was sure he had seen Nebay. He needed help to find her.

'Nebay,' he whispered towards the back of the retreating man. 'Nebay?' he repeated, a little louder. He could not explain it, but something about the sombre faces of the men that he had passed along the way, the dark circles under their eyes, saddened him. There was so much silence here. It felt wrong to break it. And yet he did. Two men turned when they heard him. He saw them stare but was only vaguely aware of their pounding footsteps. When Nebay turned towards him, Theo smiled. He could not understand the look of anger mixed with fear upon Nebay's face as he ran towards him.

The voices he heard seemed indistinct. They were shouting, both Nebay and some other men, who wore dark uniforms and waved something like sticks. It seemed unimportant now that Nebay was here to help him find Marianne. He should have asked for his help in the first place. Silly man.

There was a pain exploding somewhere inside him. It ran down his left arm like lightning and came back to rest in his chest. The feeling of falling was unexpected but the warmth of Nebay's arms was not.

CHAPTER 71

Elise had seen it all from the edge of the compound as she stepped out of the taxi; Nebay running towards her father, the security men running towards them both. Nebay and Theo colliding, crashing to the ground. She ran as fast as she could, but the air seemed to thicken around her, long seconds passing. She heard the police cars approaching as her heart fought to escape from her chest.

When she reached the fallen bodies, it looked as if Theo was sleeping soundly in Nebay's embrace, curled into the crook of his arm like a child or a lover. An arm tried to hold her as she fell to the ground and she brushed it away. She reached her hand out into the darkness to touch her father, but his body was still. Nebay's hand gripped hers.

'Elise, I am sorry.'

The security men had reached them and were rolling Theo over as if searching him, but she noticed the limpness in his body and saw his hand held up to his chest in their torchlight. They hauled Nebay to his feet and took out handcuffs.

'No!' she cried out. 'This is my father's carer. You must let him go.'

Nebay pulled out his passport, they shone the light over it and handed it back.

'Sorry, sir.'

* * *

She pulled out her phone to call Marianne. 'Meet us at the hospital,' she said quickly before following the ambulance in the car.

CHAPTER 72

On the very edge of his consciousness, Theo was aware of the machines. They were everywhere. They had taken over. He tried not to open his eyes. He did not like to see them. Something had happened. He had taken a fall. Why were they making such a fuss? He tried to move to tell them, but he was unable. He could not understand it. There were people here as well. They hovered around him. He could sense them. A hand held his, it was old like his own, he could feel the small bones and swollen knuckles.

'I'm sorry,' he whispered.

His breathing faltered.

His chest felt caved in.

The water was back. He plunged into the darkness of the river. History bruised him.

Marianne had kissed him, and he had pulled her up towards him, turning them both around so that she was sitting on the kitchen counter of the apartment in the Marais.

'Marianne Anouar, if you would stay I would ask you to be my wife.'

'And I would consider saying yes,' she said, tiredness creeping into her voice and the faintest suggestion of hope. Maybe he had been wrong. Maybe he still had a chance.

AUTHOR'S NOTE

This novel endeavours to be historically and contemporaneously accurate, only very rarely altered to fit a fictional narrative. Two such counts are the simultaneous existence of the Paris camps and the UKBA office, and the style of interviews held in this office by Elise.

The UKBA office closed when the agency was dismantled in 2013, but Paris camps have become more prevalent since 2016 after a major eviction of the Calais 'Jungle'.

The interviews conducted by Elise go further than visa applications would usually necessitate, encompassing interview techniques more commonly used in asylum applications.

ACKNOWLEDGEMENTS

It seems impossible, here, to list all those who have supported the creation of this book, but I shall try to name a few. From Aberystwyth University, where the idea first took shape, I would like to thank my supervisors Jem Poster, Jacqueline Yallop and Matthew Francis, as well as Department Head, Louise Marshall, and Creative Writing Fellow, Rosie Dub.

For early readings I would like to thank Lucie Gegg, Jo McGain, Fiona Dunbar, Alice Bowley, Eeyun Purkins, Phillippa Metcalfe and Giulio D'Errico. Residencies which have given me time and space include the Banff Centre, Camac, ComPeung and Cove Park.

Free beds and good food have been provided by many, especial thanks to those of Cefn Coch and the village of Verga. Further thanks to all my beloved friends in the UK – including those we've lost along the way – who know when I need to take a break and look in the other direction to see what's right in front of me. To Mani, a faithful four-legged friend, for the same reason.

To the community that supports me every day in Greece, the friends that have offered me encouragement and given me time even when the world is hell-bent on making sure we have none.

To the wonderful team at Legend Press for taking a chance on a new writer and supporting me through this process.

To my family, for not thinking me too mad during these years of writing, and to you, for reading.

If you enjoyed what you read,
don't keep it a secret.

Review the book online and tell
anyone who will listen.

Thanks for your support spreading
the word about Legend Press.

Follow us on Twitter
@legend_times_

Follow us on Instagram
@legend_times